NANCY DREW

girl detective ®

CH

PAPERCUT Z™

NANCY DREW
girl detective®

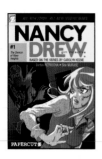

Graphic Novels
Available from Papercutz

#1 The Demon of River Heights
#2 Writ In Stone
#3 The Haunted Dollhouse
#4 The Girl Who Wasn't There
(coming February 2006)

$7.95 each in paperback
$12.95 each in hardcover

NANCY
DREW
#1
BASED ON THE SERIES BY CAROLYN KEENE
PAPERCUTZ

ALL-NEW STORY FULL-COLOR GRAPHIC NOVEL
NANCY
DREW
girl detective
#3
BASED ON THE SERIES BY CAROLYN KEENE
Stefan PETRUCHA
Sho MURASE
PAPERCUTZ

NANCY
DREW
girl detective
#4
BASED ON THE SERIES BY CAROLYN KEENE
Stefan PETRUCHA • Sho MURASE
PAPERCUTZ

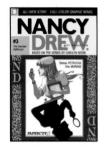

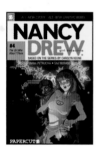

Please add $3.00 for postage and handling for the first book, add $1.00 for each additional book.

Send for our catalog:
Papercutz
555 Eighth Avenue, Suite 1202
New York, NY 10018
www.papercutz.com

NANCY DREW
#2 DREW
girl detective ®

Writ In Stone

STEFAN PETRUCHA • Writer
SHO MURASE • Artist
with 3D CG elements by RACHEL ITO
Based on the series by
CAROLYN KEENE

FFB   2007

PAPERCUTZ™
New York

Writ In Stone
STEFAN PETRUCHA – Writer
SHO MURASE – Artist
with 3D CG elements by RACHEL ITO
BRYAN SENKA – Letterer
CARLOS JOSE GUZMAN
SHO MURASE
Colorists
JIM SALICRUP
Editor-in-Chief

ISBN 10: 1-59707-002-5 paperback edition
ISBN 13: 978-1-59707-002-7 paperback edition
ISBN 10: 1-59707-006-8 hardcover edition
ISBN 13: 978-1-59707-006-5 hardcover edition

Printed in China.

10   9   8   7   6   5   4   3   2

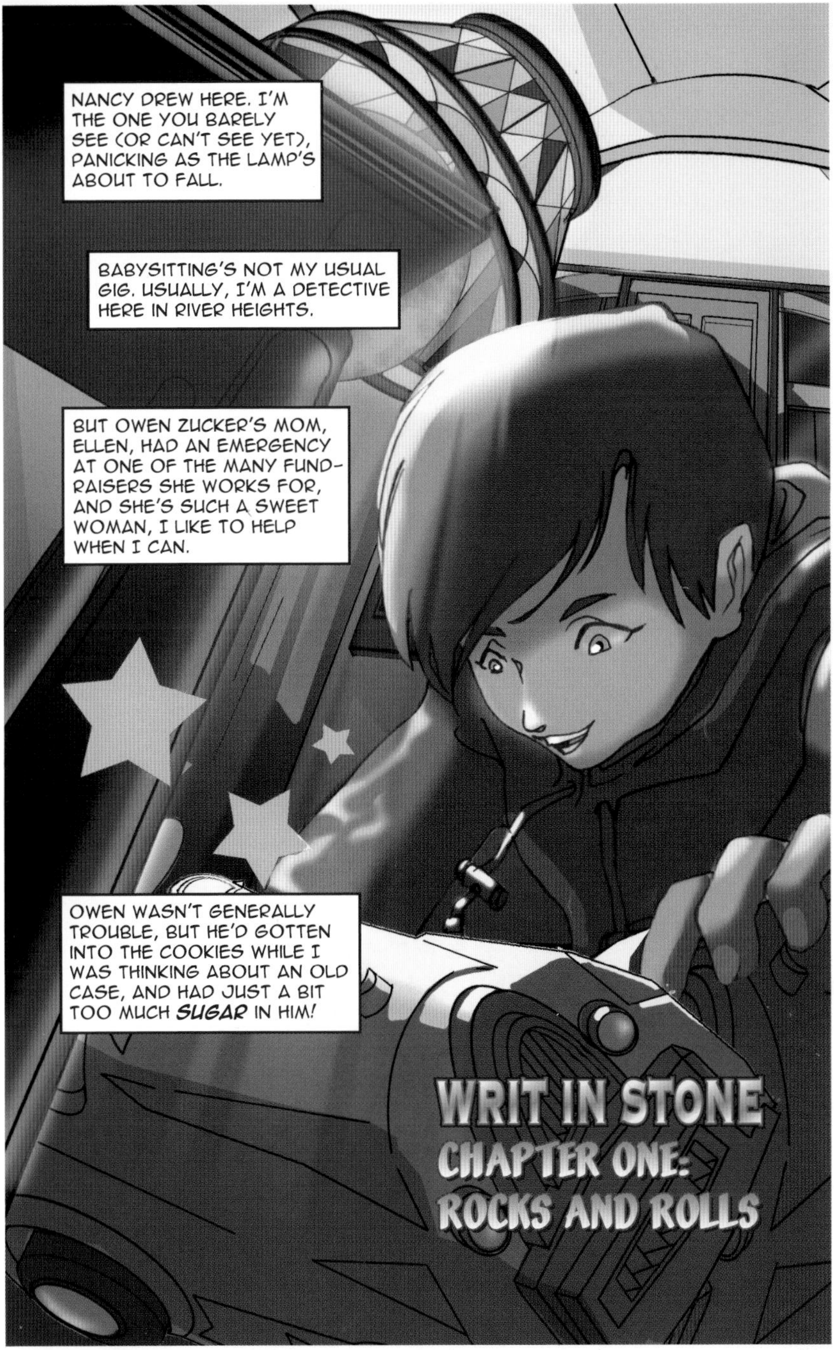
NANCY DREW HERE. I'M THE ONE YOU BARELY SEE (OR CAN'T SEE YET), PANICKING AS THE LAMP'S ABOUT TO FALL.
BABYSITTING'S NOT MY USUAL GIG. USUALLY, I'M A DETECTIVE HERE IN RIVER HEIGHTS.
BUT OWEN ZUCKER'S MOM, ELLEN, HAD AN EMERGENCY AT ONE OF THE MANY FUND-RAISERS SHE WORKS FOR, AND SHE'S SUCH A SWEET WOMAN, I LIKE TO HELP WHEN I CAN.
OWEN WASN'T GENERALLY TROUBLE, BUT HE'D GOTTEN INTO THE COOKIES WHILE I WAS THINKING ABOUT AN OLD CASE, AND HAD JUST A BIT TOO MUCH ***SUGAR*** IN HIM!
WRIT IN STONE
CHAPTER ONE:
ROCKS AND ROLLS

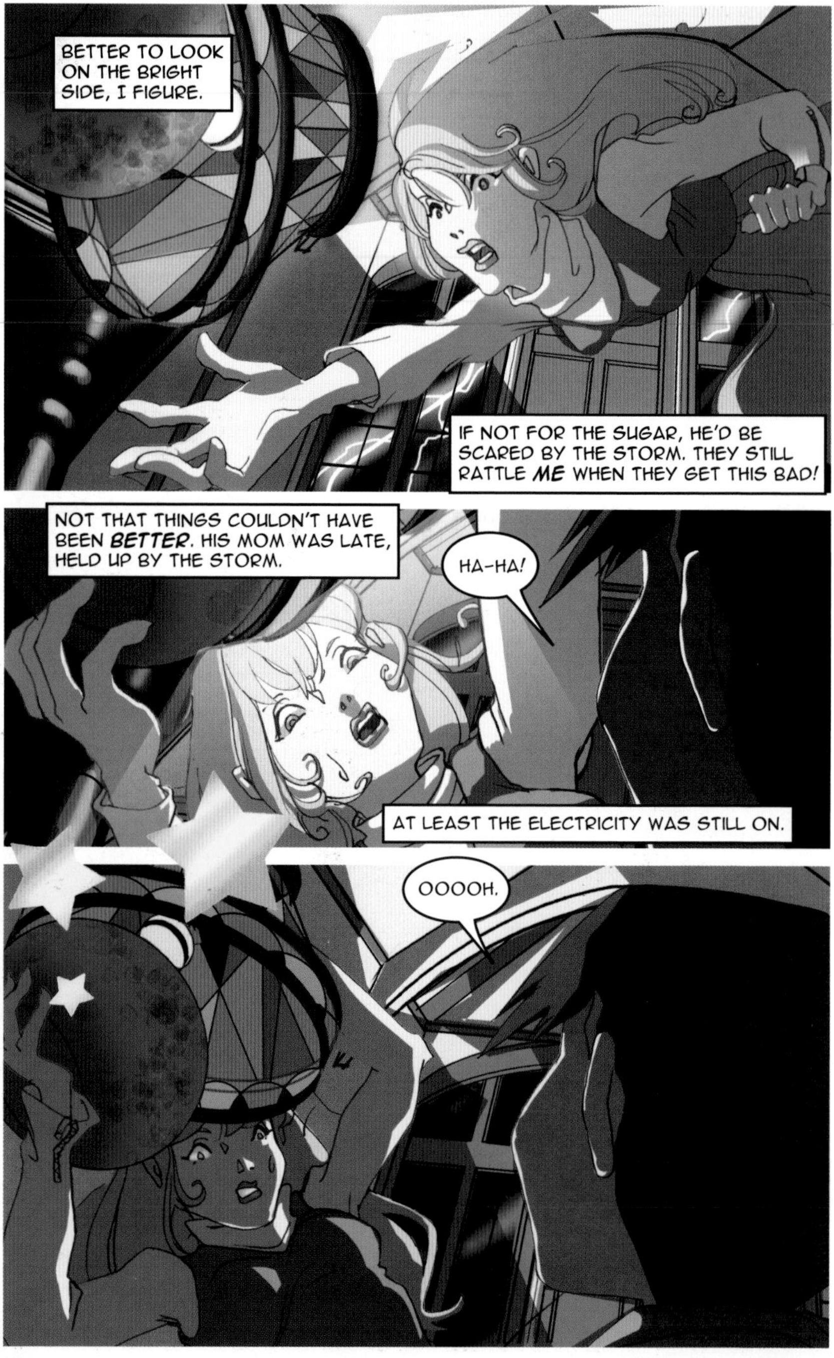
BETTER TO LOOK ON THE BRIGHT SIDE, I FIGURE.
IF NOT FOR THE SUGAR, HE'D BE SCARED BY THE STORM. THEY STILL RATTLE *ME* WHEN THEY GET THIS BAD!
NOT THAT THINGS COULDN'T HAVE BEEN *BETTER*. HIS MOM WAS LATE, HELD UP BY THE STORM.
HA-HA!
AT LEAST THE ELECTRICITY WAS STILL ON.
OOOOH.

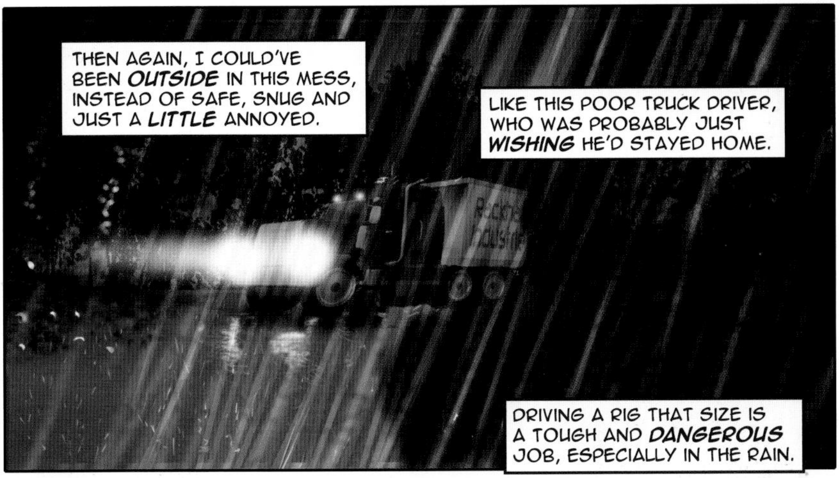
THEN AGAIN, I COULD'VE BEEN OUTSIDE IN THIS MESS, INSTEAD OF SAFE, SNUG AND JUST A LITTLE ANNOYED.
LIKE THIS POOR TRUCK DRIVER, WHO WAS PROBABLY JUST WISHING HE'D STAYED HOME.
DRIVING A RIG THAT SIZE IS A TOUGH AND DANGEROUS JOB, ESPECIALLY IN THE RAIN.

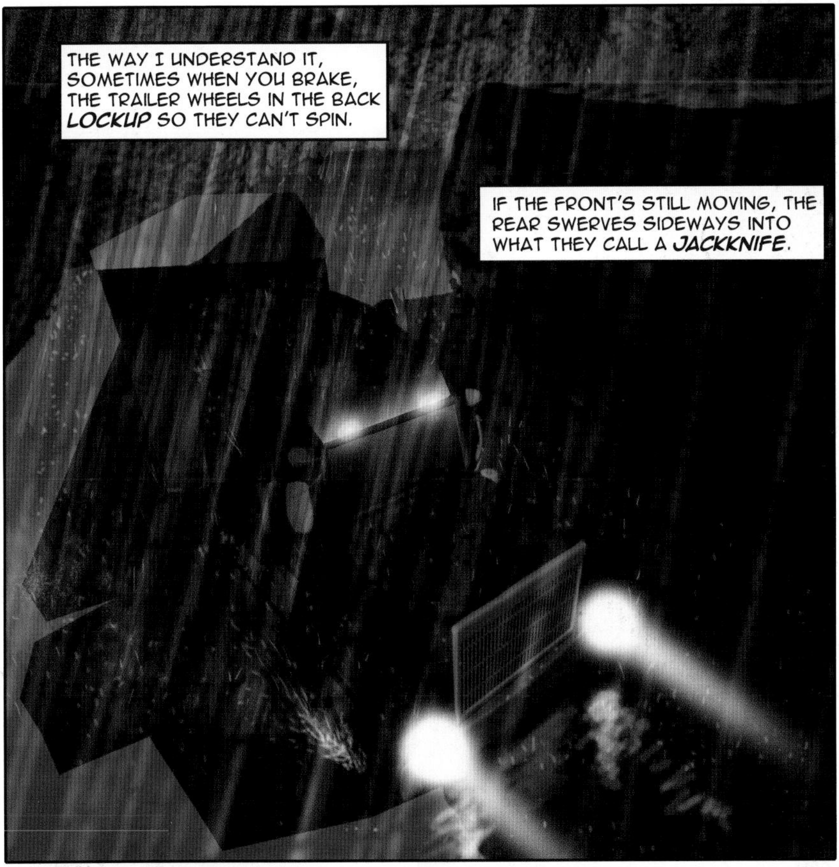
THE WAY I UNDERSTAND IT, SOMETIMES WHEN YOU BRAKE, THE TRAILER WHEELS IN THE BACK LOCKUP SO THEY CAN'T SPIN.
IF THE FRONT'S STILL MOVING, THE REAR SWERVES SIDEWAYS INTO WHAT THEY CALL A JACKKNIFE.

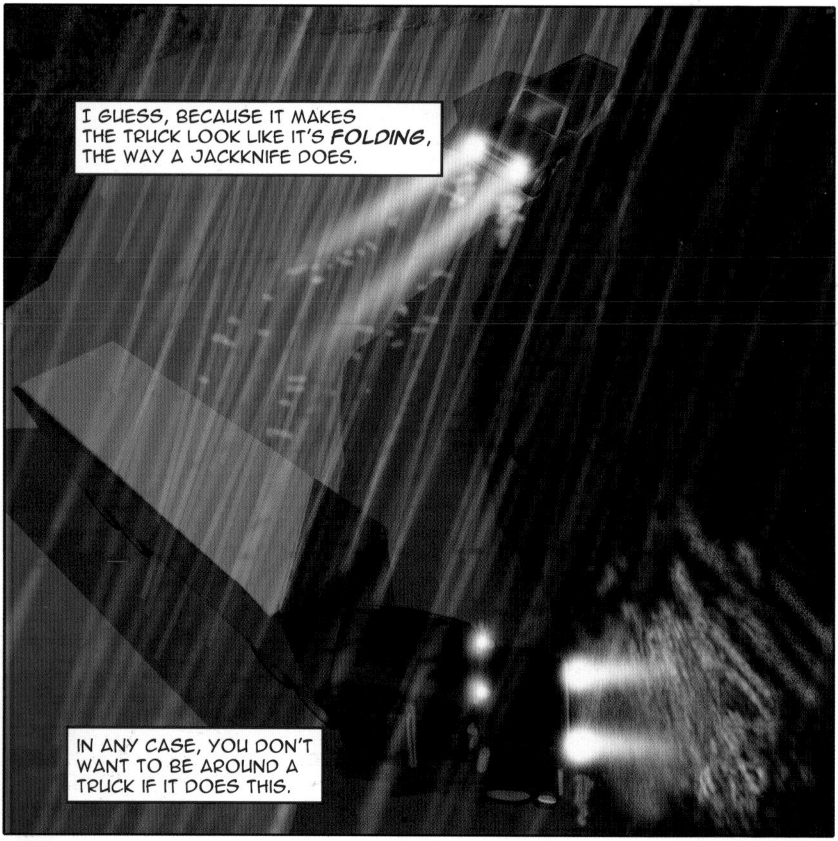
I GUESS, BECAUSE IT MAKES THE TRUCK LOOK LIKE IT'S *FOLDING*, THE WAY A JACKKNIFE DOES.
IN ANY CASE, YOU DON'T WANT TO BE AROUND A TRUCK IF IT DOES THIS.

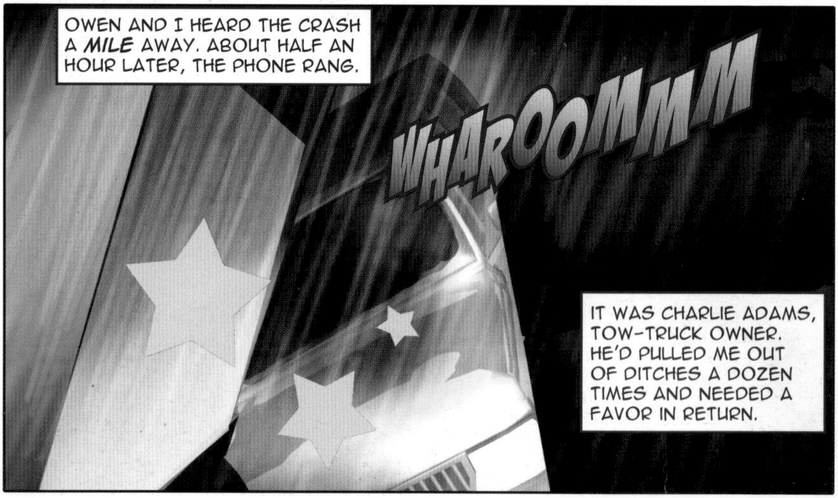
OWEN AND I HEARD THE CRASH A *MILE* AWAY. ABOUT HALF AN HOUR LATER, THE PHONE RANG.
WHAROOMMMM
IT WAS CHARLIE ADAMS, TOW-TRUCK OWNER. HE'D PULLED ME OUT OF DITCHES A DOZEN TIMES AND NEEDED A FAVOR IN RETURN.

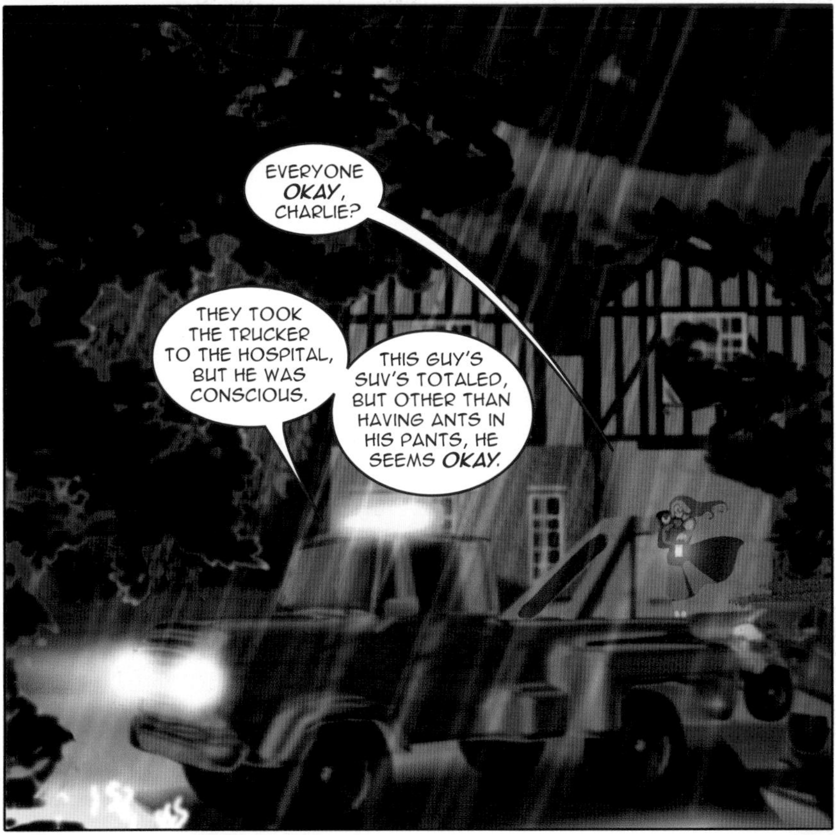
EVERYONE OKAY, CHARLIE?
THEY TOOK THE TRUCKER TO THE HOSPITAL, BUT HE WAS CONSCIOUS.
THIS GUY'S SUV'S TOTALED, BUT OTHER THAN HAVING ANTS IN HIS PANTS, HE SEEMS OKAY.

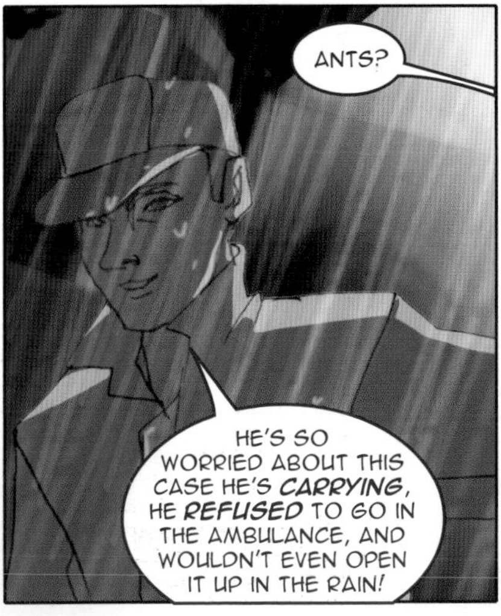
ANTS?
HE'S SO WORRIED ABOUT THIS CASE HE'S CARRYING, HE REFUSED TO GO IN THE AMBULANCE, AND WOULDN'T EVEN OPEN IT UP IN THE RAIN!

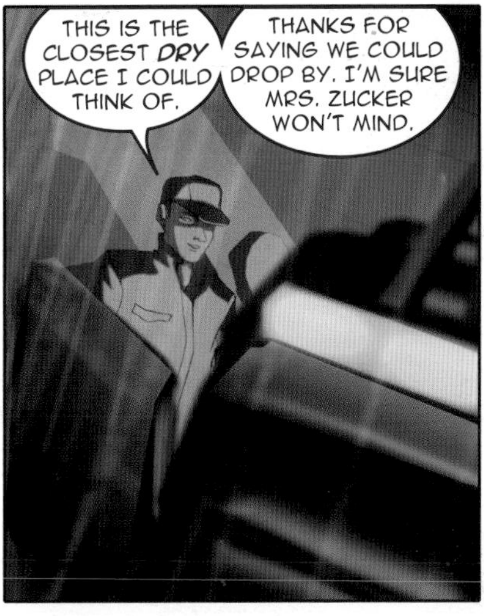
THIS IS THE CLOSEST DRY PLACE I COULD THINK OF.
THANKS FOR SAYING WE COULD DROP BY. I'M SURE MRS. ZUCKER WON'T MIND.

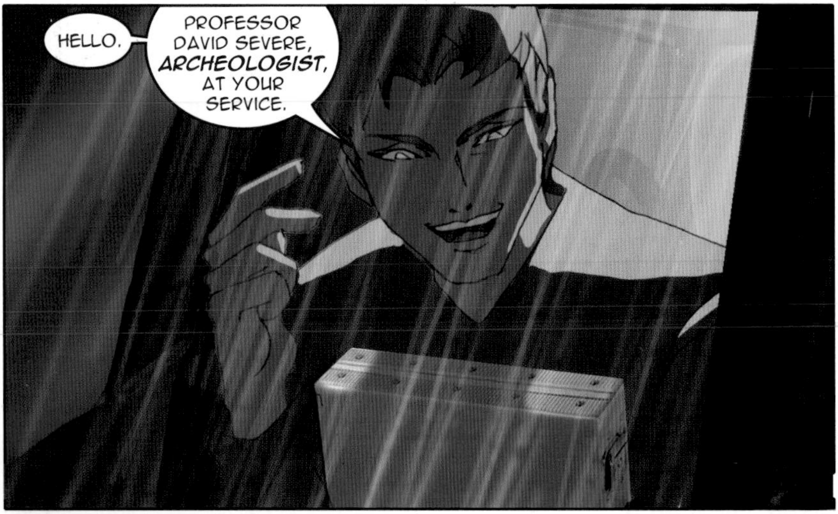
HELLO.
PROFESSOR DAVID SEVERE, ARCHEOLOGIST, AT YOUR SERVICE.

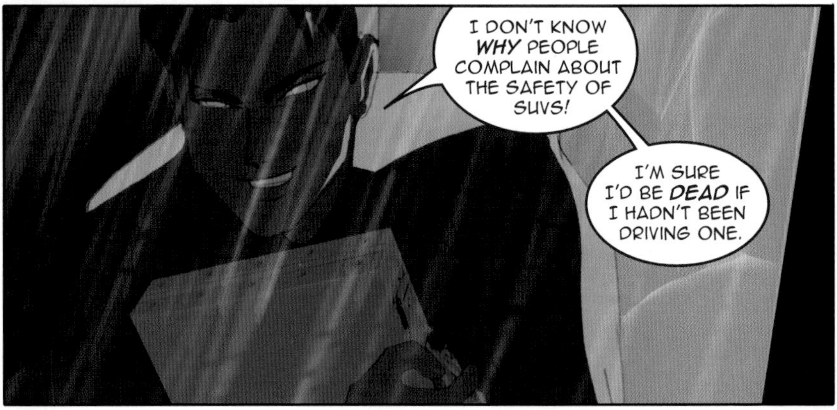
I DON'T KNOW WHY PEOPLE COMPLAIN ABOUT THE SAFETY OF SUVS!
I'M SURE I'D BE DEAD IF I HADN'T BEEN DRIVING ONE.

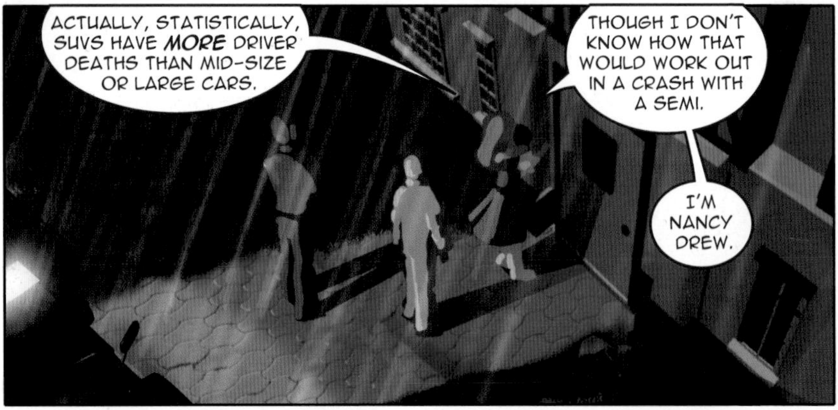
ACTUALLY, STATISTICALLY, SUVS HAVE MORE DRIVER DEATHS THAN MID-SIZE OR LARGE CARS.
THOUGH I DON'T KNOW HOW THAT WOULD WORK OUT IN A CRASH WITH A SEMI.
I'M NANCY DREW.

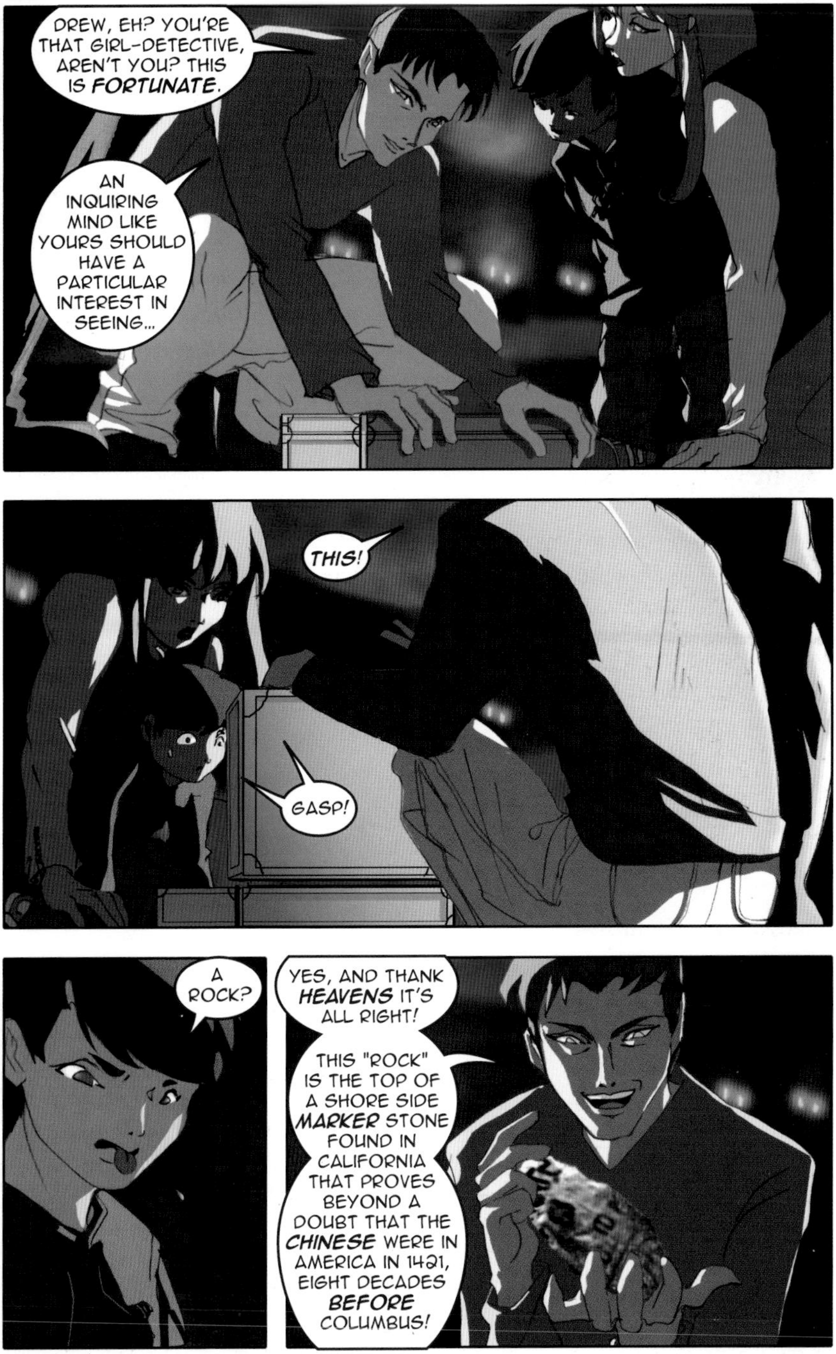
DREW, EH? YOU'RE THAT GIRL-DETECTIVE, AREN'T YOU? THIS IS FORTUNATE.
AN INQUIRING MIND LIKE YOURS SHOULD HAVE A PARTICULAR INTEREST IN SEEING...
THIS!
GASP!
A ROCK?
YES, AND THANK HEAVENS IT'S ALL RIGHT!
THIS "ROCK" IS THE TOP OF A SHORE SIDE MARKER STONE FOUND IN CALIFORNIA THAT PROVES BEYOND A DOUBT THAT THE CHINESE WERE IN AMERICA IN 1421, EIGHT DECADES BEFORE COLUMBUS!

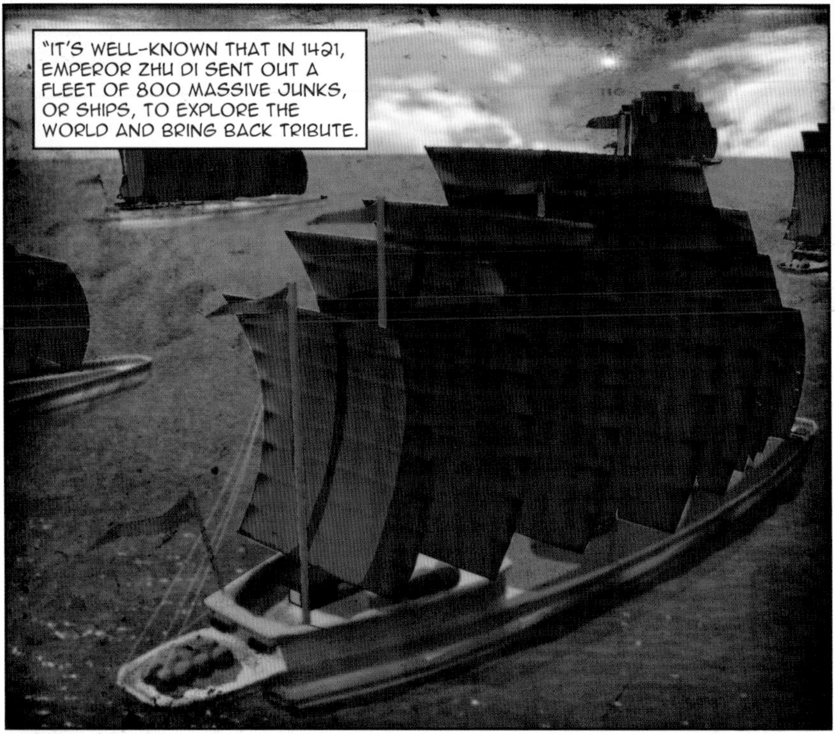
"IT'S WELL-KNOWN THAT IN 1421, EMPEROR ZHU DI SENT OUT A FLEET OF 800 MASSIVE JUNKS, OR SHIPS, TO EXPLORE THE WORLD AND BRING BACK TRIBUTE.

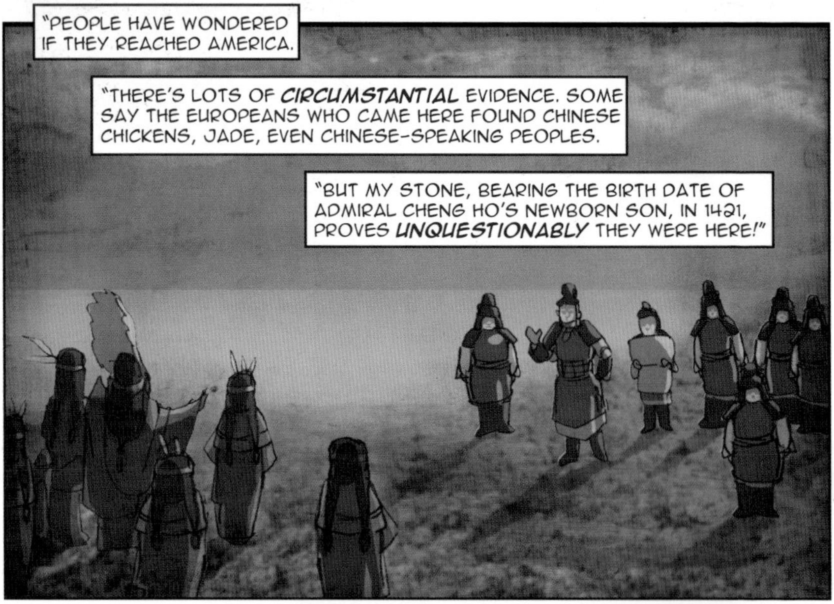
"PEOPLE HAVE WONDERED IF THEY REACHED AMERICA.
"THERE'S LOTS OF *CIRCUMSTANTIAL* EVIDENCE. SOME SAY THE EUROPEANS WHO CAME HERE FOUND CHINESE CHICKENS, JADE, EVEN CHINESE-SPEAKING PEOPLES.
"BUT MY STONE, BEARING THE BIRTH DATE OF ADMIRAL CHENG HO'S NEWBORN SON, IN 1421, PROVES *UNQUESTIONABLY* THEY WERE HERE!"

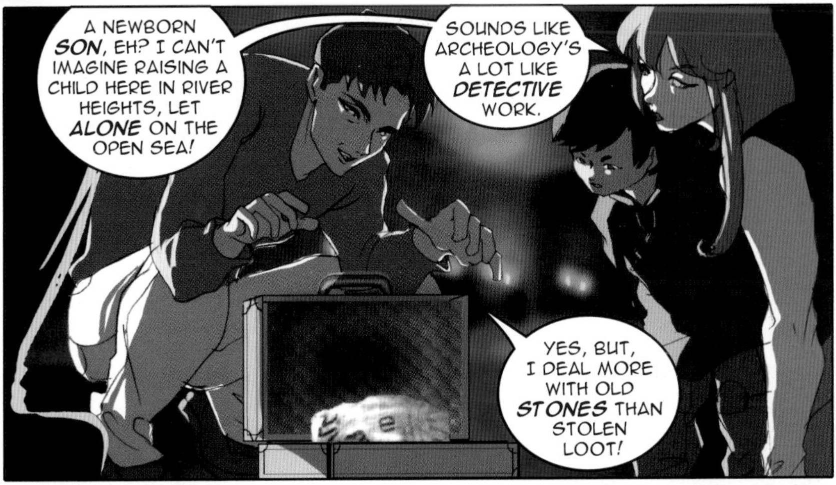
A NEWBORN SON, EH? I CAN'T IMAGINE RAISING A CHILD HERE IN RIVER HEIGHTS, LET ALONE ON THE OPEN SEA!
SOUNDS LIKE ARCHEOLOGY'S A LOT LIKE DETECTIVE WORK.
YES, BUT, I DEAL MORE WITH OLD STONES THAN STOLEN LOOT!

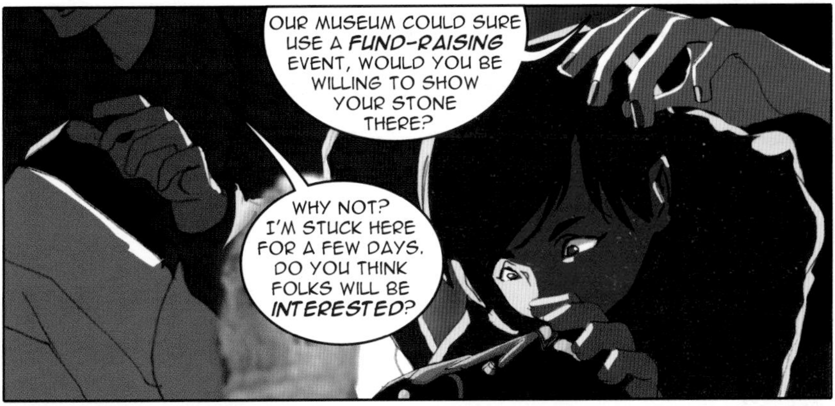
OUR MUSEUM COULD SURE USE A FUND-RAISING EVENT, WOULD YOU BE WILLING TO SHOW YOUR STONE THERE?
WHY NOT? I'M STUCK HERE FOR A FEW DAYS. DO YOU THINK FOLKS WILL BE INTERESTED?

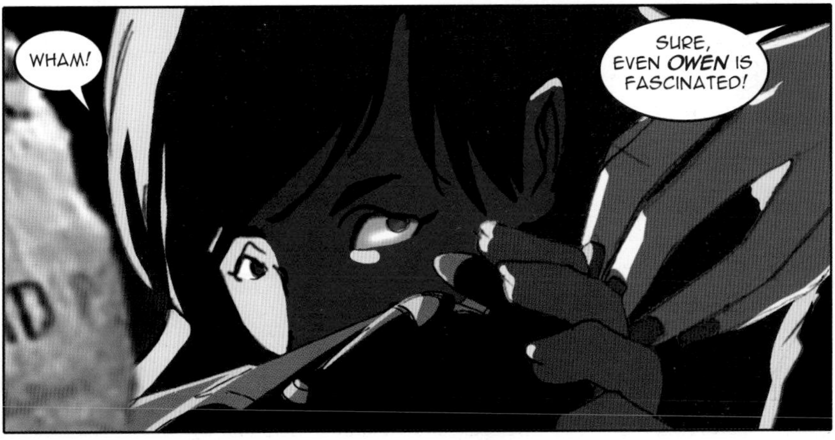
WHAM!
SURE, EVEN OWEN IS FASCINATED!

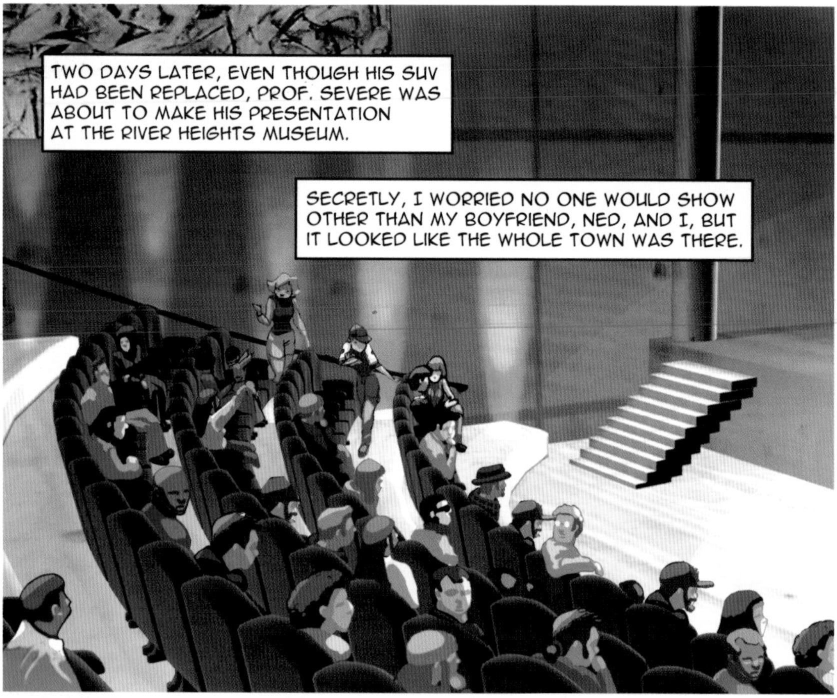
TWO DAYS LATER, EVEN THOUGH HIS SUV HAD BEEN REPLACED, PROF. SEVERE WAS ABOUT TO MAKE HIS PRESENTATION AT THE RIVER HEIGHTS MUSEUM.
SECRETLY, I WORRIED NO ONE WOULD SHOW OTHER THAN MY BOYFRIEND, NED, AND I, BUT IT LOOKED LIKE THE WHOLE TOWN WAS THERE.

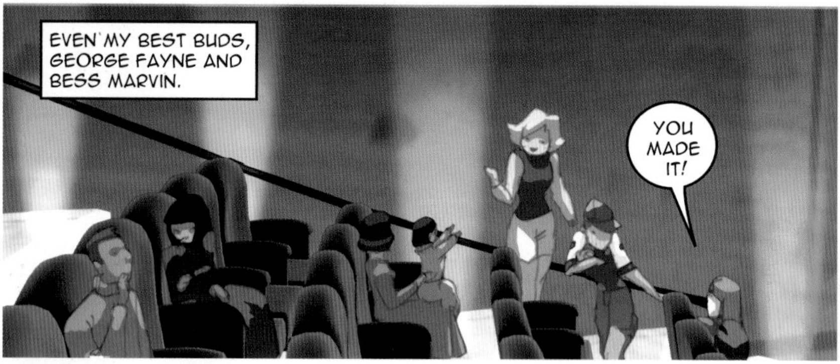
EVEN MY BEST BUDS, GEORGE FAYNE AND BESS MARVIN.
YOU MADE IT!

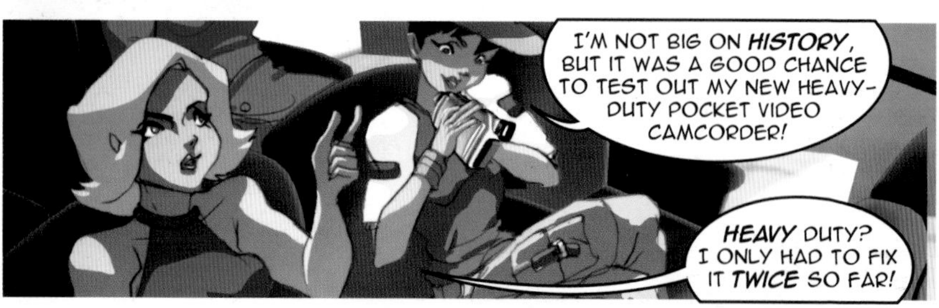
I'M NOT BIG ON ***HISTORY***, BUT IT WAS A GOOD CHANCE TO TEST OUT MY NEW HEAVY-DUTY POCKET VIDEO CAMCORDER!
HEAVY DUTY? I ONLY HAD TO FIX IT ***TWICE*** SO FAR!

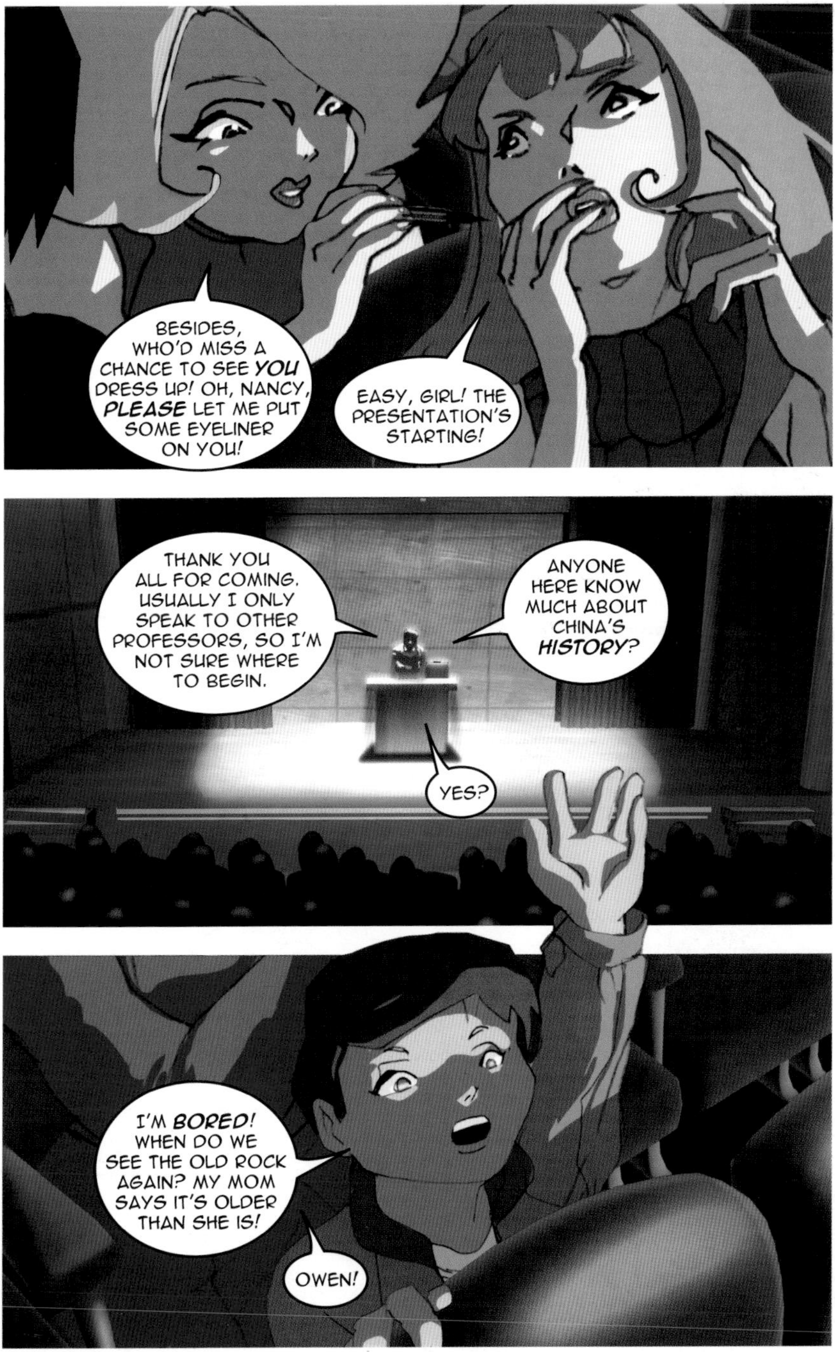
BESIDES, WHO'D MISS A CHANCE TO SEE *YOU* DRESS UP! OH, NANCY, *PLEASE* LET ME PUT SOME EYELINER ON YOU!
EASY, GIRL! THE PRESENTATION'S STARTING!
THANK YOU ALL FOR COMING. USUALLY I ONLY SPEAK TO OTHER PROFESSORS, SO I'M NOT SURE WHERE TO BEGIN.
ANYONE HERE KNOW MUCH ABOUT CHINA'S *HISTORY*?
YES?
I'M *BORED*! WHEN DO WE SEE THE OLD ROCK AGAIN? MY MOM SAYS IT'S OLDER THAN SHE IS!
OWEN!

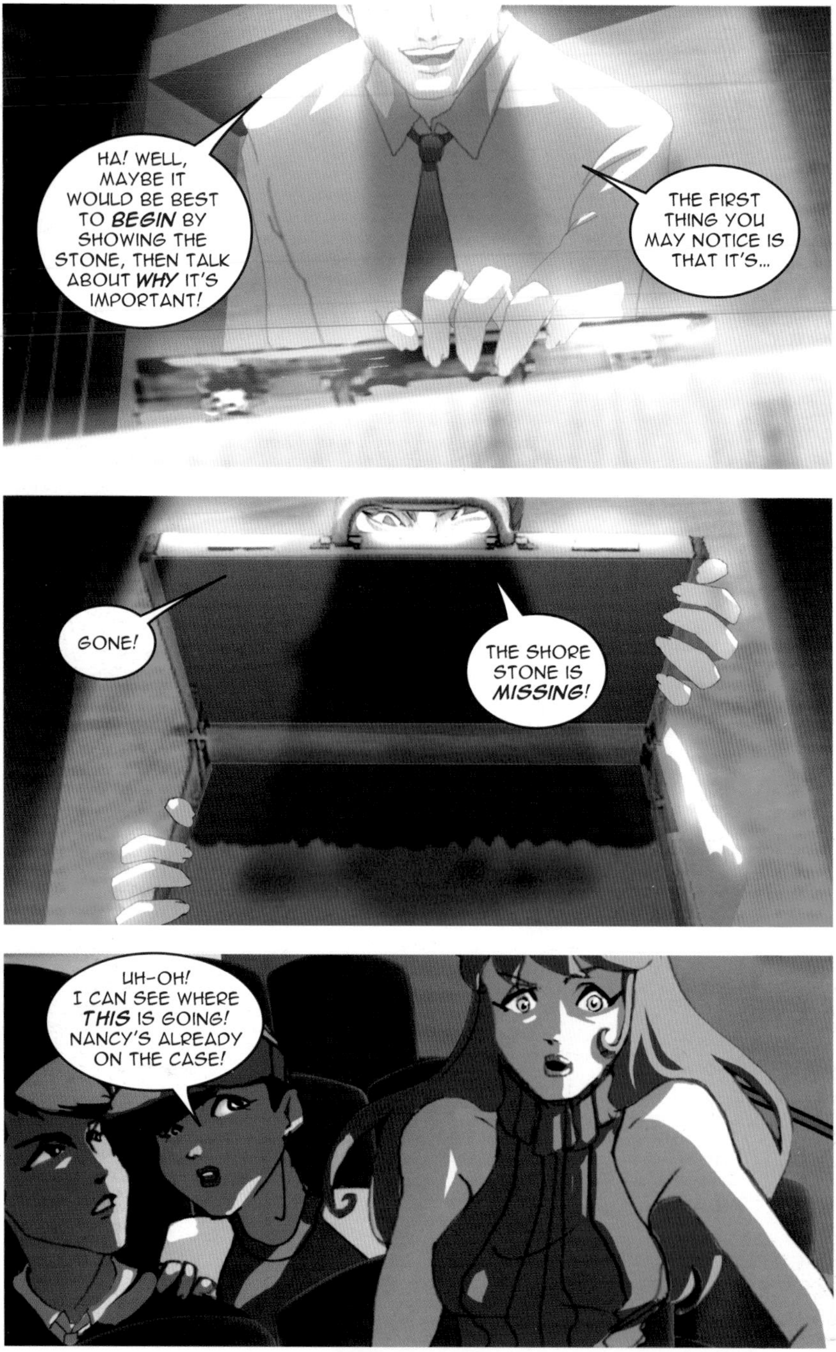
HA! WELL, MAYBE IT WOULD BE BEST TO *BEGIN* BY SHOWING THE STONE, THEN TALK ABOUT *WHY* IT'S IMPORTANT!
THE FIRST THING YOU MAY NOTICE IS THAT IT'S...
GONE!
THE SHORE STONE IS *MISSING*!
UH-OH! I CAN SEE WHERE *THIS* IS GOING! NANCY'S ALREADY ON THE CASE!

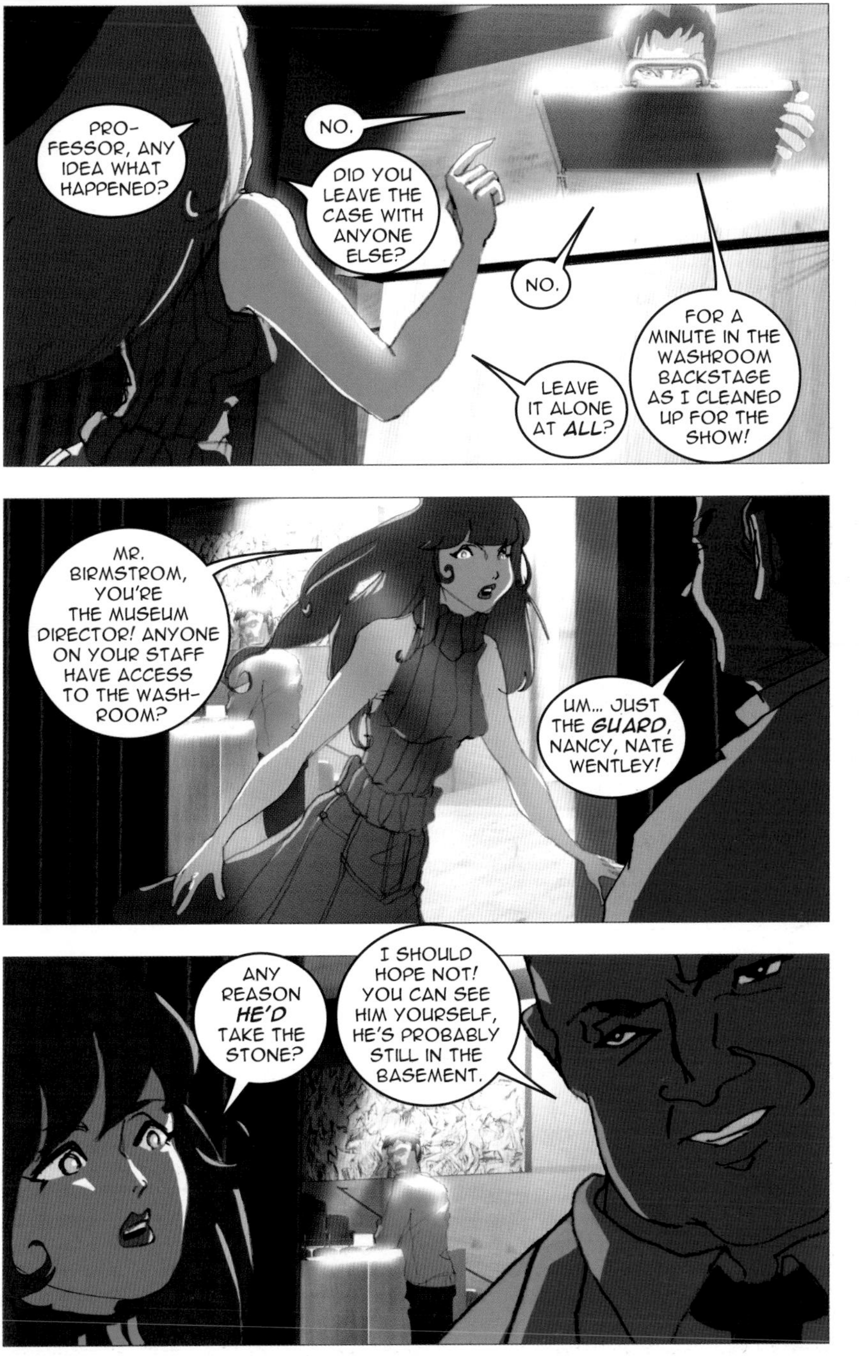
PRO-FESSOR, ANY IDEA WHAT HAPPENED?
NO.
DID YOU LEAVE THE CASE WITH ANYONE ELSE?
NO.
LEAVE IT ALONE AT *ALL*?
FOR A MINUTE IN THE WASHROOM BACKSTAGE AS I CLEANED UP FOR THE SHOW!
MR. BIRMSTROM, YOU'RE THE MUSEUM DIRECTOR! ANYONE ON YOUR STAFF HAVE ACCESS TO THE WASH-ROOM?
UM... JUST THE *GUARD*, NANCY, NATE WENTLEY!
ANY REASON *HE'D* TAKE THE STONE?
I SHOULD HOPE NOT! YOU CAN SEE HIM YOURSELF, HE'S PROBABLY STILL IN THE BASEMENT.

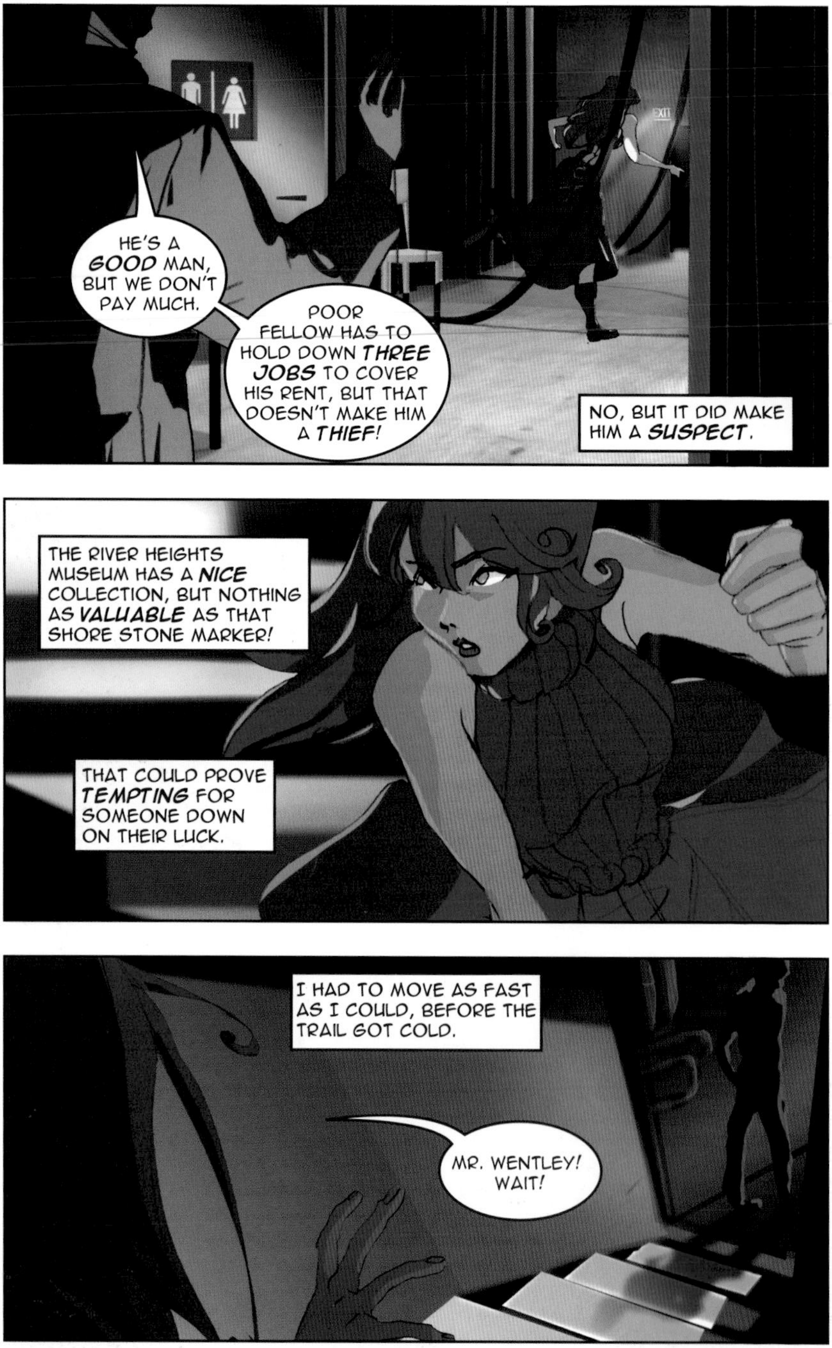
HE'S A GOOD MAN, BUT WE DON'T PAY MUCH.
POOR FELLOW HAS TO HOLD DOWN THREE JOBS TO COVER HIS RENT, BUT THAT DOESN'T MAKE HIM A THIEF!
NO, BUT IT DID MAKE HIM A SUSPECT.
THE RIVER HEIGHTS MUSEUM HAS A NICE COLLECTION, BUT NOTHING AS VALUABLE AS THAT SHORE STONE MARKER!
THAT COULD PROVE TEMPTING FOR SOMEONE DOWN ON THEIR LUCK.
I HAD TO MOVE AS FAST AS I COULD, BEFORE THE TRAIL GOT COLD.
MR. WENTLEY! WAIT!

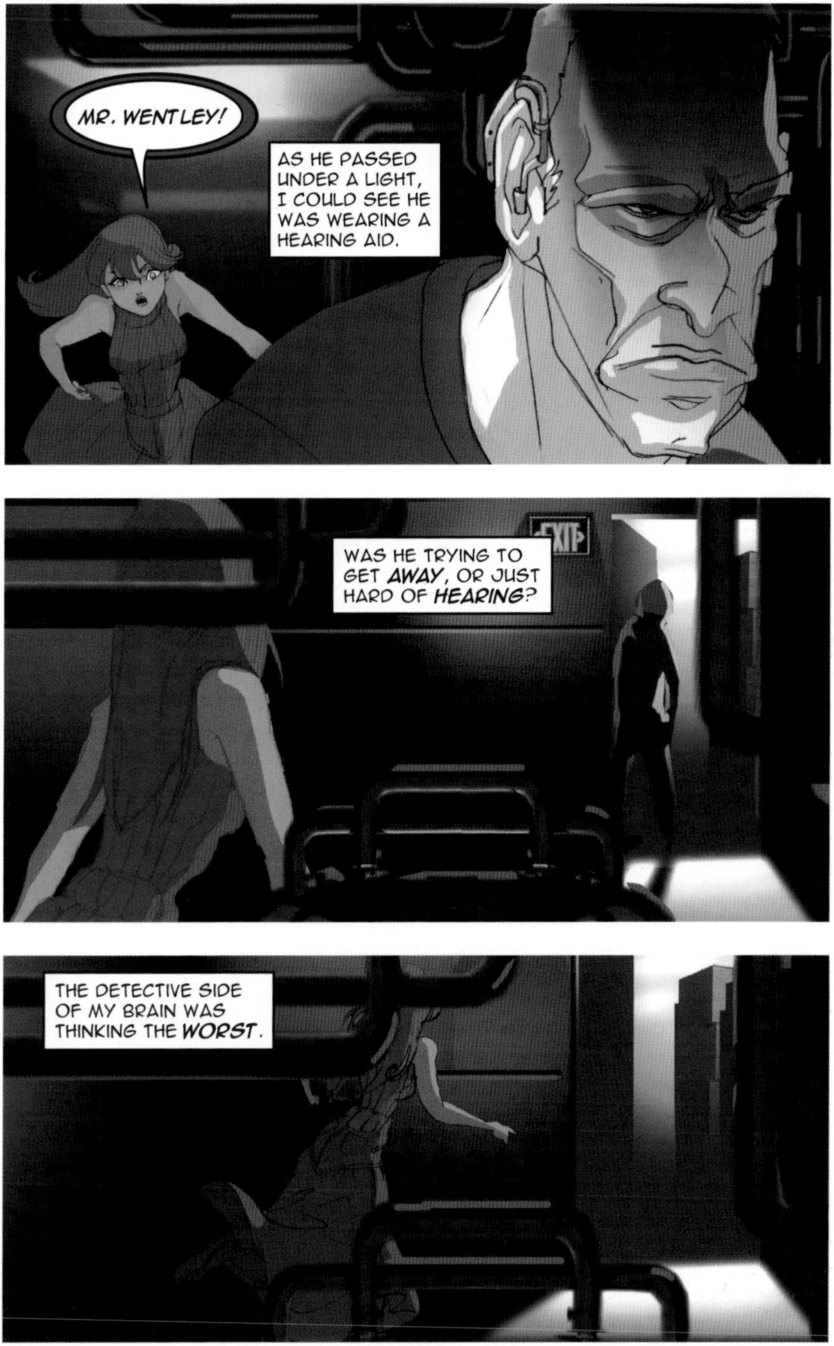
MR. WENTLEY!
AS HE PASSED UNDER A LIGHT, I COULD SEE HE WAS WEARING A HEARING AID.
EXIT
WAS HE TRYING TO GET AWAY, OR JUST HARD OF HEARING?
THE DETECTIVE SIDE OF MY BRAIN WAS THINKING THE WORST.

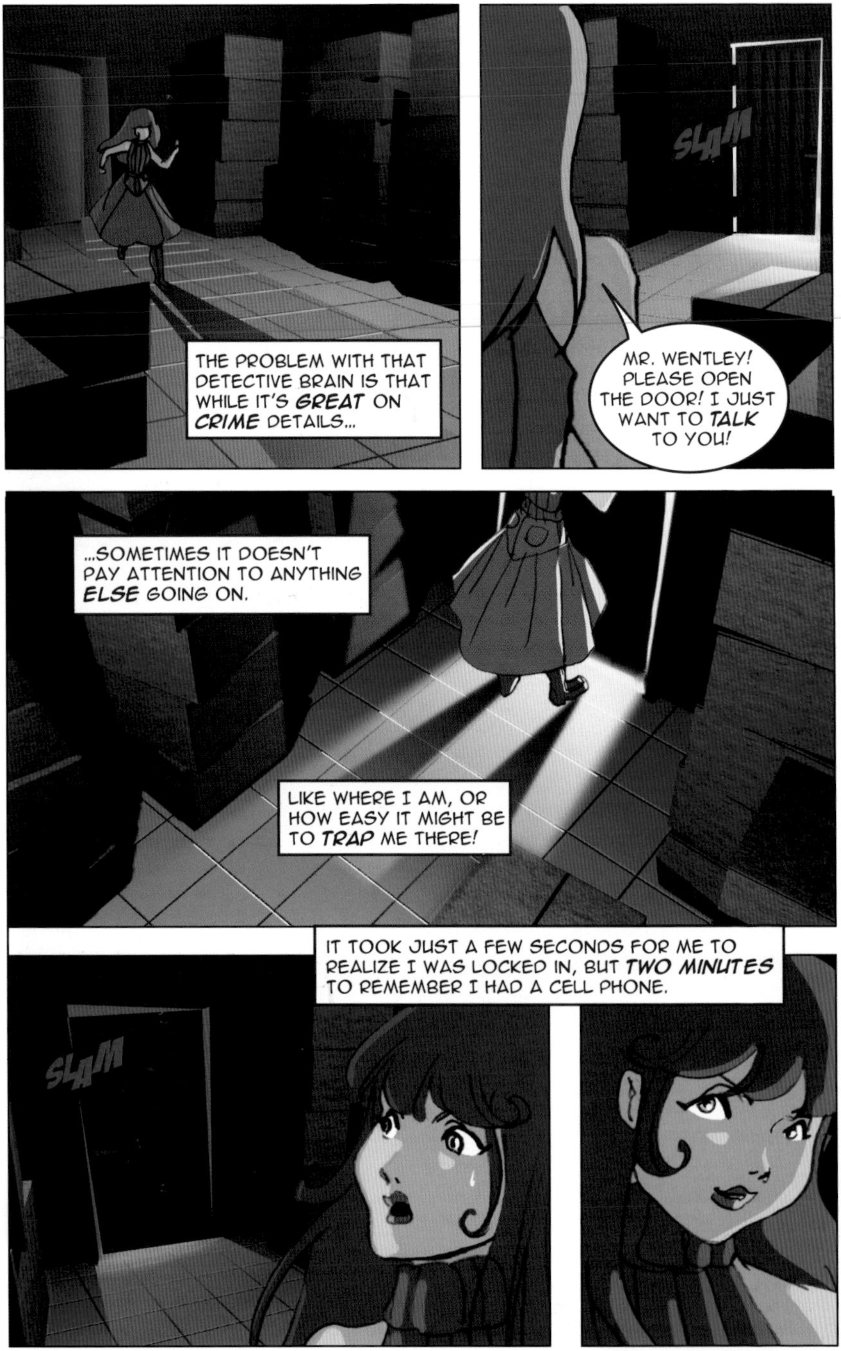
THE PROBLEM WITH THAT DETECTIVE BRAIN IS THAT WHILE IT'S GREAT ON CRIME DETAILS...
SLAM
MR. WENTLEY! PLEASE OPEN THE DOOR! I JUST WANT TO TALK TO YOU!
...SOMETIMES IT DOESN'T PAY ATTENTION TO ANYTHING ELSE GOING ON.
LIKE WHERE I AM, OR HOW EASY IT MIGHT BE TO TRAP ME THERE!
IT TOOK JUST A FEW SECONDS FOR ME TO REALIZE I WAS LOCKED IN, BUT TWO MINUTES TO REMEMBER I HAD A CELL PHONE.
SLAM

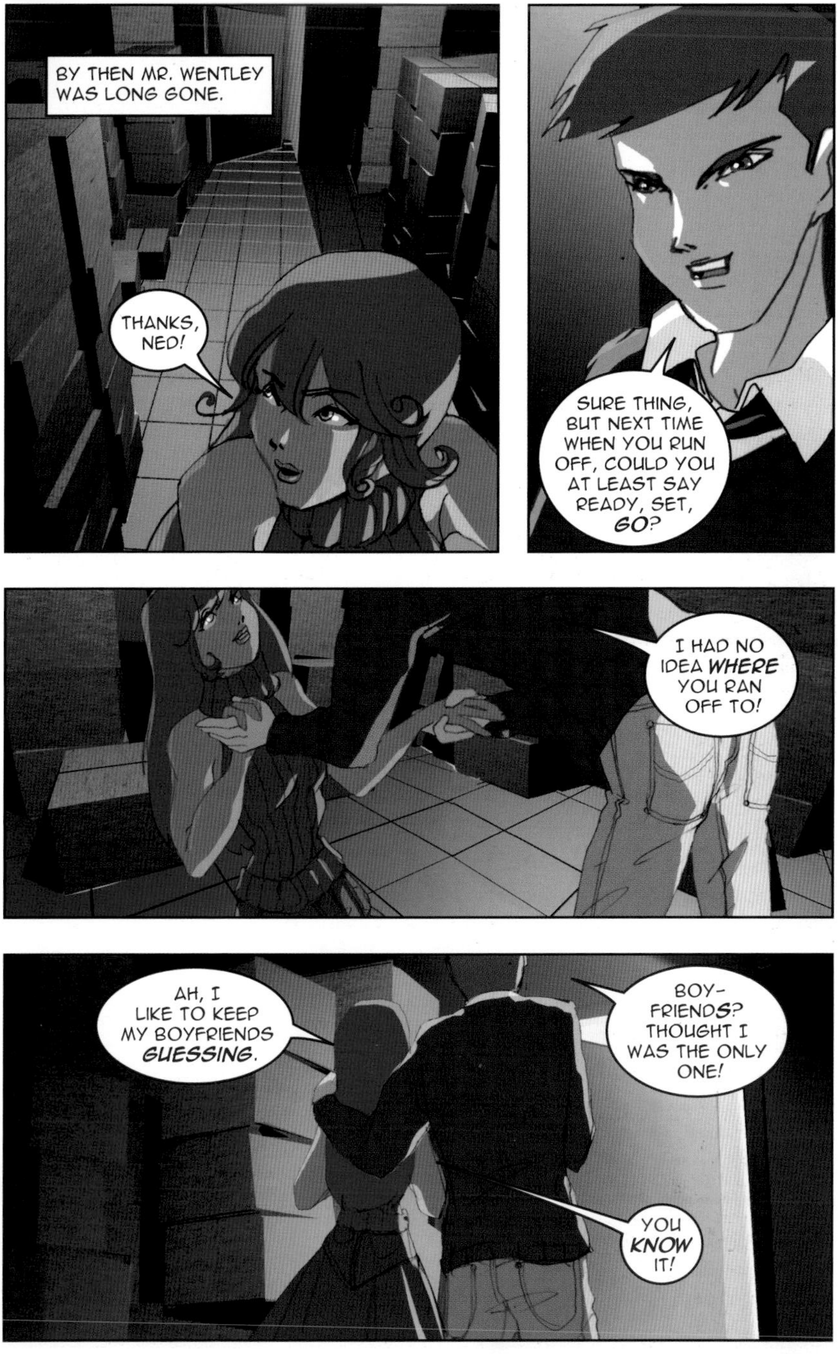
BY THEN MR. WENTLEY WAS LONG GONE.
THANKS, NED!
SURE THING, BUT NEXT TIME WHEN YOU RUN OFF, COULD YOU AT LEAST SAY READY, SET, GO?
I HAD NO IDEA WHERE YOU RAN OFF TO!
AH, I LIKE TO KEEP MY BOYFRIENDS GUESSING.
BOY-FRIENDS? THOUGHT I WAS THE ONLY ONE!
YOU KNOW IT!

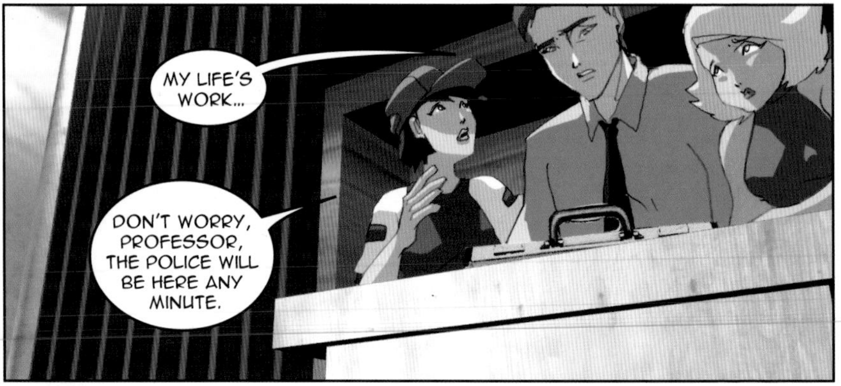
MY LIFE'S WORK...
DON'T WORRY, PROFESSOR, THE POLICE WILL BE HERE ANY MINUTE.

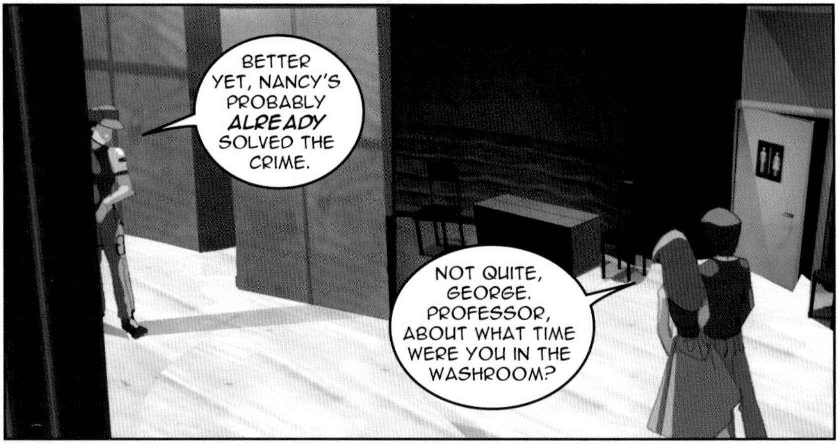
BETTER YET, NANCY'S PROBABLY ALREADY SOLVED THE CRIME.
NOT QUITE, GEORGE. PROFESSOR, ABOUT WHAT TIME WERE YOU IN THE WASHROOM?

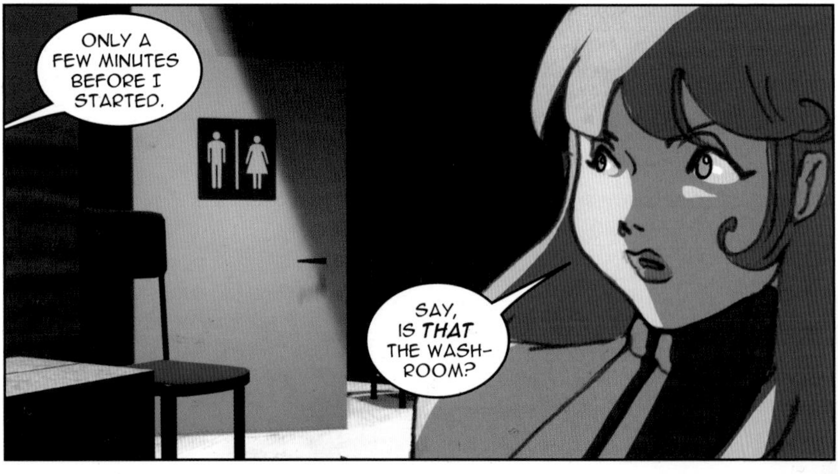
ONLY A FEW MINUTES BEFORE I STARTED.
SAY, IS THAT THE WASH-ROOM?

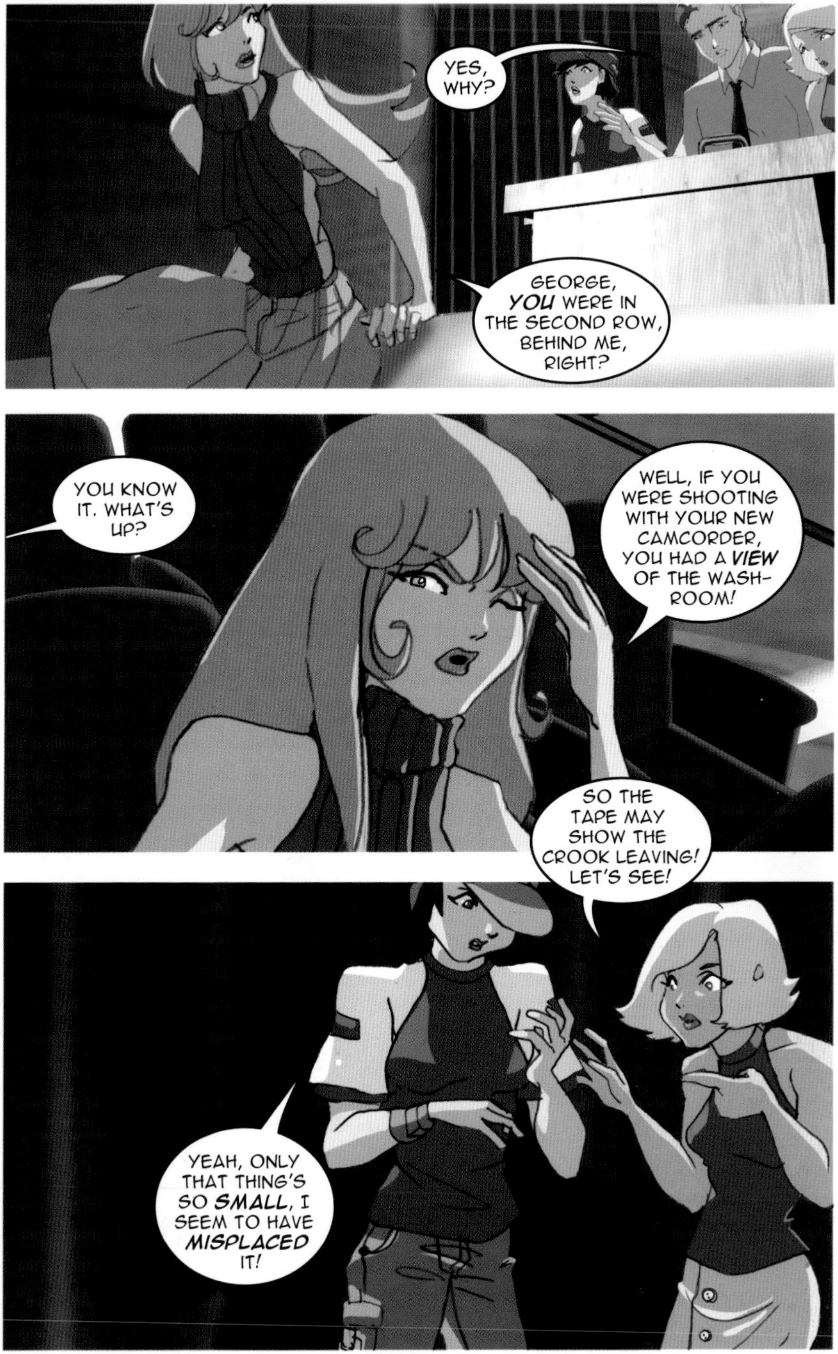
YES, WHY?
GEORGE, YOU WERE IN THE SECOND ROW, BEHIND ME, RIGHT?
YOU KNOW IT. WHAT'S UP?
WELL, IF YOU WERE SHOOTING WITH YOUR NEW CAMCORDER, YOU HAD A VIEW OF THE WASH-ROOM!
SO THE TAPE MAY SHOW THE CROOK LEAVING! LET'S SEE!
YEAH, ONLY THAT THING'S SO SMALL, I SEEM TO HAVE MISPLACED IT!

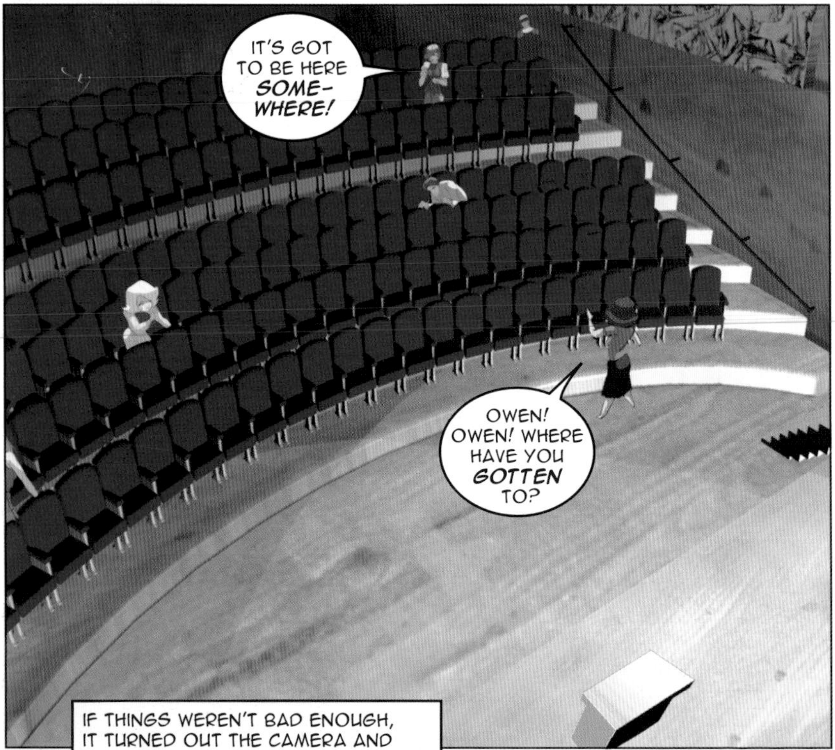
IT'S GOT TO BE HERE *SOME-WHERE!*
OWEN! OWEN! WHERE HAVE YOU *GOTTEN* TO?
IF THINGS WEREN'T BAD ENOUGH, IT TURNED OUT THE CAMERA AND THE SHORE STONE MARKER WEREN'T THE *ONLY* THINGS MISSING...

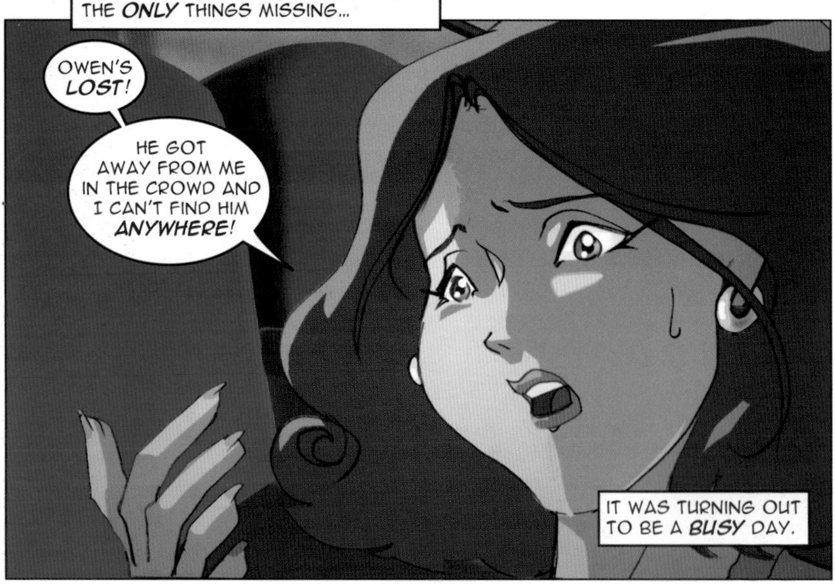
OWEN'S *LOST!*
HE GOT AWAY FROM ME IN THE CROWD AND I CAN'T FIND HIM *ANYWHERE!*
IT WAS TURNING OUT TO BE A *BUSY* DAY.

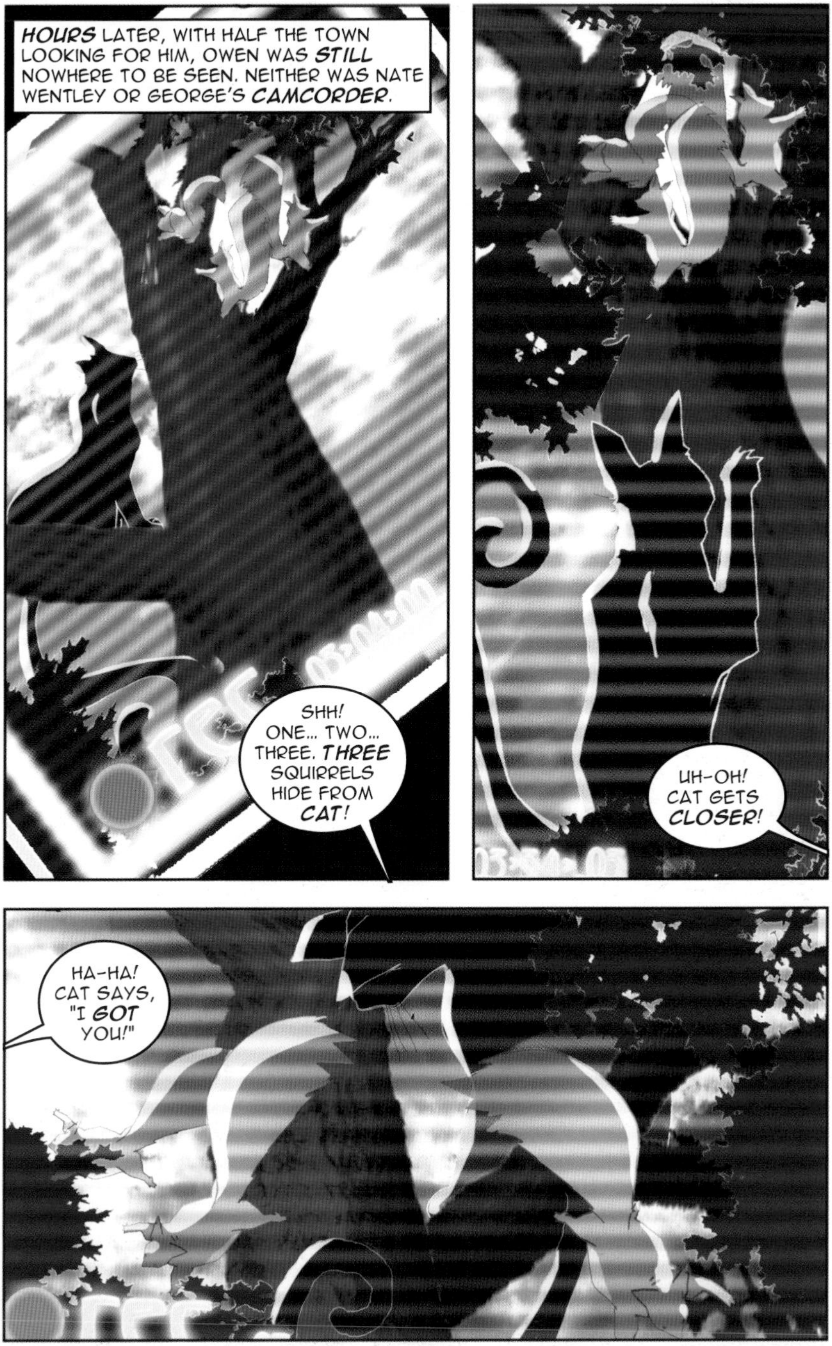
HOURS LATER, WITH HALF THE TOWN LOOKING FOR HIM, OWEN WAS STILL NOWHERE TO BE SEEN. NEITHER WAS NATE WENTLEY OR GEORGE'S CAMCORDER.
SHH! ONE... TWO... THREE. THREE SQUIRRELS HIDE FROM CAT!
UH-OH! CAT GETS CLOSER!
HA-HA! CAT SAYS, "I GOT YOU!"

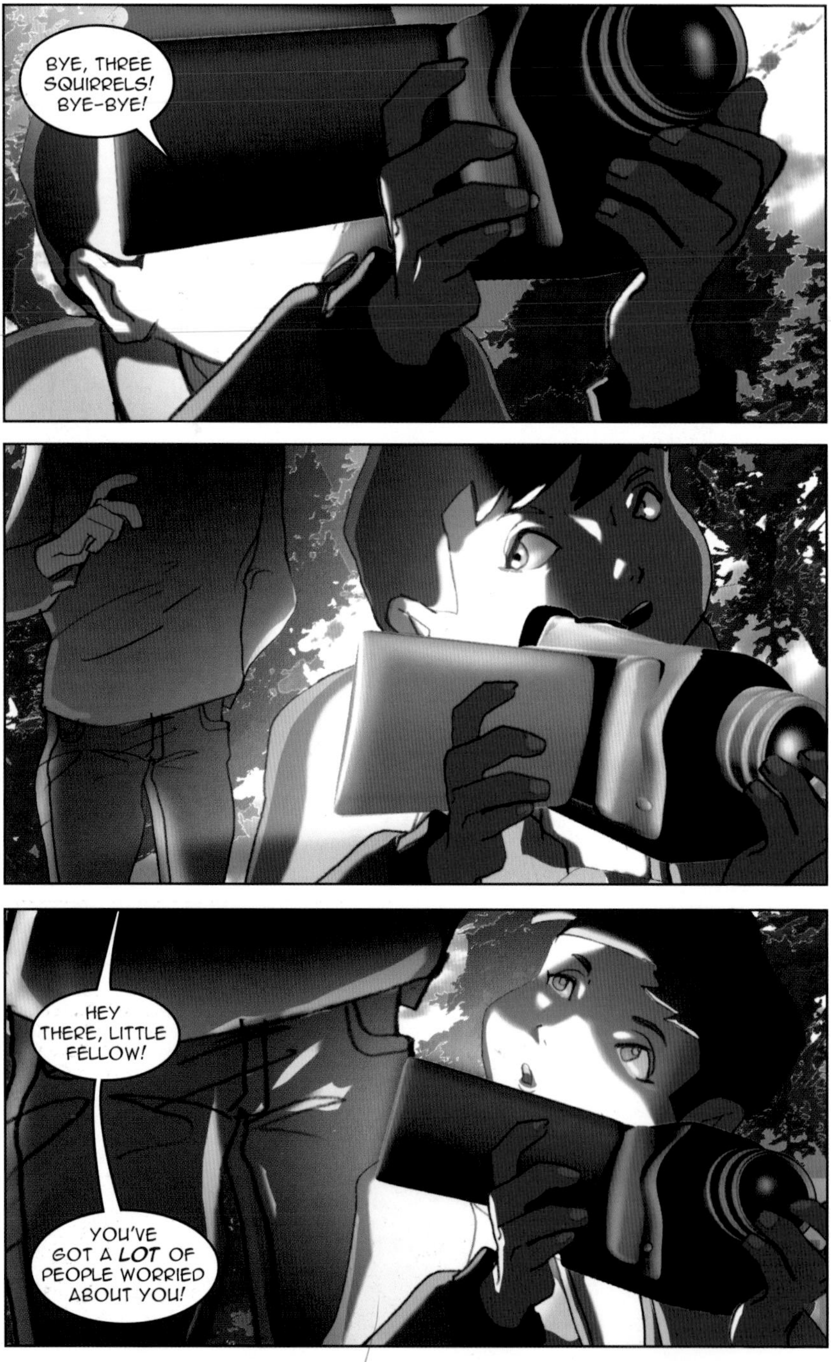
BYE, THREE SQUIRRELS! BYE-BYE!
HEY THERE, LITTLE FELLOW!
YOU'VE GOT A ***LOT*** OF PEOPLE WORRIED ABOUT YOU!

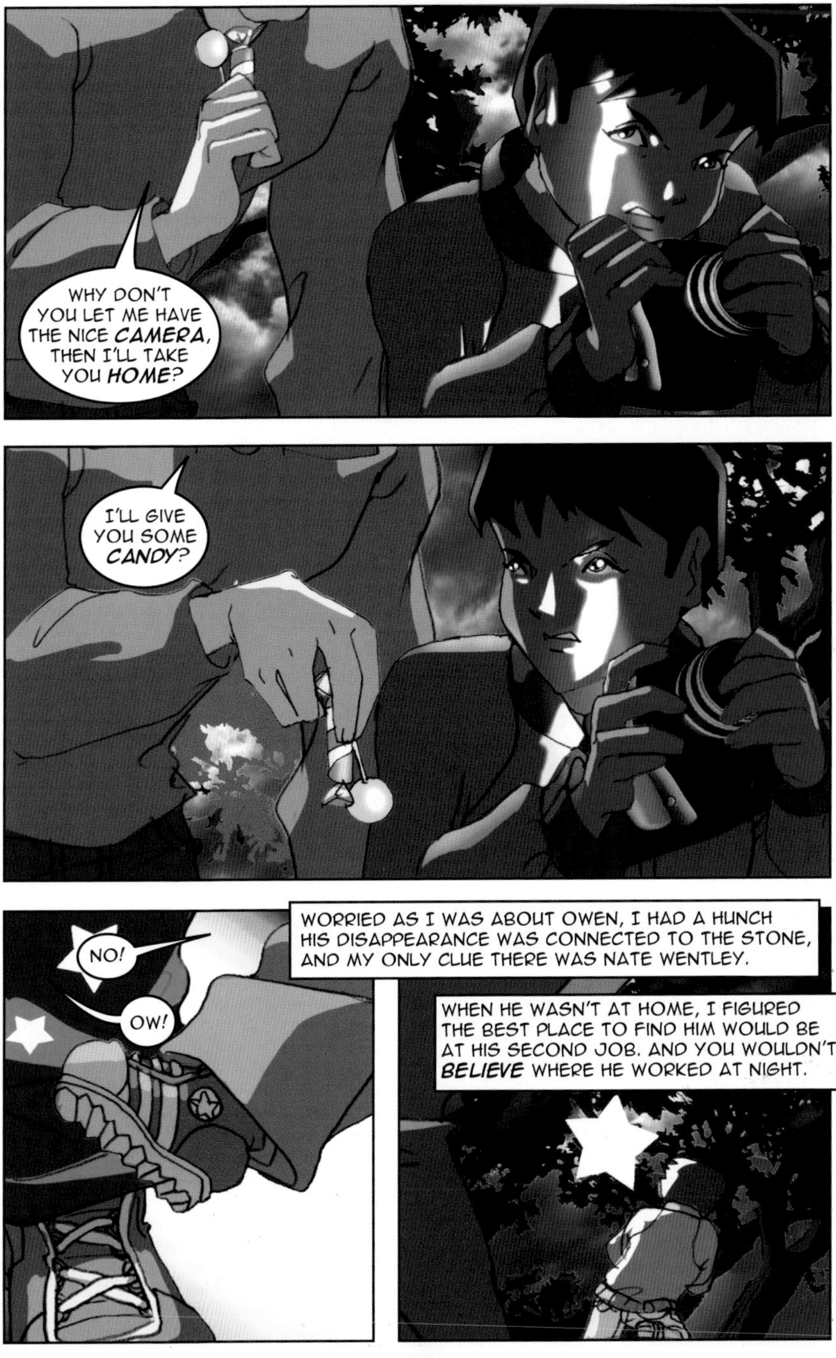
WHY DON'T YOU LET ME HAVE THE NICE CAMERA, THEN I'LL TAKE YOU HOME?
I'LL GIVE YOU SOME CANDY?
NO!
OW!
WORRIED AS I WAS ABOUT OWEN, I HAD A HUNCH HIS DISAPPEARANCE WAS CONNECTED TO THE STONE, AND MY ONLY CLUE THERE WAS NATE WENTLEY.
WHEN HE WASN'T AT HOME, I FIGURED THE BEST PLACE TO FIND HIM WOULD BE AT HIS SECOND JOB. AND YOU WOULDN'T BELIEVE WHERE HE WORKED AT NIGHT.

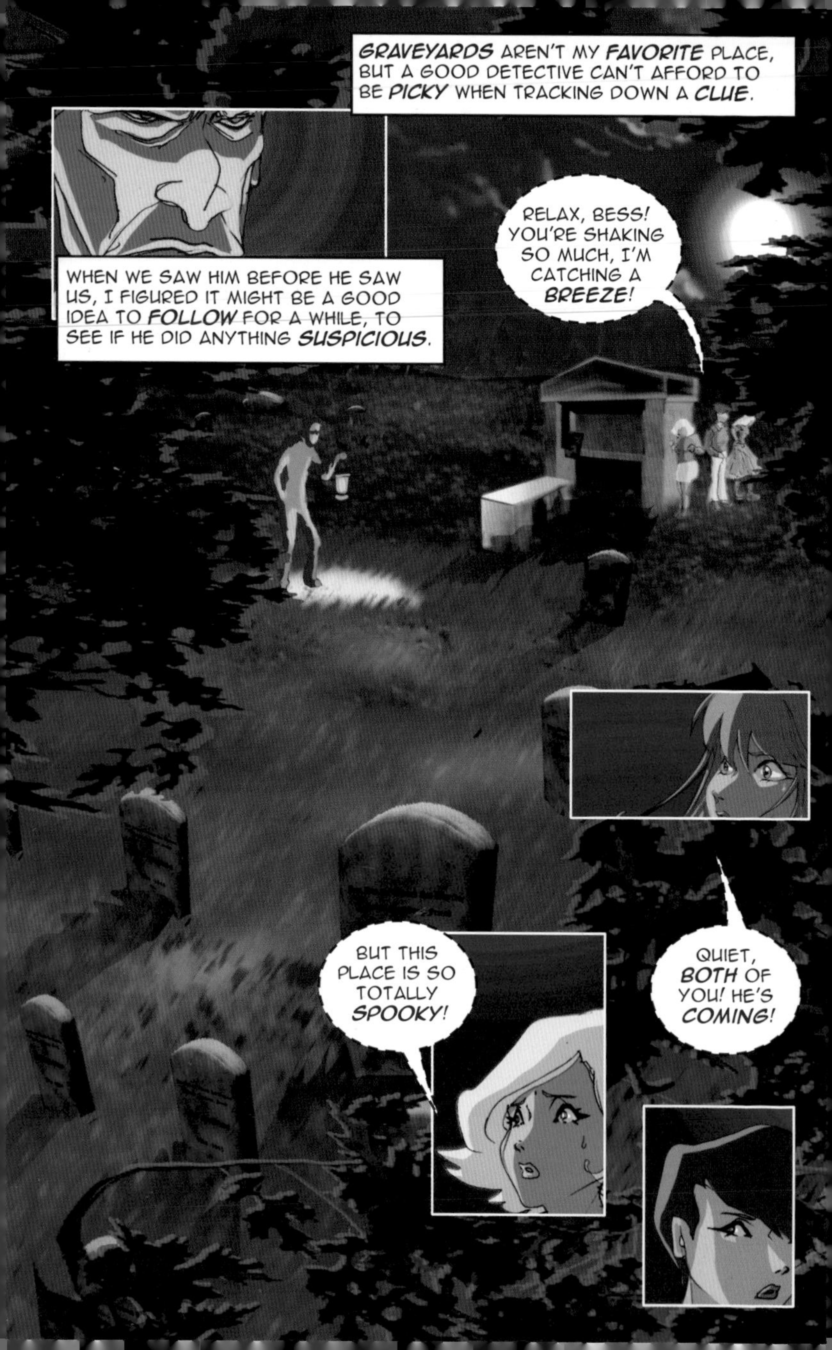
GRAVEYARDS AREN'T MY FAVORITE PLACE, BUT A GOOD DETECTIVE CAN'T AFFORD TO BE PICKY WHEN TRACKING DOWN A CLUE.
WHEN WE SAW HIM BEFORE HE SAW US, I FIGURED IT MIGHT BE A GOOD IDEA TO FOLLOW FOR A WHILE, TO SEE IF HE DID ANYTHING SUSPICIOUS.
RELAX, BESS! YOU'RE SHAKING SO MUCH, I'M CATCHING A BREEZE!
BUT THIS PLACE IS SO TOTALLY SPOOKY!
QUIET, BOTH OF YOU! HE'S COMING!

HE HAD A LIGHT STEP, BUT I COULD HEAR EARTH CRUNCH BENEATH HIS FEET, AND THE LIGHT FROM HIS LANTERN SWAYED AS HE MOVED.

SO I COULD KIND OF TELL *WHERE* HE WAS.

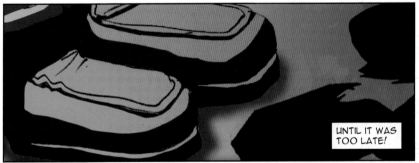

UNTIL THE SOUNDS JUST *STOPPED!*

AND I COULDN'T FIGURE OUT *WHY*...

UNTIL IT WAS TOO LATE!

AHHHH!

AHHHH!

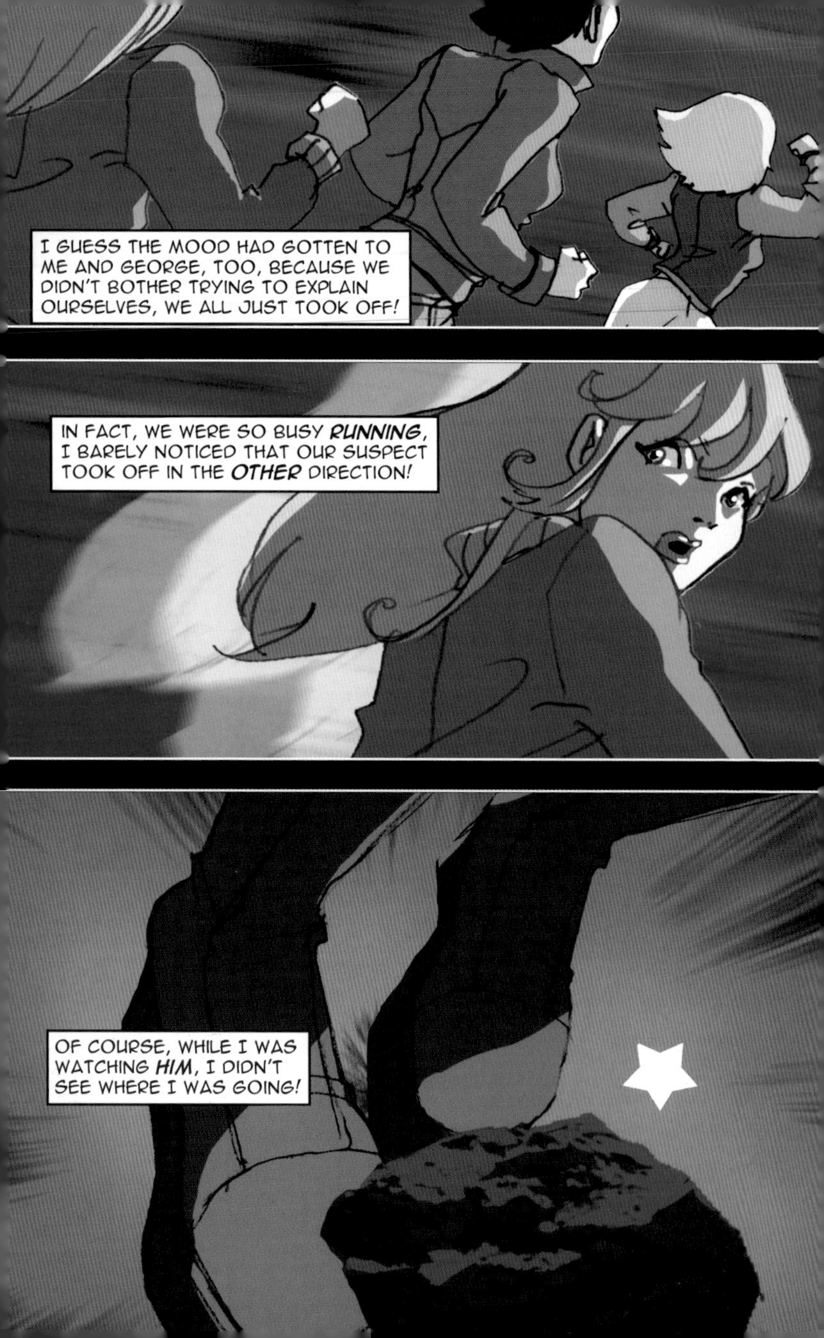
I GUESS THE MOOD HAD GOTTEN TO ME AND GEORGE, TOO, BECAUSE WE DIDN'T BOTHER TRYING TO EXPLAIN OURSELVES, WE ALL JUST TOOK OFF!
IN FACT, WE WERE SO BUSY RUNNING, I BARELY NOTICED THAT OUR SUSPECT TOOK OFF IN THE OTHER DIRECTION!
OF COURSE, WHILE I WAS WATCHING HIM, I DIDN'T SEE WHERE I WAS GOING!

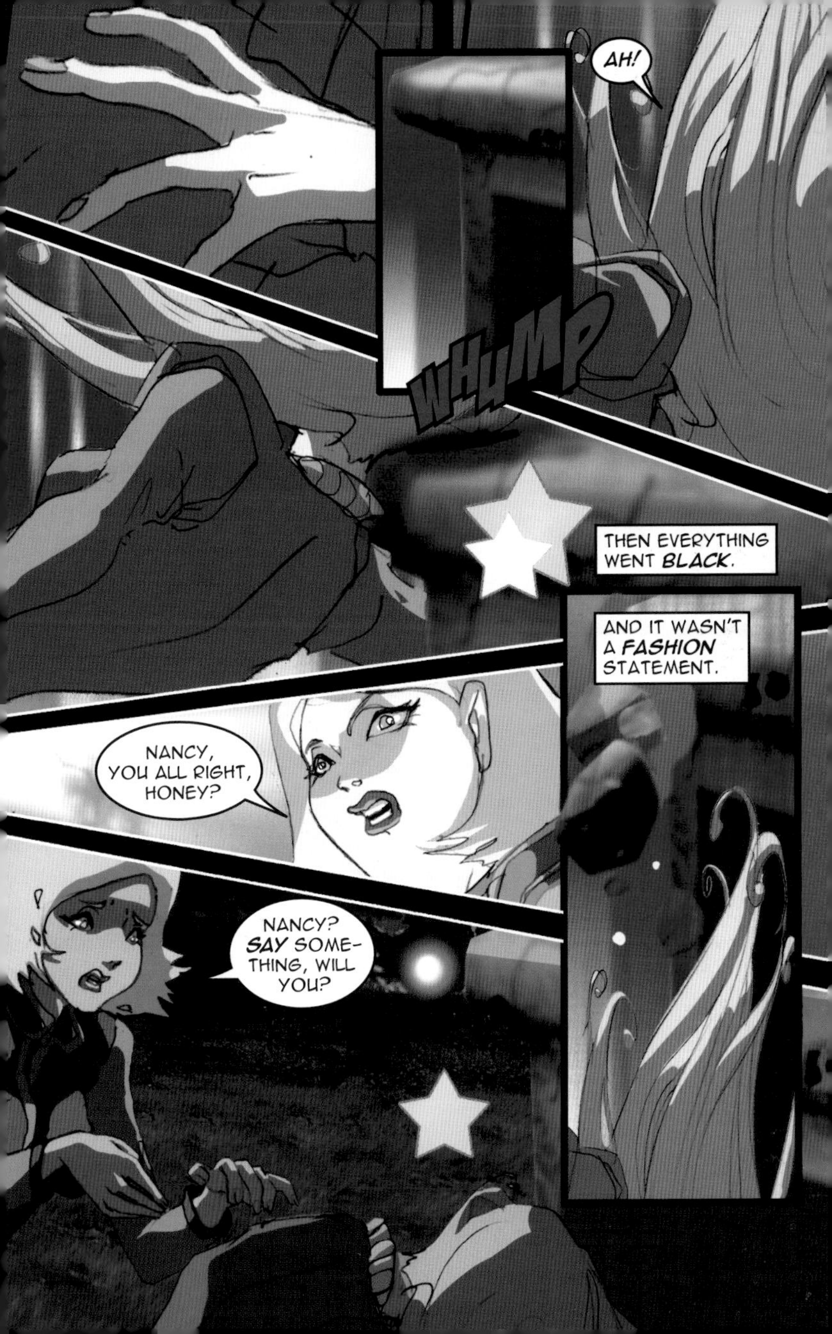
AH!
WHUMP
THEN EVERYTHING WENT BLACK.
AND IT WASN'T A FASHION STATEMENT.
NANCY, YOU ALL RIGHT, HONEY?
NANCY? SAY SOMETHING, WILL YOU?

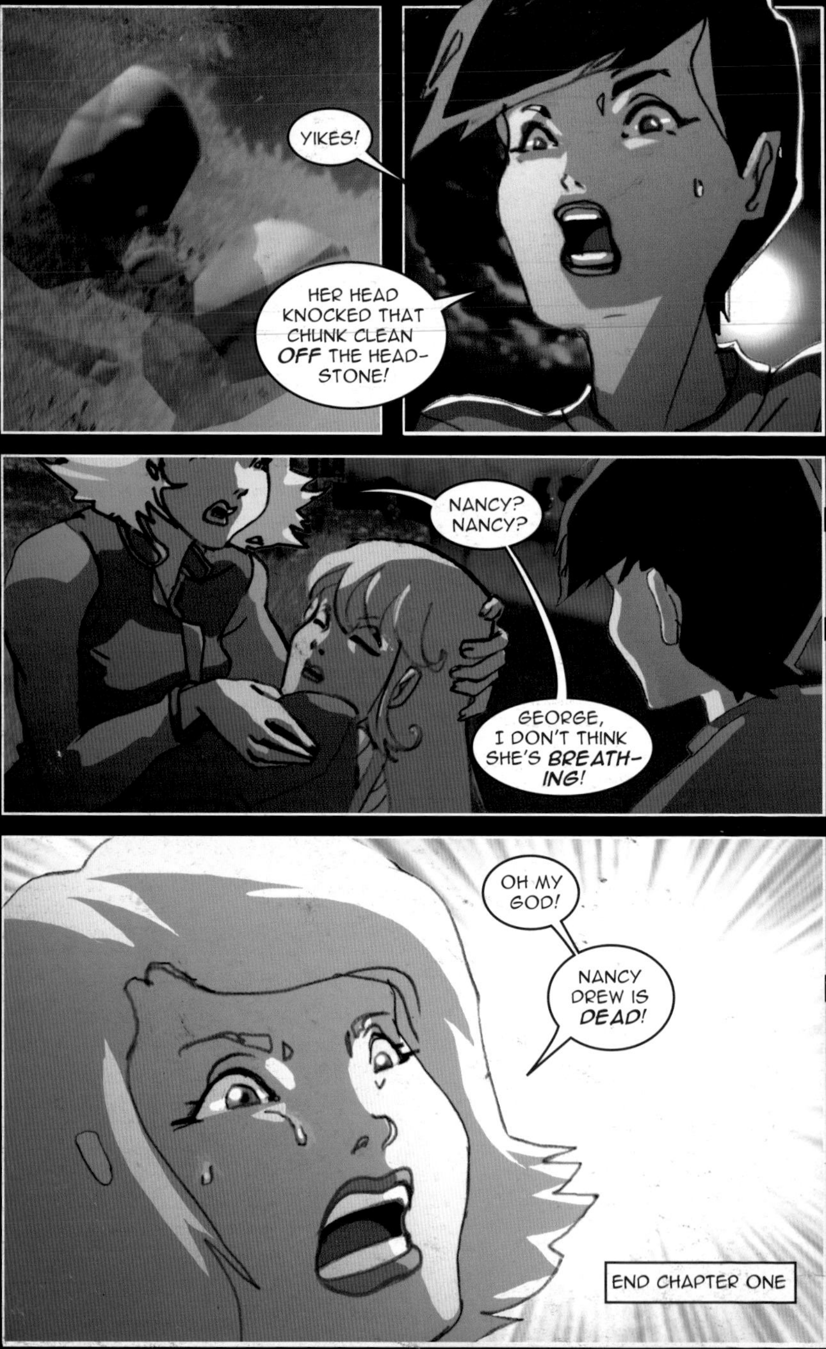
YIKES!
HER HEAD KNOCKED THAT CHUNK CLEAN OFF THE HEAD-STONE!
NANCY? NANCY?
GEORGE, I DON'T THINK SHE'S BREATH-ING!
OH MY GOD!
NANCY DREW IS DEAD!
END CHAPTER ONE

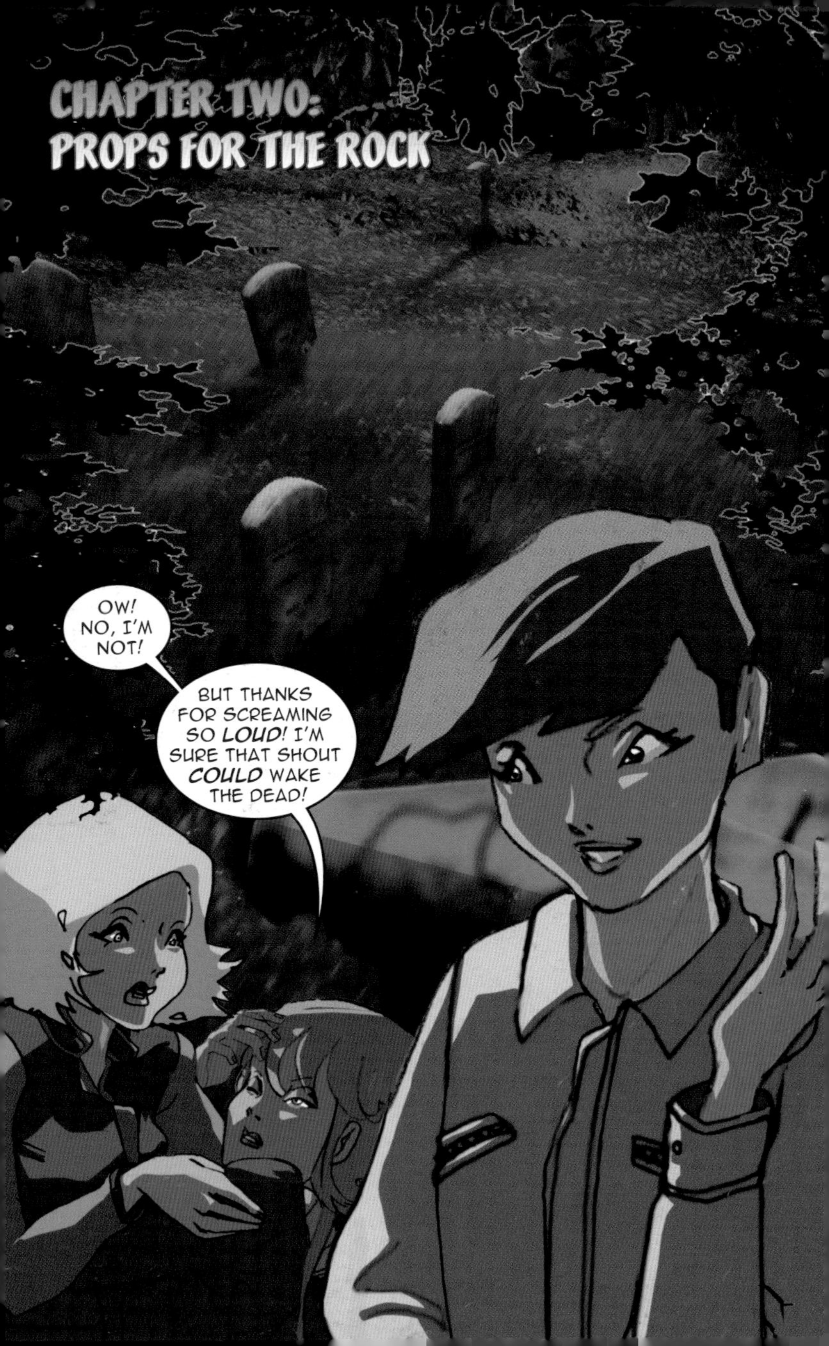
CHAPTER TWO:
PROPS FOR THE ROCK
OW! NO, I'M NOT!
BUT THANKS FOR SCREAMING SO LOUD! I'M SURE THAT SHOUT COULD WAKE THE DEAD!

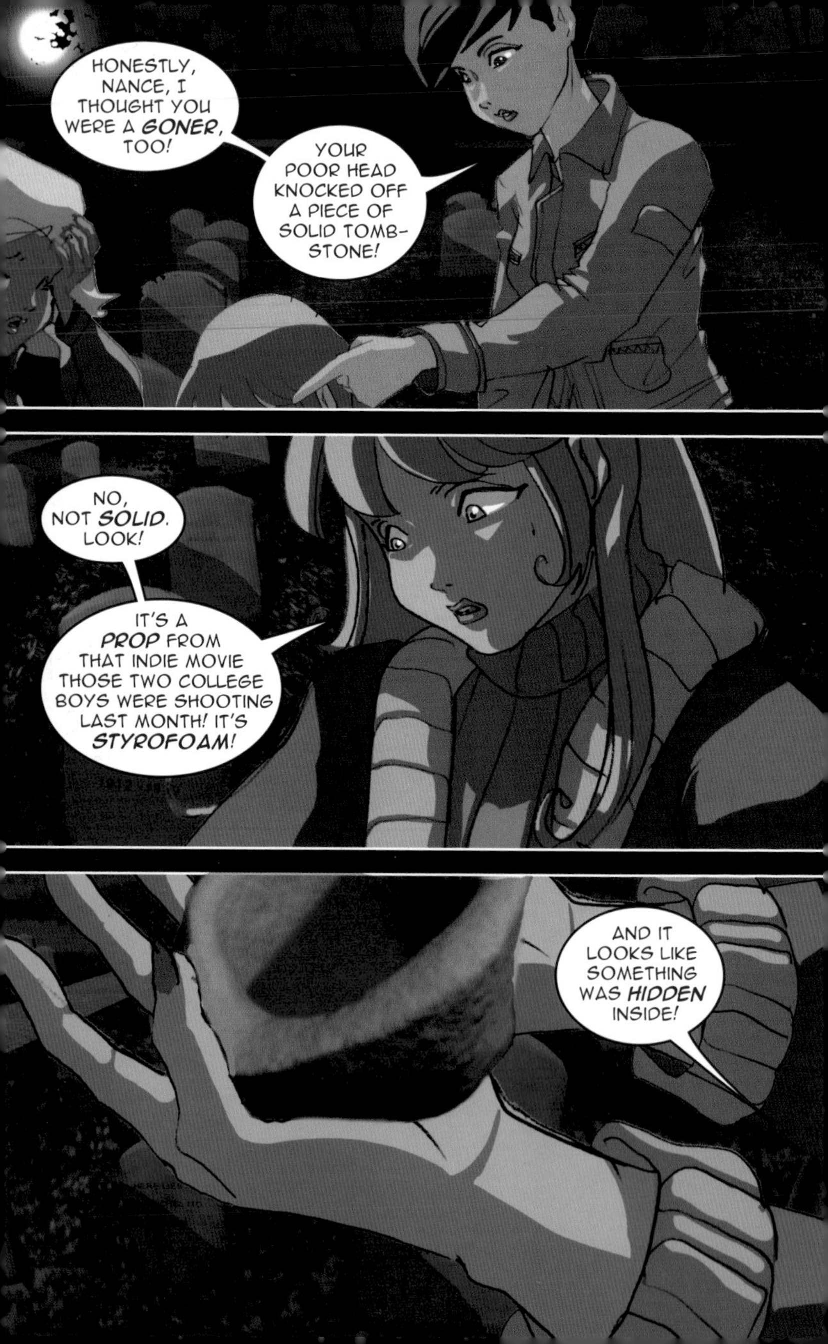
HONESTLY, NANCE, I THOUGHT YOU WERE A GONER, TOO!
YOUR POOR HEAD KNOCKED OFF A PIECE OF SOLID TOMB-STONE!
NO, NOT SOLID. LOOK!
IT'S A PROP FROM THAT INDIE MOVIE THOSE TWO COLLEGE BOYS WERE SHOOTING LAST MONTH! IT'S STYROFOAM!
AND IT LOOKS LIKE SOMETHING WAS HIDDEN INSIDE!

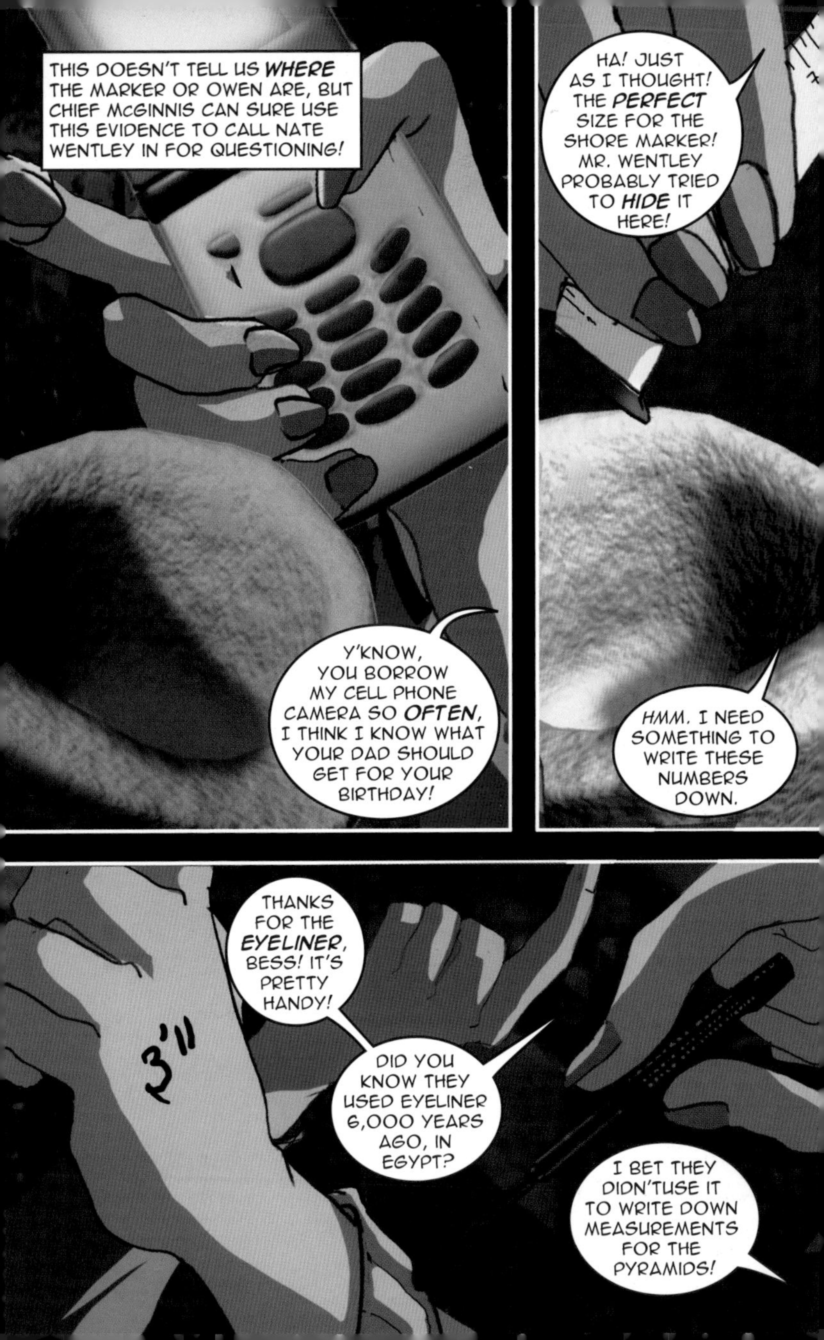
THIS DOESN'T TELL US WHERE THE MARKER OR OWEN ARE, BUT CHIEF McGINNIS CAN SURE USE THIS EVIDENCE TO CALL NATE WENTLEY IN FOR QUESTIONING!
Y'KNOW, YOU BORROW MY CELL PHONE CAMERA SO OFTEN, I THINK I KNOW WHAT YOUR DAD SHOULD GET FOR YOUR BIRTHDAY!
HA! JUST AS I THOUGHT! THE PERFECT SIZE FOR THE SHORE MARKER! MR. WENTLEY PROBABLY TRIED TO HIDE IT HERE!
HMM. I NEED SOMETHING TO WRITE THESE NUMBERS DOWN.
THANKS FOR THE EYELINER, BESS! IT'S PRETTY HANDY!
3'11
DID YOU KNOW THEY USED EYELINER 6,000 YEARS AGO, IN EGYPT?
I BET THEY DIDN'T USE IT TO WRITE DOWN MEASUREMENTS FOR THE PYRAMIDS!

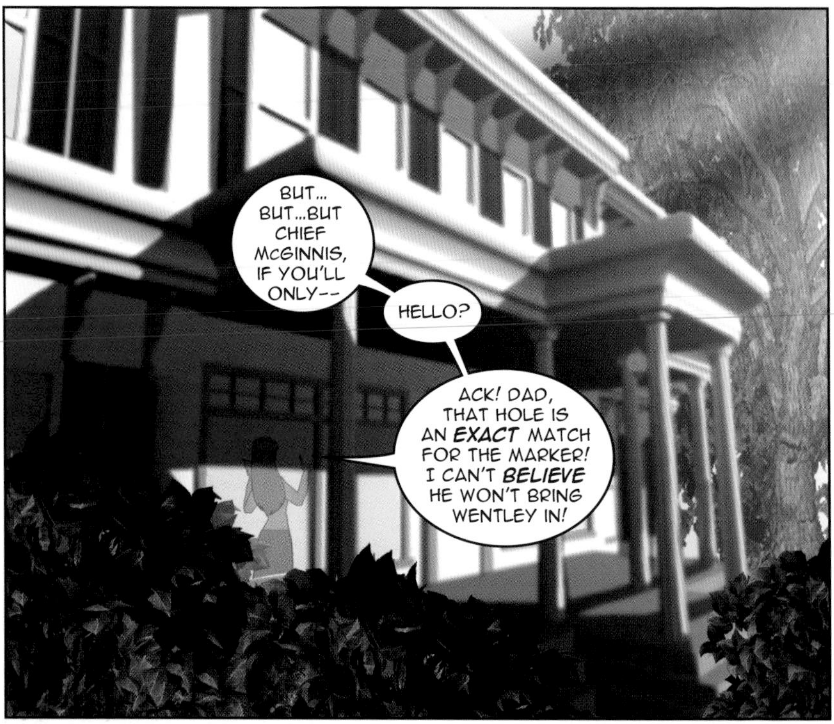
BUT... BUT...BUT CHIEF McGINNIS, IF YOU'LL ONLY--
HELLO?
ACK! DAD, THAT HOLE IS AN EXACT MATCH FOR THE MARKER! I CAN'T BELIEVE HE WON'T BRING WENTLEY IN!

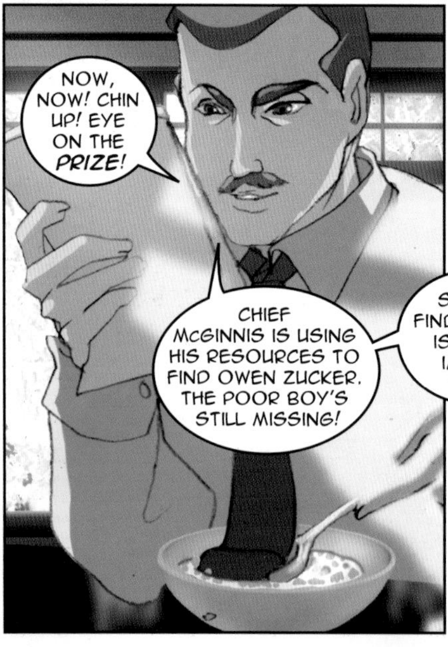
NOW, NOW! CHIN UP! EYE ON THE PRIZE!
CHIEF McGINNIS IS USING HIS RESOURCES TO FIND OWEN ZUCKER. THE POOR BOY'S STILL MISSING!
SURELY FINDING HIM IS MORE IMPOR-TANT!

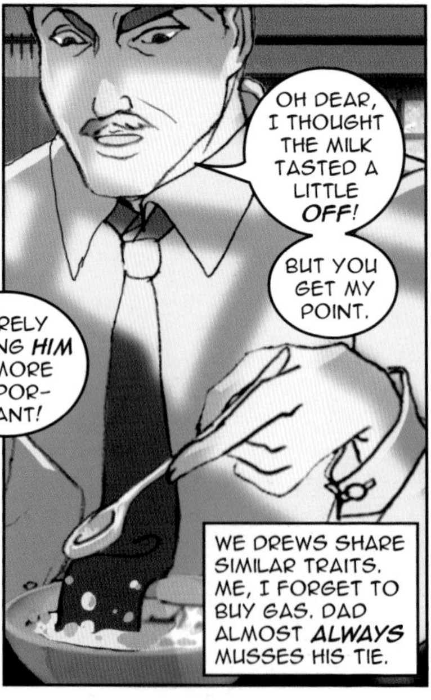
OH DEAR, I THOUGHT THE MILK TASTED A LITTLE OFF!
BUT YOU GET MY POINT.
WE DREWS SHARE SIMILAR TRAITS. ME, I FORGET TO BUY GAS. DAD ALMOST ALWAYS MUSSES HIS TIE.

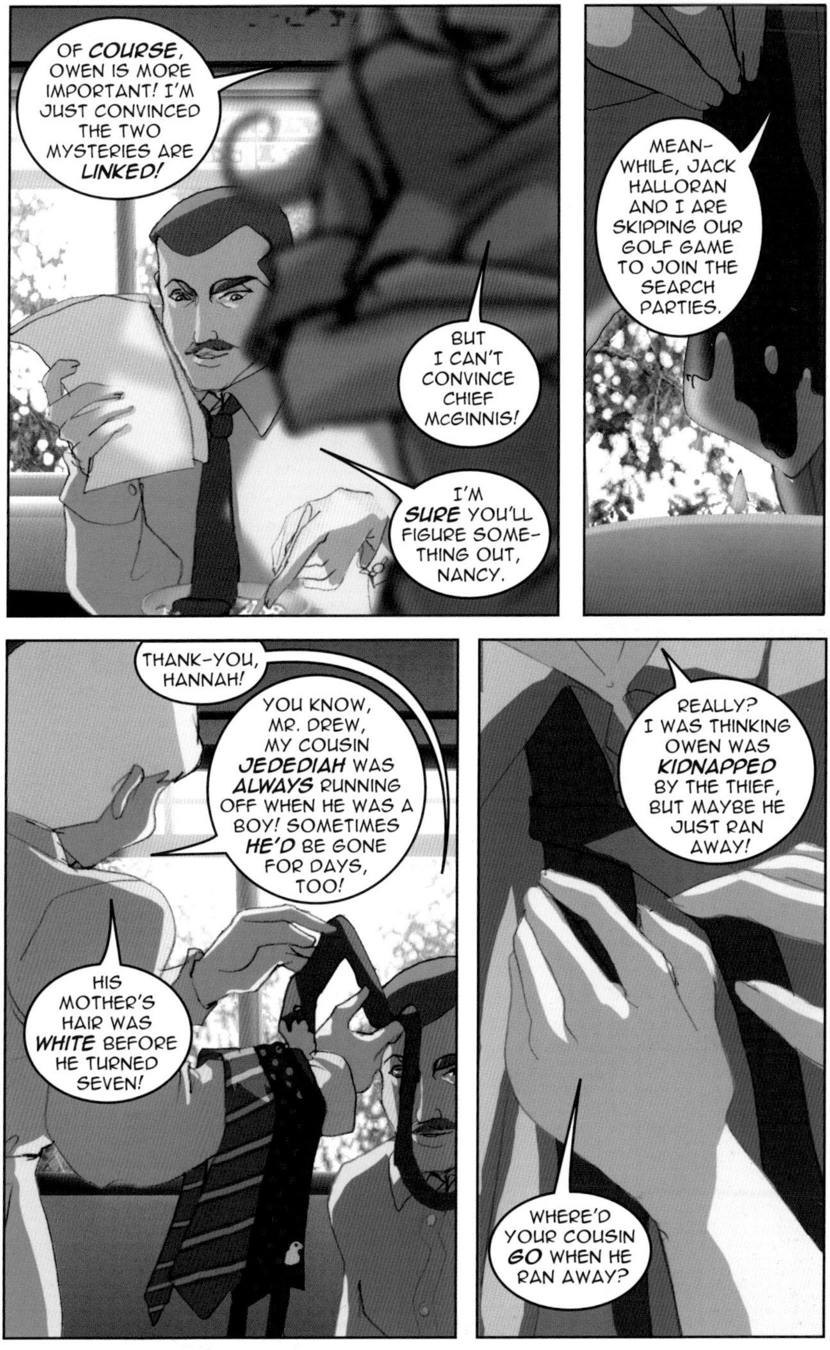

OF COURSE, OWEN IS MORE IMPORTANT! I'M JUST CONVINCED THE TWO MYSTERIES ARE LINKED!
BUT I CAN'T CONVINCE CHIEF MCGINNIS!
I'M SURE YOU'LL FIGURE SOME-THING OUT, NANCY.
MEAN-WHILE, JACK HALLORAN AND I ARE SKIPPING OUR GOLF GAME TO JOIN THE SEARCH PARTIES.
THANK-YOU, HANNAH!
YOU KNOW, MR. DREW, MY COUSIN JEDEDIAH WAS ALWAYS RUNNING OFF WHEN HE WAS A BOY! SOMETIMES HE'D BE GONE FOR DAYS, TOO!
HIS MOTHER'S HAIR WAS WHITE BEFORE HE TURNED SEVEN!
REALLY? I WAS THINKING OWEN WAS KIDNAPPED BY THE THIEF, BUT MAYBE HE JUST RAN AWAY!
WHERE'D YOUR COUSIN GO WHEN HE RAN AWAY?

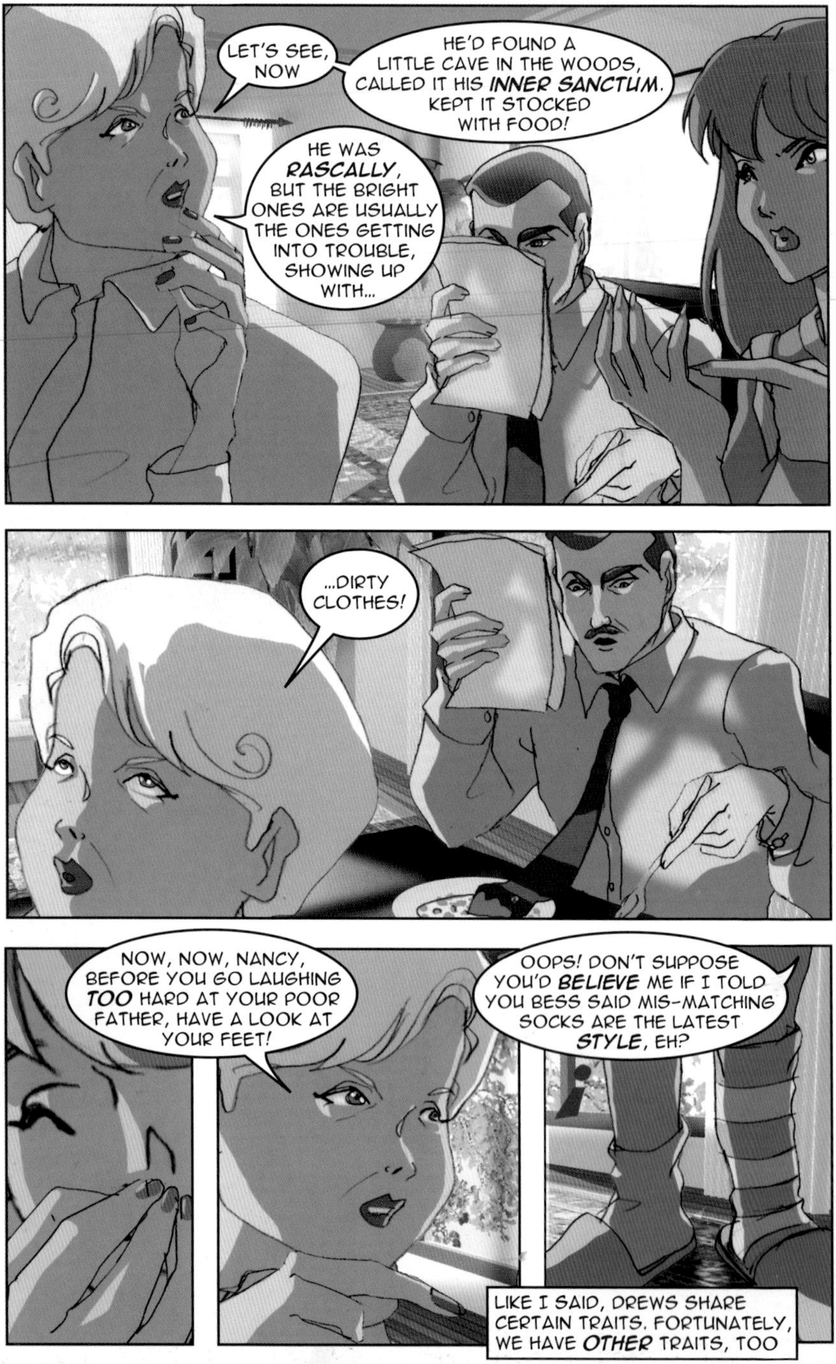
LET'S SEE, NOW
HE'D FOUND A LITTLE CAVE IN THE WOODS, CALLED IT HIS INNER SANCTUM. KEPT IT STOCKED WITH FOOD!
HE WAS RASCALLY, BUT THE BRIGHT ONES ARE USUALLY THE ONES GETTING INTO TROUBLE, SHOWING UP WITH...
...DIRTY CLOTHES!
NOW, NOW, NANCY, BEFORE YOU GO LAUGHING TOO HARD AT YOUR POOR FATHER, HAVE A LOOK AT YOUR FEET!
OOPS! DON'T SUPPOSE YOU'D BELIEVE ME IF I TOLD YOU BESS SAID MIS-MATCHING SOCKS ARE THE LATEST STYLE, EH?
LIKE I SAID, DREWS SHARE CERTAIN TRAITS. FORTUNATELY, WE HAVE OTHER TRAITS, TOO

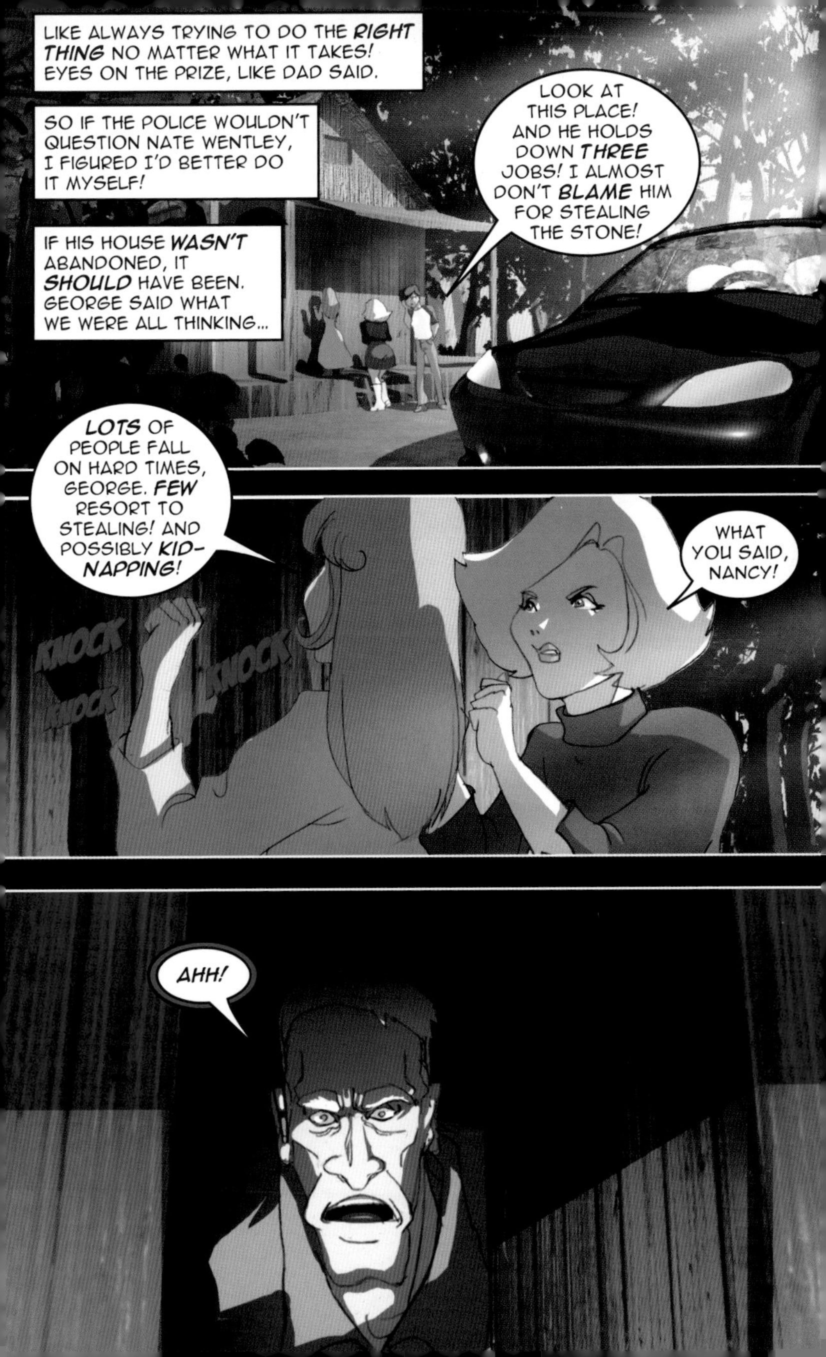
LIKE ALWAYS TRYING TO DO THE RIGHT THING NO MATTER WHAT IT TAKES! EYES ON THE PRIZE, LIKE DAD SAID.
SO IF THE POLICE WOULDN'T QUESTION NATE WENTLEY, I FIGURED I'D BETTER DO IT MYSELF!
IF HIS HOUSE WASN'T ABANDONED, IT SHOULD HAVE BEEN. GEORGE SAID WHAT WE WERE ALL THINKING...
LOOK AT THIS PLACE! AND HE HOLDS DOWN THREE JOBS! I ALMOST DON'T BLAME HIM FOR STEALING THE STONE!
LOTS OF PEOPLE FALL ON HARD TIMES, GEORGE. FEW RESORT TO STEALING! AND POSSIBLY KID-NAPPING!
WHAT YOU SAID, NANCY!
KNOCK KNOCK KNOCK
AHH!

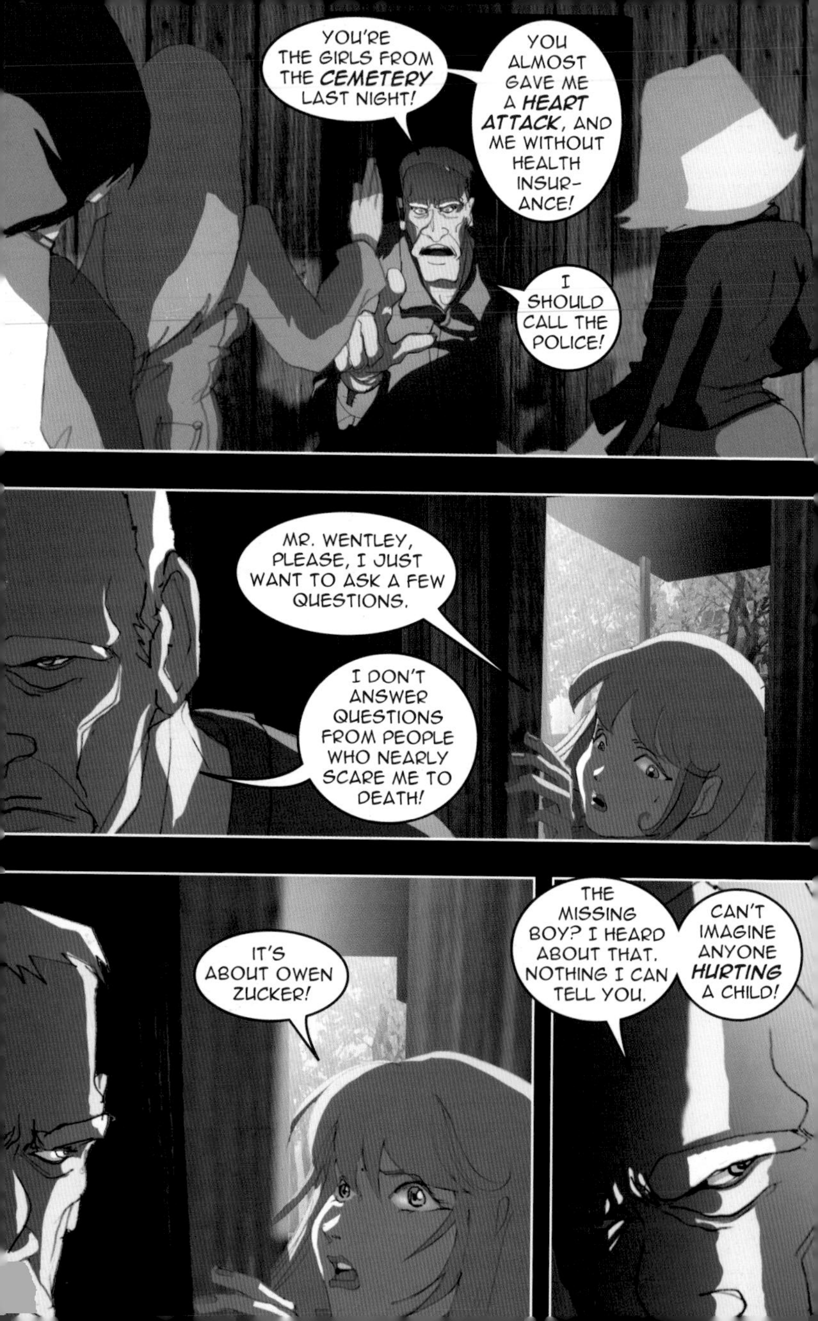
YOU'RE THE GIRLS FROM THE *CEMETERY* LAST NIGHT!
YOU ALMOST GAVE ME A ***HEART ATTACK***, AND ME WITHOUT HEALTH INSUR-ANCE!
I SHOULD CALL THE POLICE!
MR. WENTLEY, PLEASE, I JUST WANT TO ASK A FEW QUESTIONS.
I DON'T ANSWER QUESTIONS FROM PEOPLE WHO NEARLY SCARE ME TO DEATH!
IT'S ABOUT OWEN ZUCKER!
THE MISSING BOY? I HEARD ABOUT THAT. NOTHING I CAN TELL YOU.
CAN'T IMAGINE ANYONE ***HURTING*** A CHILD!

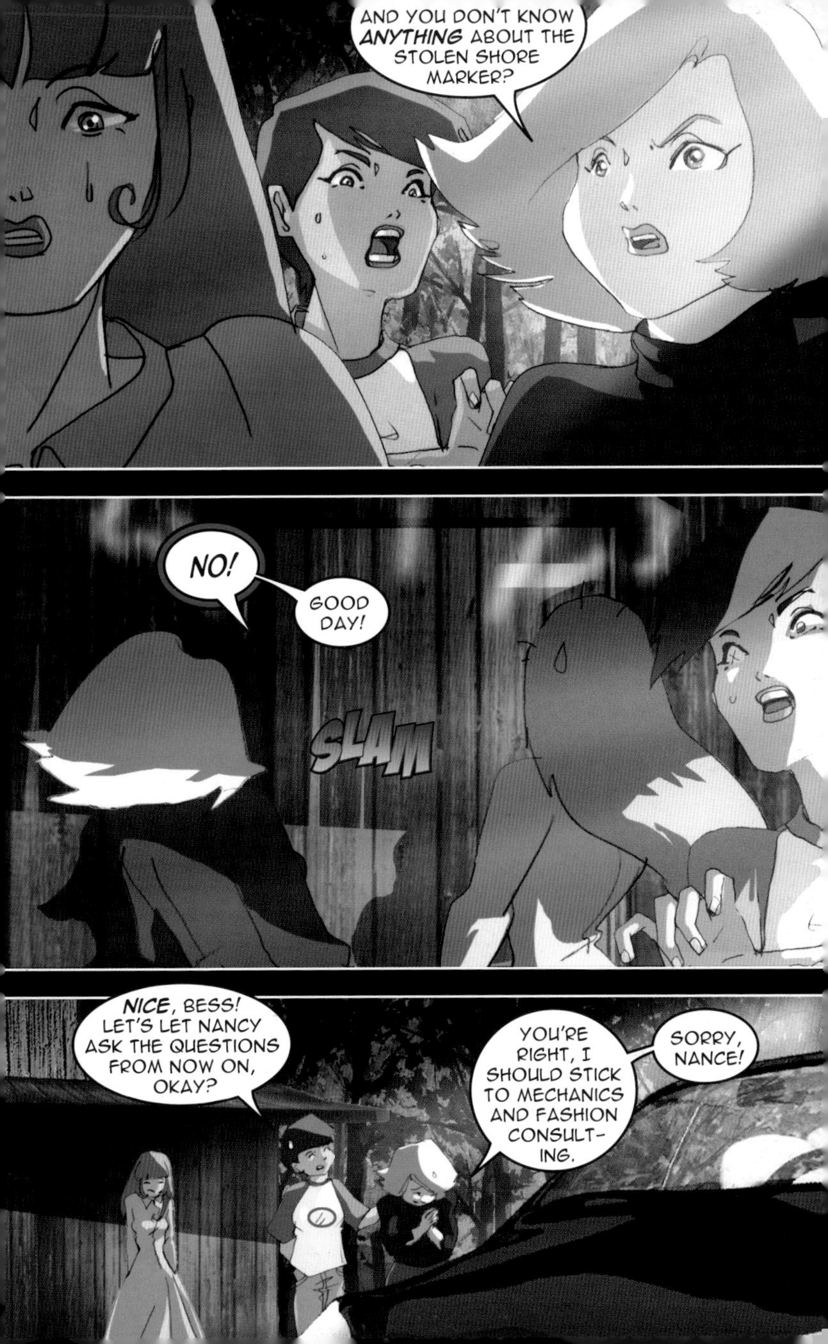
AND YOU DON'T KNOW ANYTHING ABOUT THE STOLEN SHORE MARKER?
NO!
GOOD DAY!
SLAM
NICE, BESS! LET'S LET NANCY ASK THE QUESTIONS FROM NOW ON, OKAY?
SORRY, NANCE!
YOU'RE RIGHT, I SHOULD STICK TO MECHANICS AND FASHION CONSULT-ING.

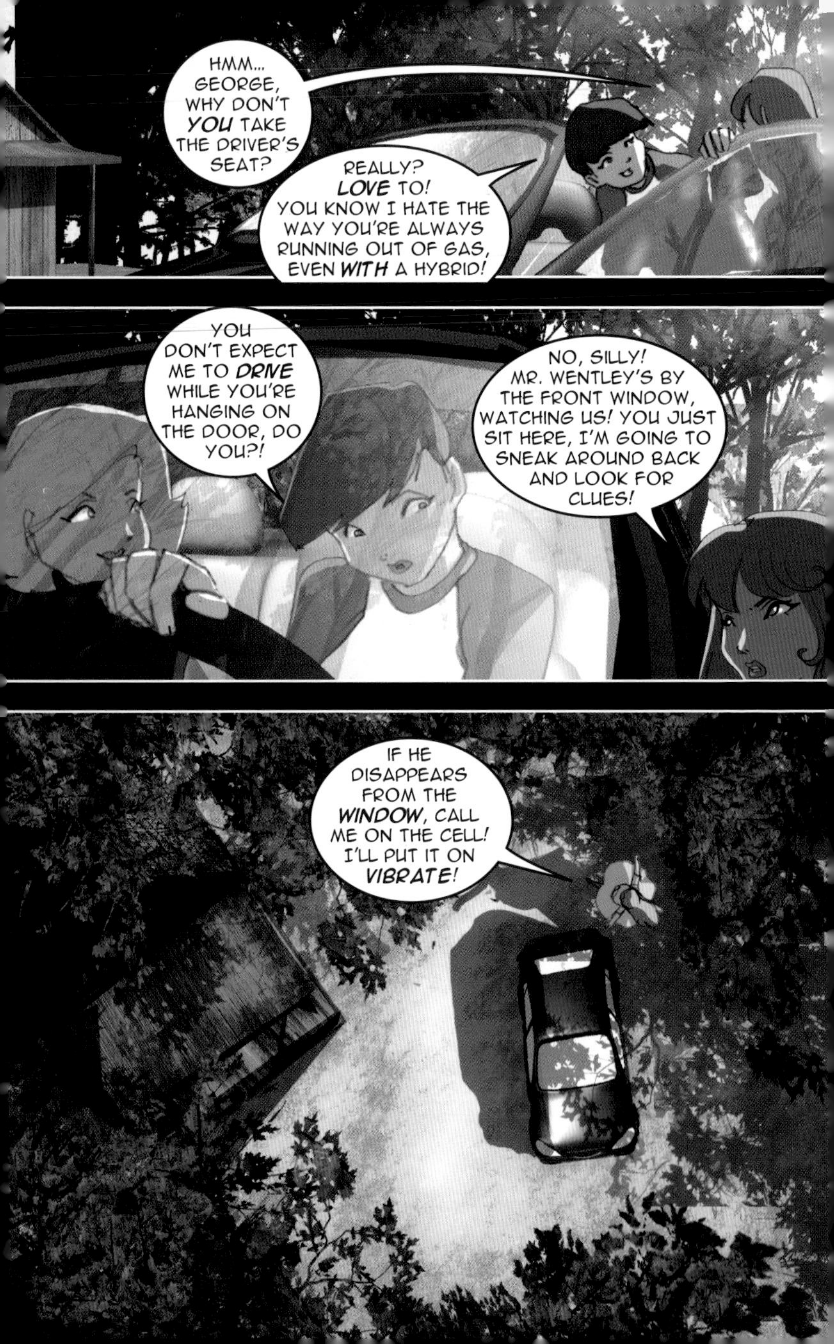
HMM... GEORGE, WHY DON'T YOU TAKE THE DRIVER'S SEAT?
REALLY? LOVE TO! YOU KNOW I HATE THE WAY YOU'RE ALWAYS RUNNING OUT OF GAS, EVEN WITH A HYBRID!
YOU DON'T EXPECT ME TO DRIVE WHILE YOU'RE HANGING ON THE DOOR, DO YOU?!
NO, SILLY! MR. WENTLEY'S BY THE FRONT WINDOW, WATCHING US! YOU JUST SIT HERE, I'M GOING TO SNEAK AROUND BACK AND LOOK FOR CLUES!
IF HE DISAPPEARS FROM THE WINDOW, CALL ME ON THE CELL! I'LL PUT IT ON VIBRATE!

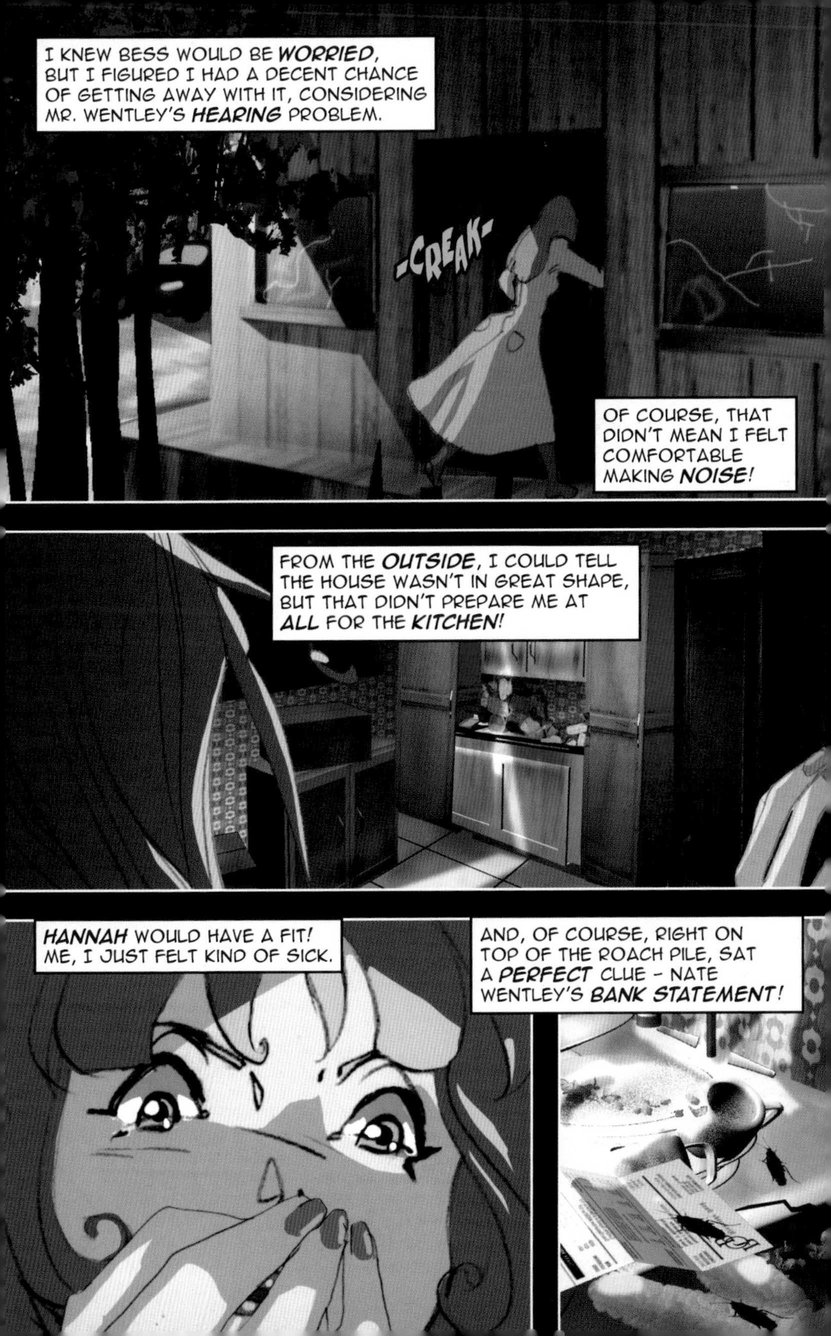
I KNEW BESS WOULD BE WORRIED, BUT I FIGURED I HAD A DECENT CHANCE OF GETTING AWAY WITH IT, CONSIDERING MR. WENTLEY'S HEARING PROBLEM.
-CREAK-
OF COURSE, THAT DIDN'T MEAN I FELT COMFORTABLE MAKING NOISE!
FROM THE OUTSIDE, I COULD TELL THE HOUSE WASN'T IN GREAT SHAPE, BUT THAT DIDN'T PREPARE ME AT ALL FOR THE KITCHEN!
HANNAH WOULD HAVE A FIT! ME, I JUST FELT KIND OF SICK.
AND, OF COURSE, RIGHT ON TOP OF THE ROACH PILE, SAT A PERFECT CLUE - NATE WENTLEY'S BANK STATEMENT!

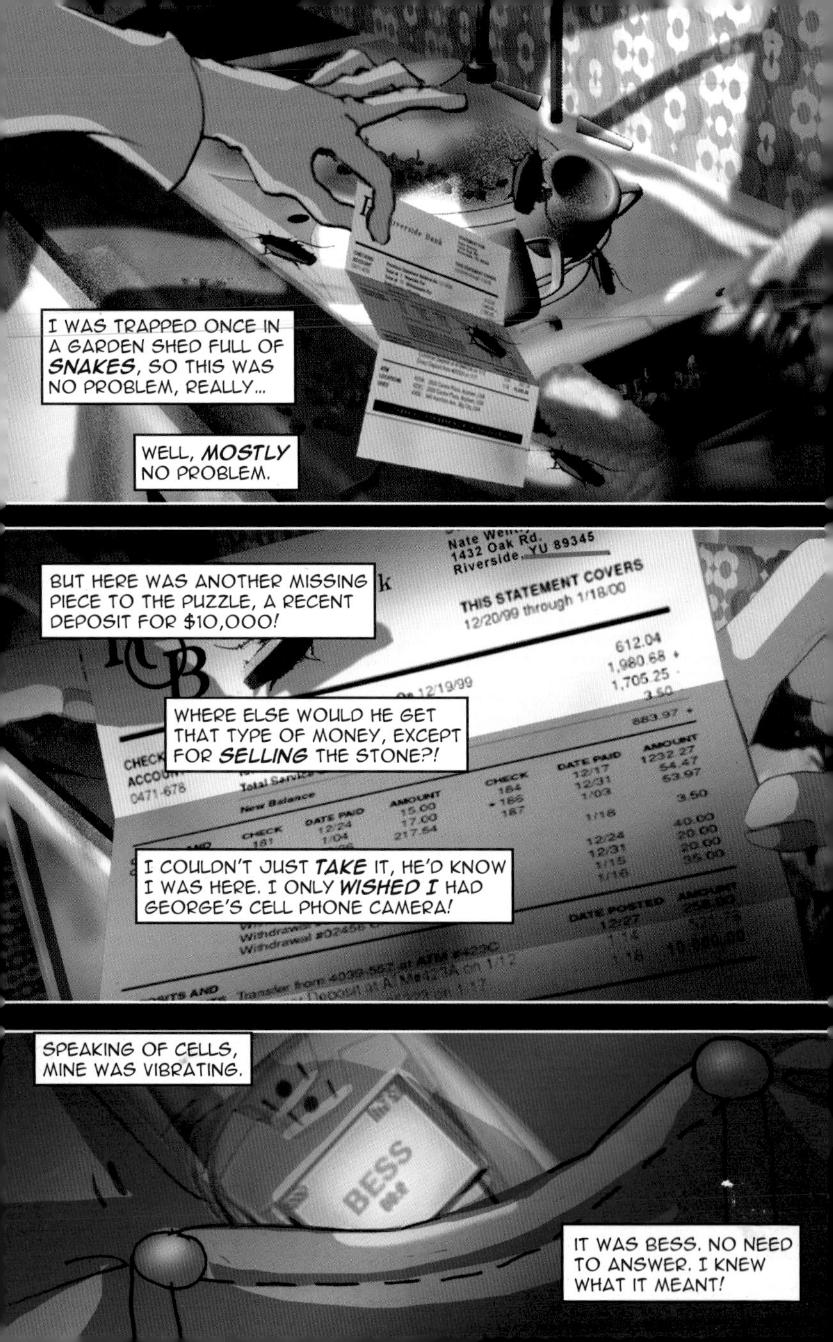
I WAS TRAPPED ONCE IN A GARDEN SHED FULL OF SNAKES, SO THIS WAS NO PROBLEM, REALLY...
WELL, MOSTLY NO PROBLEM.
BUT HERE WAS ANOTHER MISSING PIECE TO THE PUZZLE, A RECENT DEPOSIT FOR $10,000!
1432 Oak Rd.
THIS STATEMENT COVERS
12/20/99 through 1/18/00
WHERE ELSE WOULD HE GET THAT TYPE OF MONEY, EXCEPT FOR SELLING THE STONE?!
I COULDN'T JUST TAKE IT, HE'D KNOW I WAS HERE. I ONLY WISHED I HAD GEORGE'S CELL PHONE CAMERA!
SPEAKING OF CELLS, MINE WAS VIBRATING.
BESS
IT WAS BESS. NO NEED TO ANSWER. I KNEW WHAT IT MEANT!

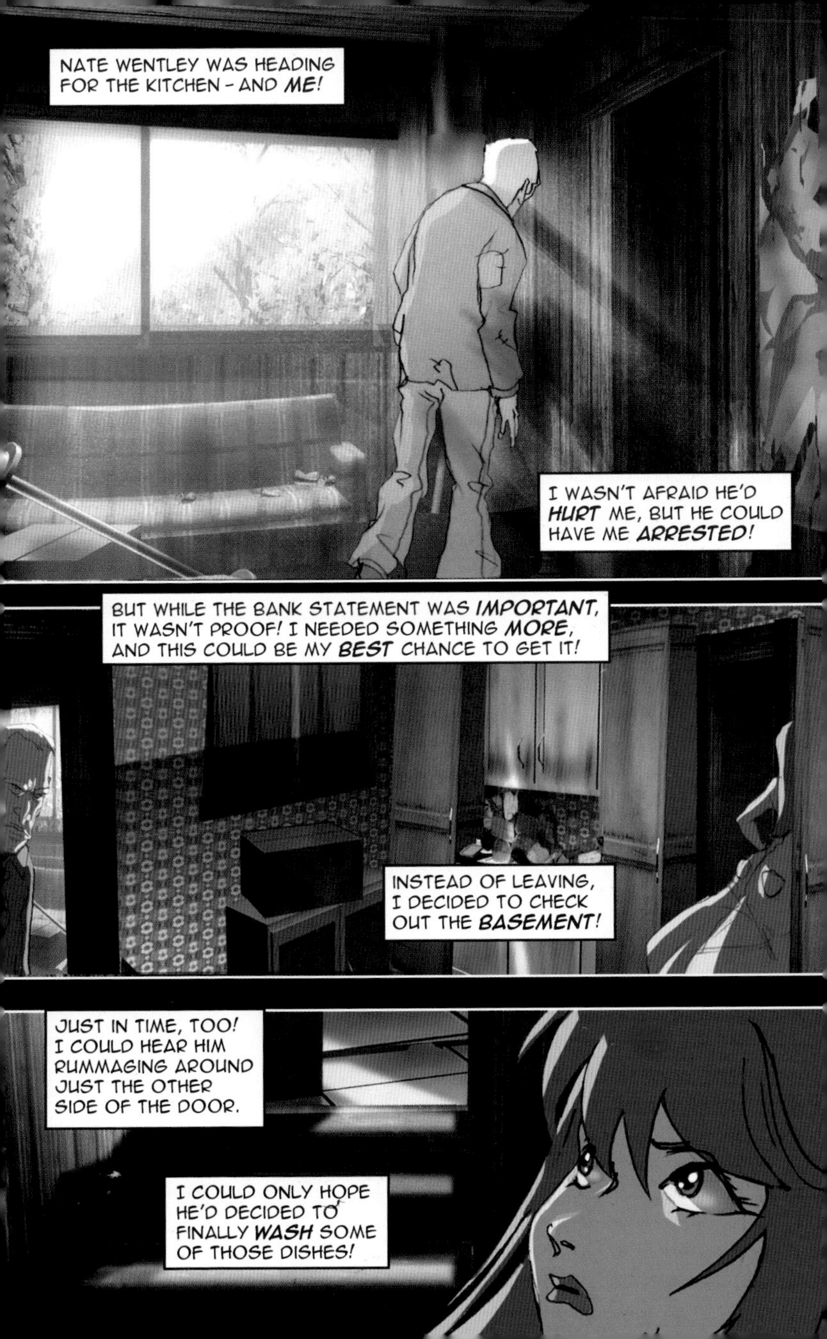
NATE WENTLEY WAS HEADING FOR THE KITCHEN - AND *ME*!
I WASN'T AFRAID HE'D *HURT* ME, BUT HE COULD HAVE ME *ARRESTED*!
BUT WHILE THE BANK STATEMENT WAS *IMPORTANT*, IT WASN'T PROOF! I NEEDED SOMETHING *MORE*, AND THIS COULD BE MY *BEST* CHANCE TO GET IT!
INSTEAD OF LEAVING, I DECIDED TO CHECK OUT THE *BASEMENT*!
JUST IN TIME, TOO! I COULD HEAR HIM RUMMAGING AROUND JUST THE OTHER SIDE OF THE DOOR.
I COULD ONLY HOPE HE'D DECIDED TO FINALLY *WASH* SOME OF THOSE DISHES!

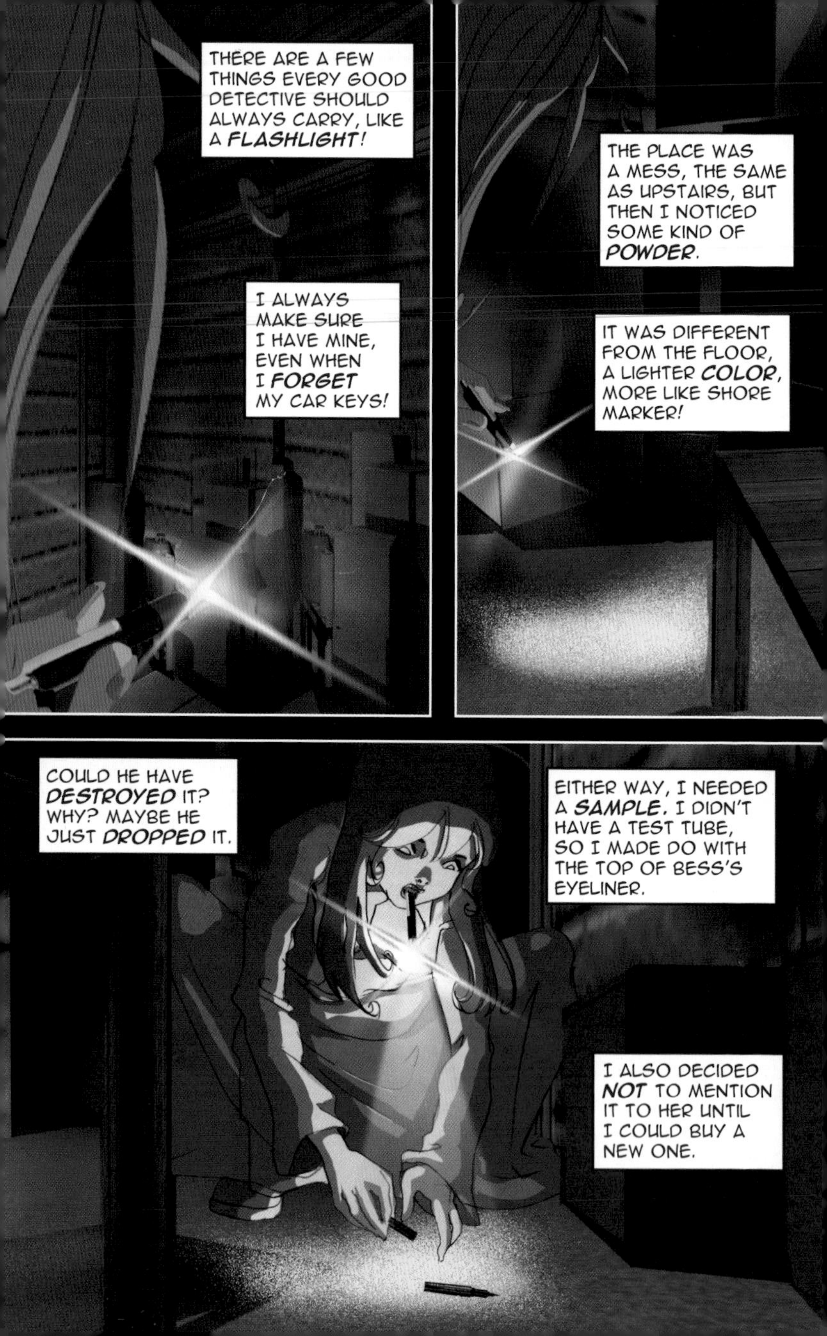
THERE ARE A FEW THINGS EVERY GOOD DETECTIVE SHOULD ALWAYS CARRY, LIKE A FLASHLIGHT!
I ALWAYS MAKE SURE I HAVE MINE, EVEN WHEN I FORGET MY CAR KEYS!
THE PLACE WAS A MESS, THE SAME AS UPSTAIRS, BUT THEN I NOTICED SOME KIND OF POWDER.
IT WAS DIFFERENT FROM THE FLOOR, A LIGHTER COLOR, MORE LIKE SHORE MARKER!
COULD HE HAVE DESTROYED IT? WHY? MAYBE HE JUST DROPPED IT.
EITHER WAY, I NEEDED A SAMPLE. I DIDN'T HAVE A TEST TUBE, SO I MADE DO WITH THE TOP OF BESS'S EYELINER.
I ALSO DECIDED NOT TO MENTION IT TO HER UNTIL I COULD BUY A NEW ONE.

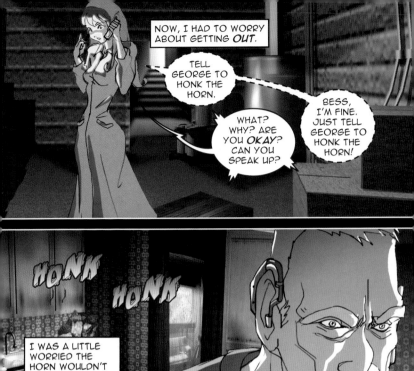

NOW, I HAD TO WORRY ABOUT GETTING *OUT*.

TELL GEORGE TO HONK THE HORN.

WHAT? WHY? ARE YOU *OKAY*? CAN YOU SPEAK UP?

BESS, I'M FINE. JUST TELL GEORGE TO HONK THE HORN!

HONK

HONK

I WAS A LITTLE WORRIED THE HORN WOULDN'T BE LOUD ENOUGH, BUT IT *WAS*!

IF I COULD PROVE THE DUST WAS FROM THE SHORE STONE, HALF THE CASE WOULD BE SOLVED!

FORTUNATELY, WE STILL HAD A VISITOR IN RIVER HEIGHTS WHO WAS AN *EXPERT* ON THE MARKER!

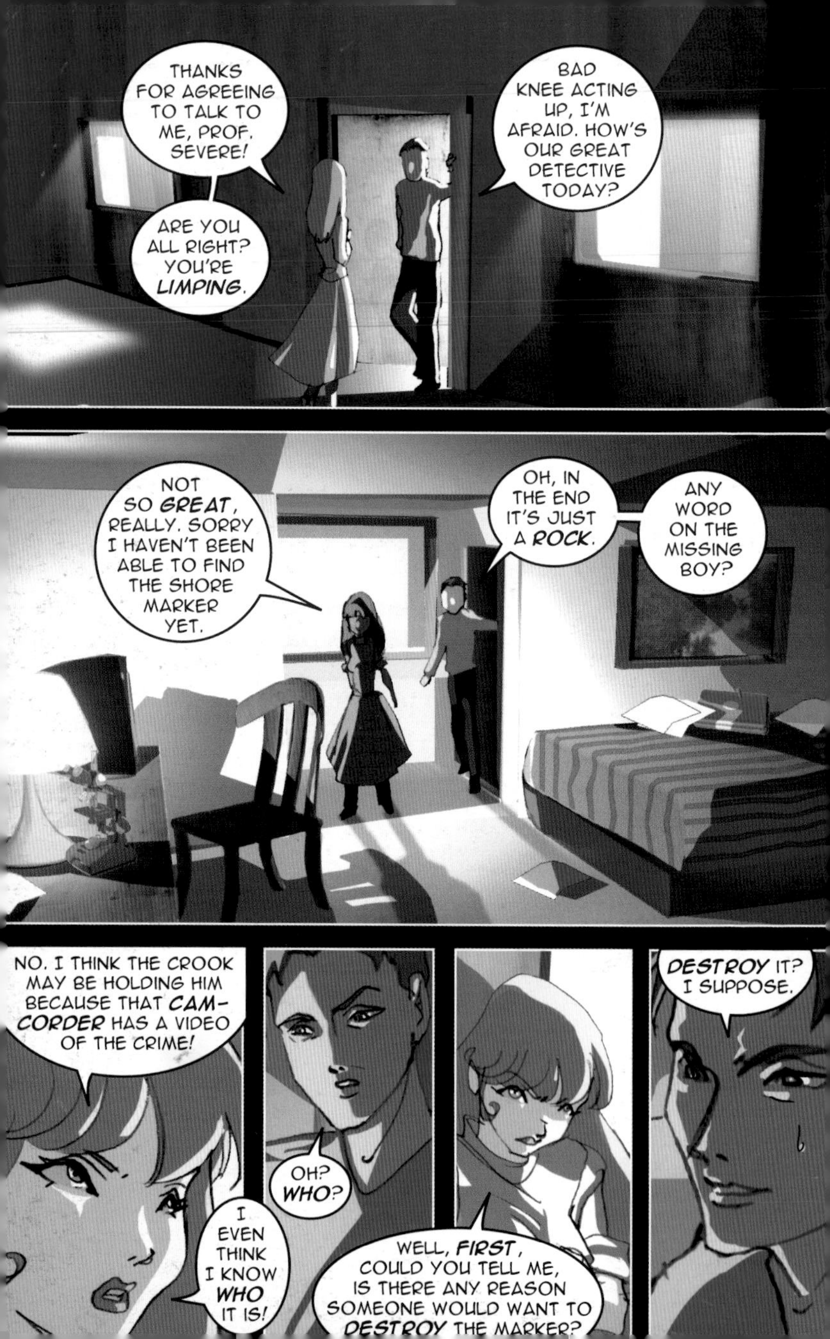
THANKS FOR AGREEING TO TALK TO ME, PROF. SEVERE!
ARE YOU ALL RIGHT? YOU'RE *LIMPING*.
BAD KNEE ACTING UP, I'M AFRAID. HOW'S OUR GREAT DETECTIVE TODAY?
NOT SO *GREAT*, REALLY. SORRY I HAVEN'T BEEN ABLE TO FIND THE SHORE MARKER YET.
OH, IN THE END IT'S JUST A *ROCK*.
ANY WORD ON THE MISSING BOY?
NO. I THINK THE CROOK MAY BE HOLDING HIM BECAUSE THAT *CAM-CORDER* HAS A VIDEO OF THE CRIME!
I EVEN THINK I KNOW *WHO* IT IS!
OH? *WHO*?
WELL, *FIRST*, COULD YOU TELL ME, IS THERE ANY REASON SOMEONE WOULD WANT TO *DESTROY* THE MARKER?
DESTROY IT? I SUPPOSE.

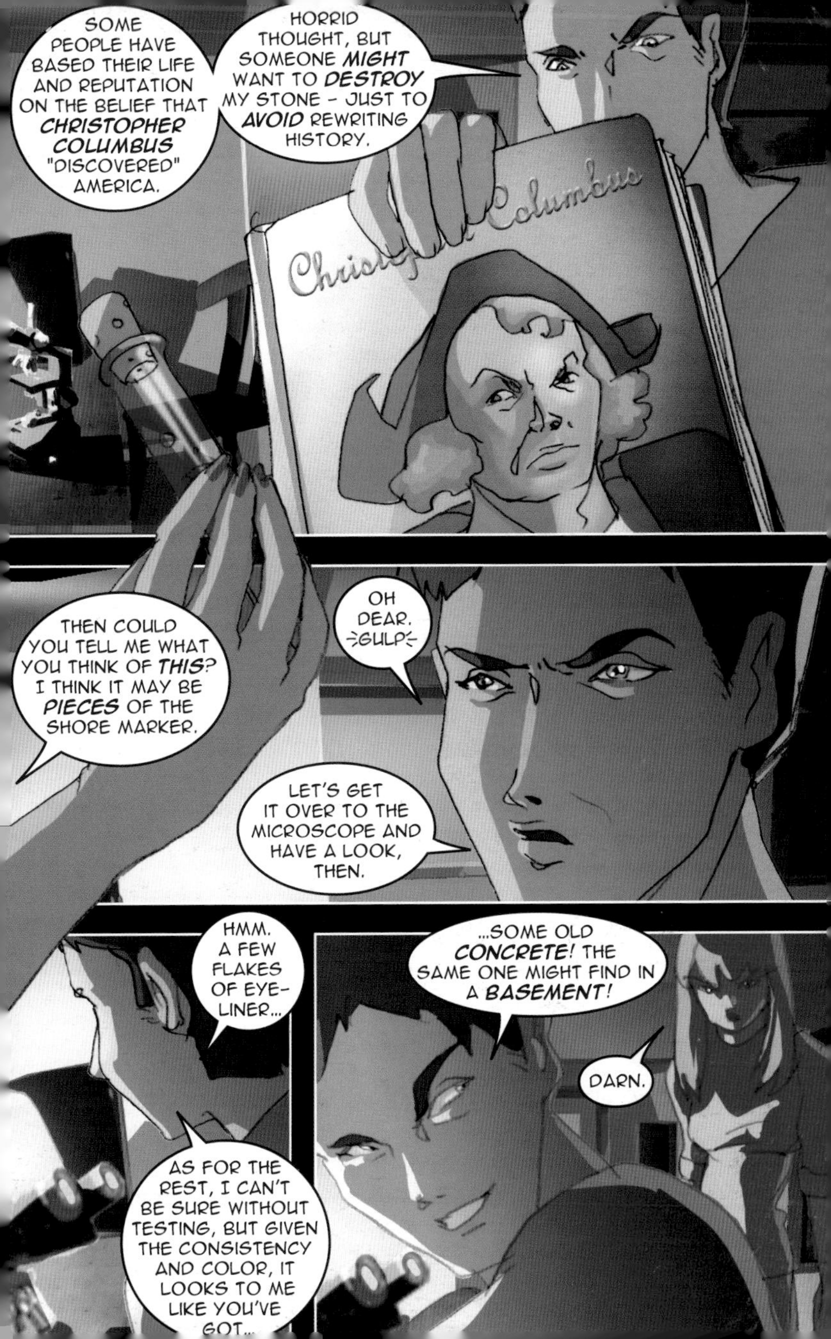
SOME PEOPLE HAVE BASED THEIR LIFE AND REPUTATION ON THE BELIEF THAT CHRISTOPHER COLUMBUS "DISCOVERED" AMERICA.
HORRID THOUGHT, BUT SOMEONE MIGHT WANT TO DESTROY MY STONE - JUST TO AVOID REWRITING HISTORY.
Christopher Columbus
THEN COULD YOU TELL ME WHAT YOU THINK OF THIS? I THINK IT MAY BE PIECES OF THE SHORE MARKER.
OH DEAR. GULP
LET'S GET IT OVER TO THE MICROSCOPE AND HAVE A LOOK, THEN.
HMM. A FEW FLAKES OF EYE-LINER...
AS FOR THE REST, I CAN'T BE SURE WITHOUT TESTING, BUT GIVEN THE CONSISTENCY AND COLOR, IT LOOKS TO ME LIKE YOU'VE GOT...
...SOME OLD CONCRETE! THE SAME ONE MIGHT FIND IN A BASEMENT!
DARN.

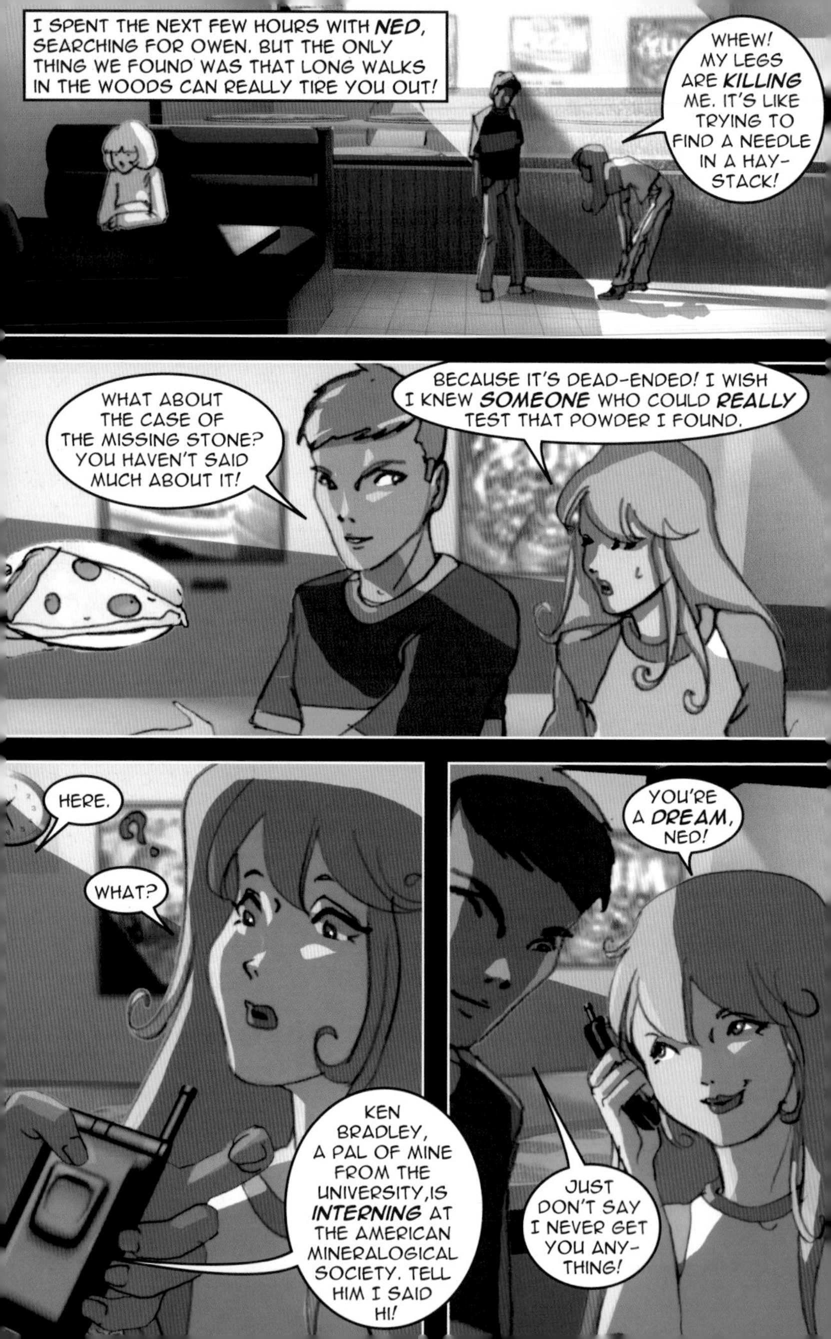
I SPENT THE NEXT FEW HOURS WITH NED, SEARCHING FOR OWEN. BUT THE ONLY THING WE FOUND WAS THAT LONG WALKS IN THE WOODS CAN REALLY TIRE YOU OUT!
WHEW! MY LEGS ARE KILLING ME. IT'S LIKE TRYING TO FIND A NEEDLE IN A HAY-STACK!
WHAT ABOUT THE CASE OF THE MISSING STONE? YOU HAVEN'T SAID MUCH ABOUT IT!
BECAUSE IT'S DEAD-ENDED! I WISH I KNEW SOMEONE WHO COULD REALLY TEST THAT POWDER I FOUND.
HERE.
WHAT?
KEN BRADLEY, A PAL OF MINE FROM THE UNIVERSITY, IS INTERNING AT THE AMERICAN MINERALOGICAL SOCIETY. TELL HIM I SAID HI!
YOU'RE A DREAM, NED!
JUST DON'T SAY I NEVER GET YOU ANY-THING!

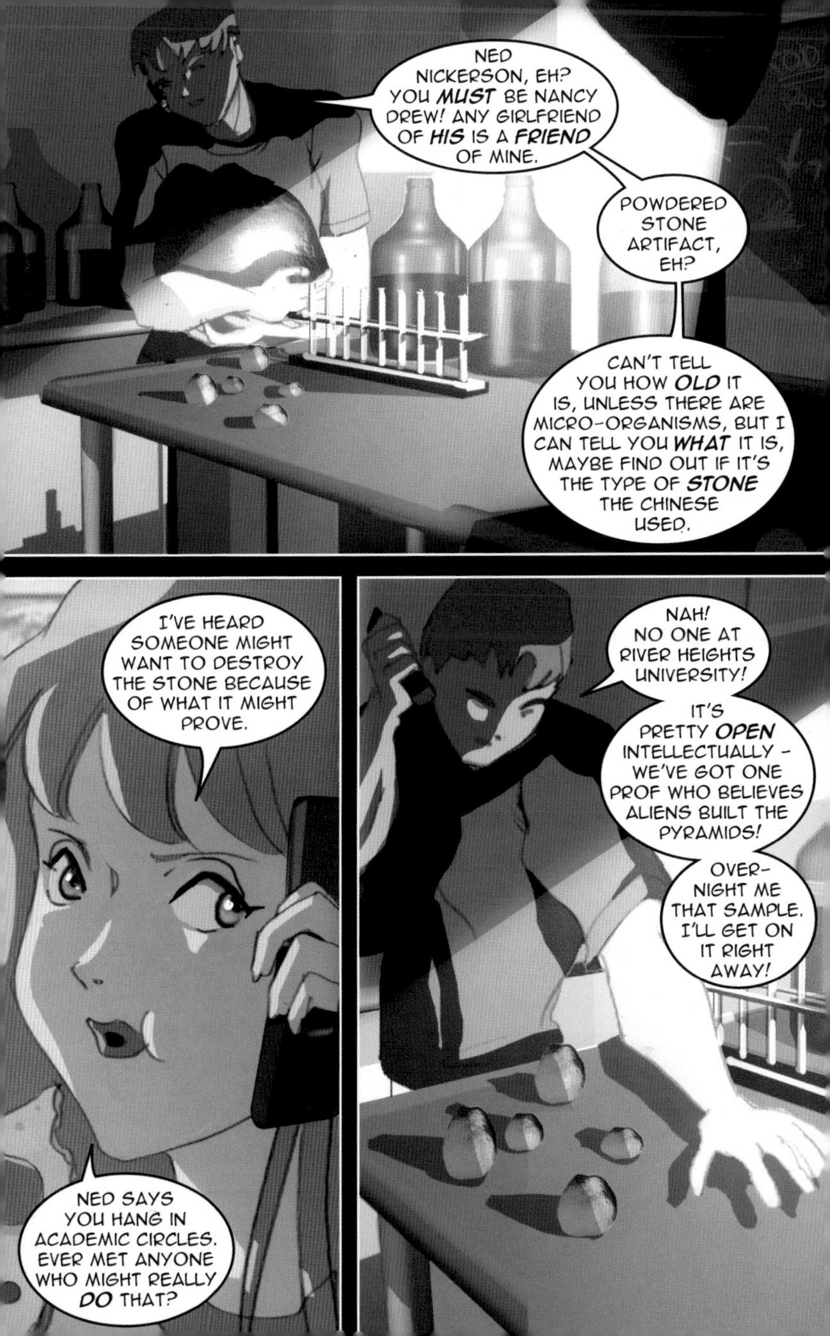

NED NICKERSON, EH? YOU MUST BE NANCY DREW! ANY GIRLFRIEND OF HIS IS A FRIEND OF MINE.
POWDERED STONE ARTIFACT, EH?
CAN'T TELL YOU HOW OLD IT IS, UNLESS THERE ARE MICRO-ORGANISMS, BUT I CAN TELL YOU WHAT IT IS, MAYBE FIND OUT IF IT'S THE TYPE OF STONE THE CHINESE USED.
I'VE HEARD SOMEONE MIGHT WANT TO DESTROY THE STONE BECAUSE OF WHAT IT MIGHT PROVE.
NED SAYS YOU HANG IN ACADEMIC CIRCLES. EVER MET ANYONE WHO MIGHT REALLY DO THAT?
NAH! NO ONE AT RIVER HEIGHTS UNIVERSITY!
IT'S PRETTY OPEN INTELLECTUALLY - WE'VE GOT ONE PROF WHO BELIEVES ALIENS BUILT THE PYRAMIDS!
OVER-NIGHT ME THAT SAMPLE. I'LL GET ON IT RIGHT AWAY!

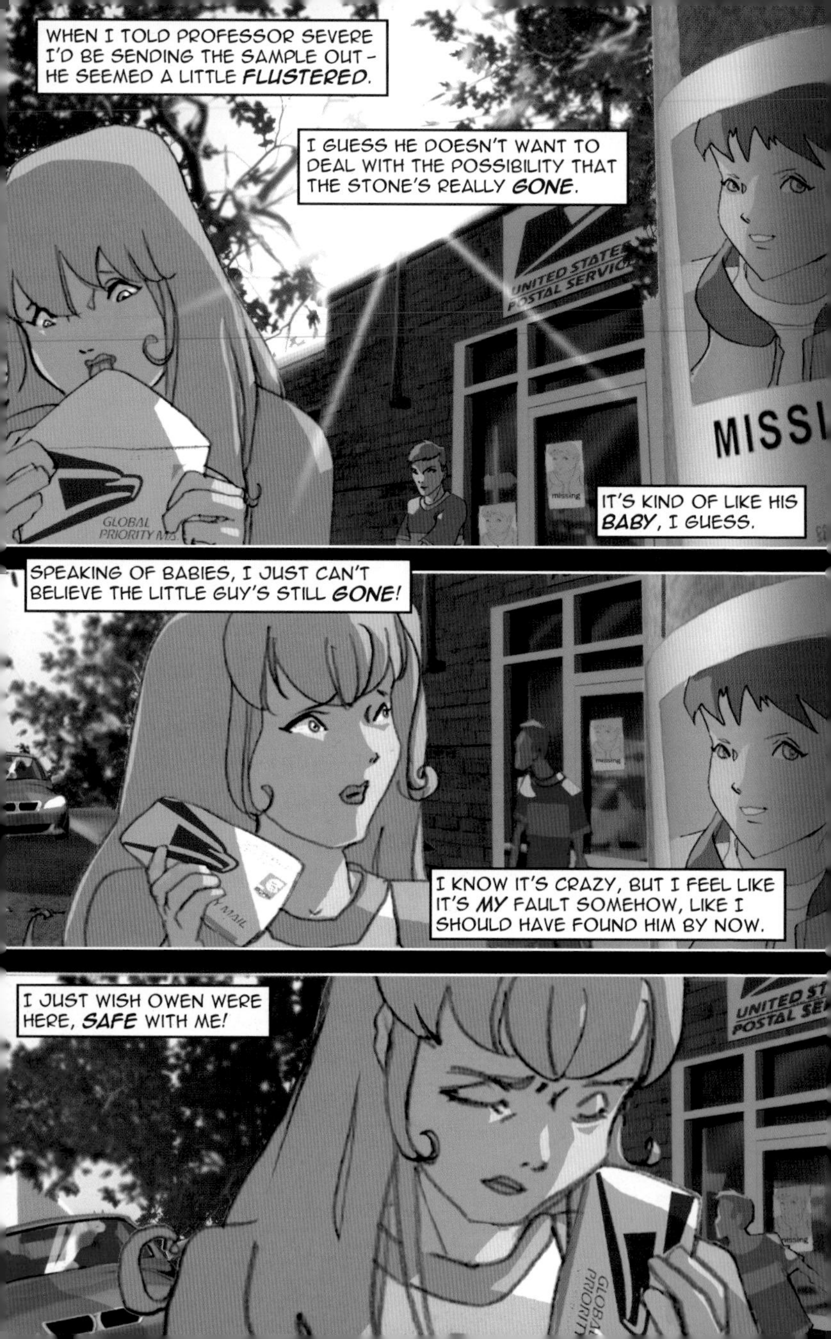
WHEN I TOLD PROFESSOR SEVERE I'D BE SENDING THE SAMPLE OUT – HE SEEMED A LITTLE FLUSTERED.
I GUESS HE DOESN'T WANT TO DEAL WITH THE POSSIBILITY THAT THE STONE'S REALLY GONE.
IT'S KIND OF LIKE HIS BABY, I GUESS.
SPEAKING OF BABIES, I JUST CAN'T BELIEVE THE LITTLE GUY'S STILL GONE!
I KNOW IT'S CRAZY, BUT I FEEL LIKE IT'S MY FAULT SOMEHOW, LIKE I SHOULD HAVE FOUND HIM BY NOW.
I JUST WISH OWEN WERE HERE, SAFE WITH ME!

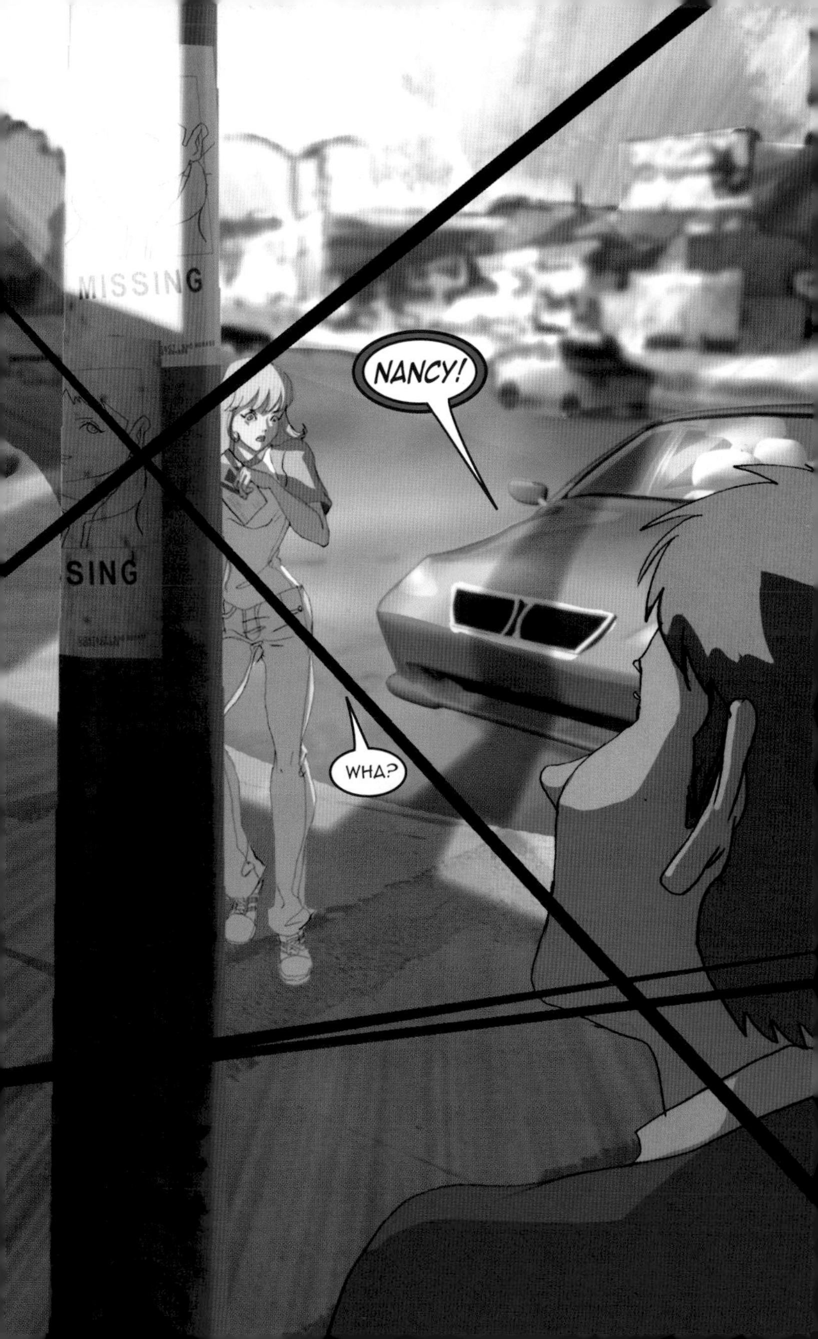
MISSING
SING
NANCY!
WHA?

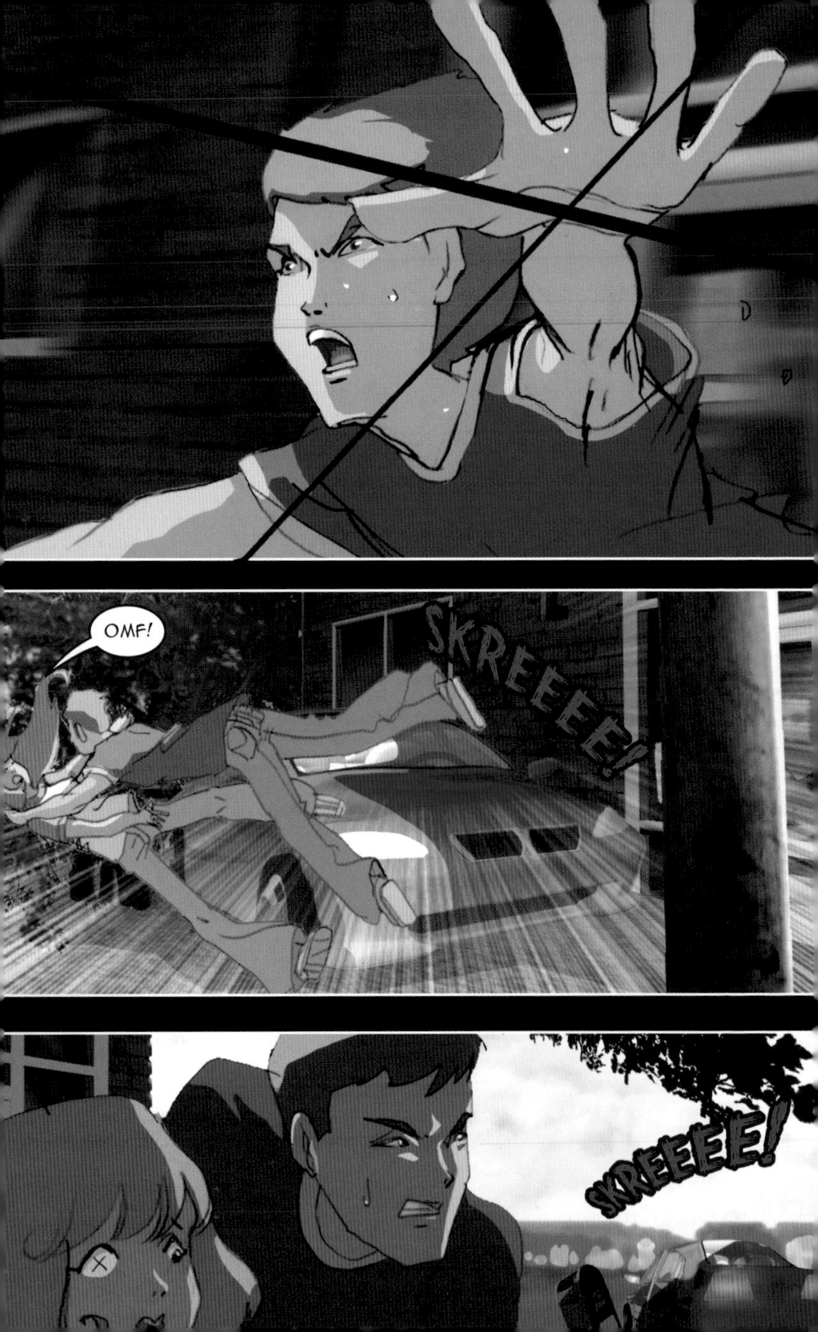
OMF!
SKREEEEE!
SKREEEEE!

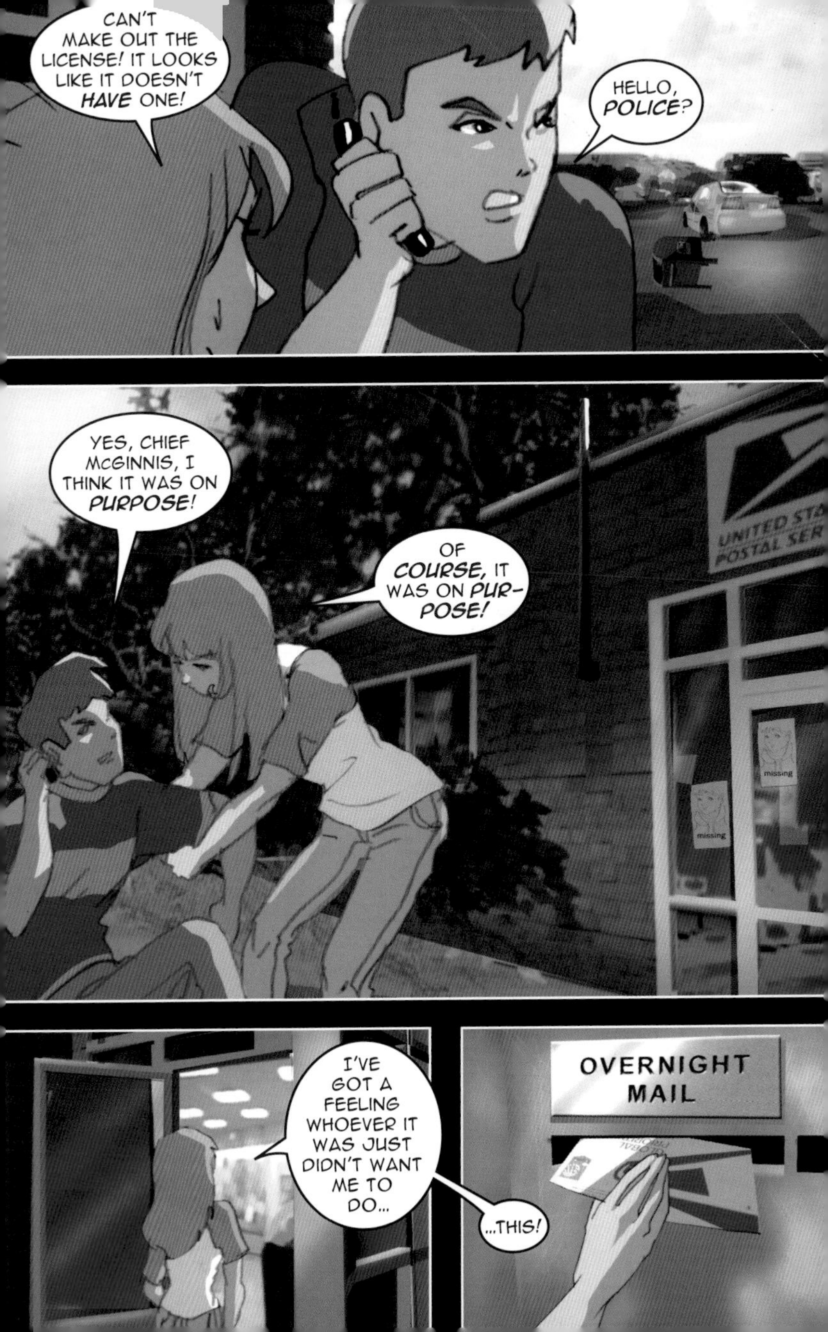
CAN'T MAKE OUT THE LICENSE! IT LOOKS LIKE IT DOESN'T HAVE ONE!
HELLO, POLICE?
YES, CHIEF MCGINNIS, I THINK IT WAS ON PURPOSE!
OF COURSE, IT WAS ON PURPOSE!
UNITED STA
POSTAL SER
missing
missing
I'VE GOT A FEELING WHOEVER IT WAS JUST DIDN'T WANT ME TO DO...
OVERNIGHT MAIL
...THIS!

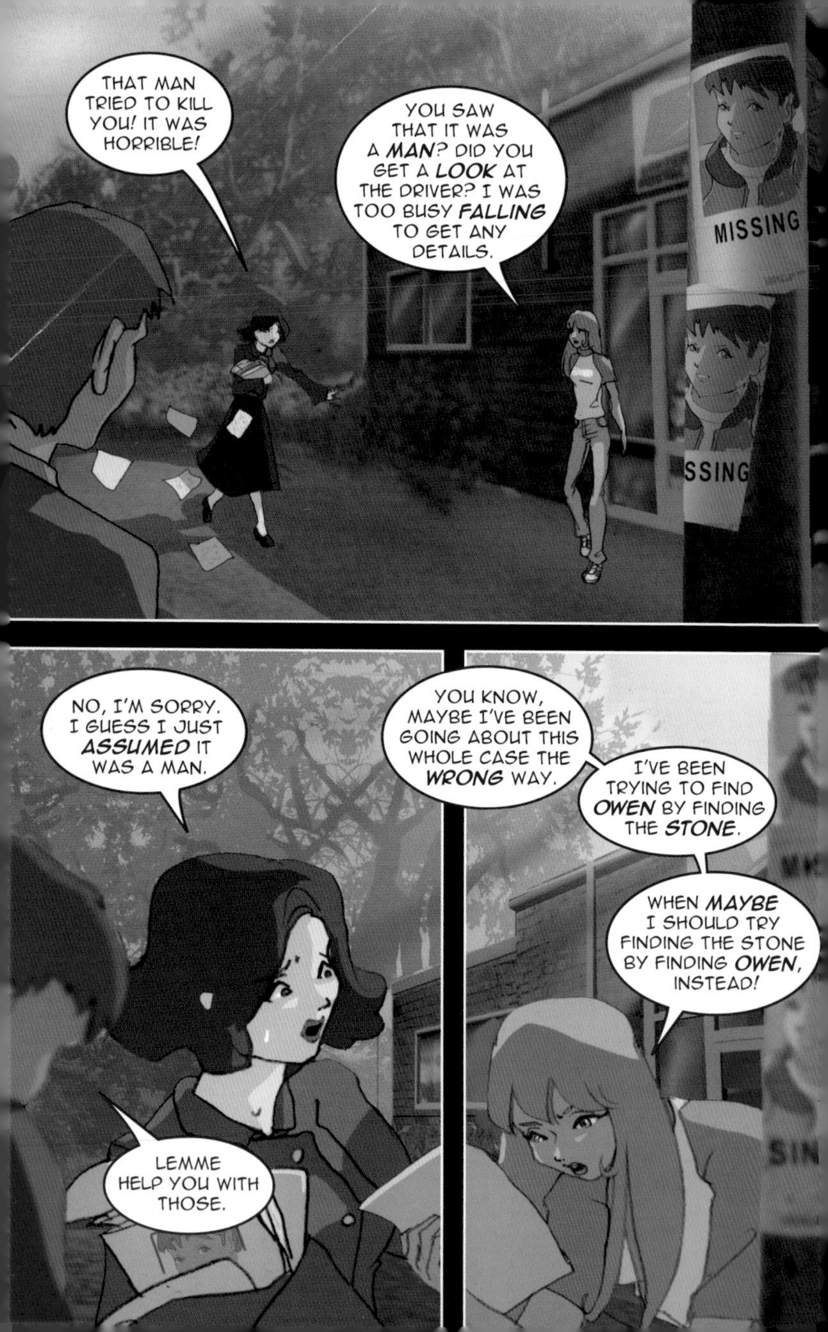
THAT MAN TRIED TO KILL YOU! IT WAS HORRIBLE!
YOU SAW THAT IT WAS A MAN? DID YOU GET A LOOK AT THE DRIVER? I WAS TOO BUSY FALLING TO GET ANY DETAILS.
MISSING
SSING
NO, I'M SORRY. I GUESS I JUST ASSUMED IT WAS A MAN.
LEMME HELP YOU WITH THOSE.
YOU KNOW, MAYBE I'VE BEEN GOING ABOUT THIS WHOLE CASE THE WRONG WAY.
I'VE BEEN TRYING TO FIND OWEN BY FINDING THE STONE.
WHEN MAYBE I SHOULD TRY FINDING THE STONE BY FINDING OWEN, INSTEAD!

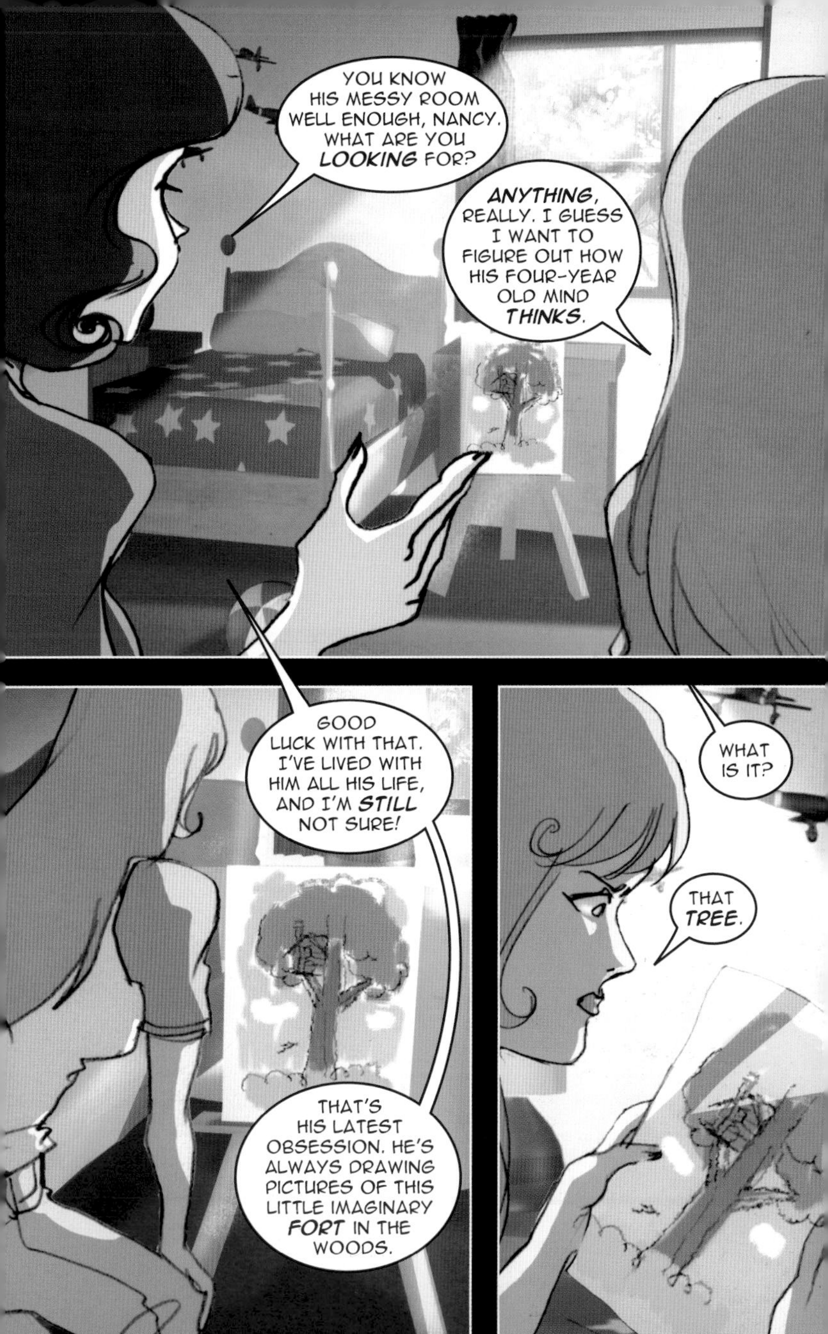

YOU KNOW HIS MESSY ROOM WELL ENOUGH, NANCY. WHAT ARE YOU LOOKING FOR?
ANYTHING, REALLY. I GUESS I WANT TO FIGURE OUT HOW HIS FOUR-YEAR OLD MIND THINKS.
GOOD LUCK WITH THAT. I'VE LIVED WITH HIM ALL HIS LIFE, AND I'M STILL NOT SURE!
THAT'S HIS LATEST OBSESSION. HE'S ALWAYS DRAWING PICTURES OF THIS LITTLE IMAGINARY FORT IN THE WOODS.
WHAT IS IT?
THAT TREE.

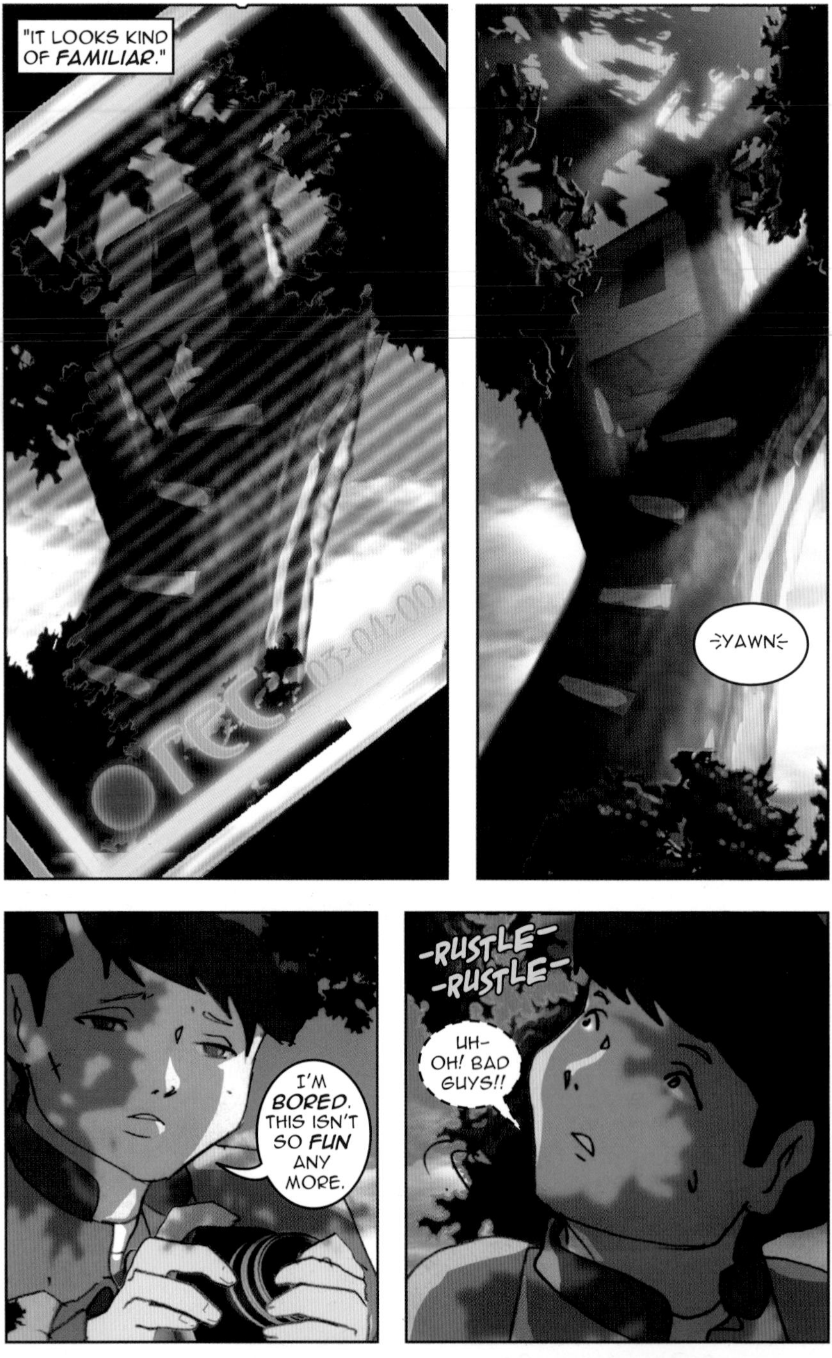
"IT LOOKS KIND OF FAMILIAR."
YAWN
I'M BORED. THIS ISN'T SO FUN ANY MORE.
-RUSTLE- -RUSTLE-
UH-OH! BAD GUYS!!

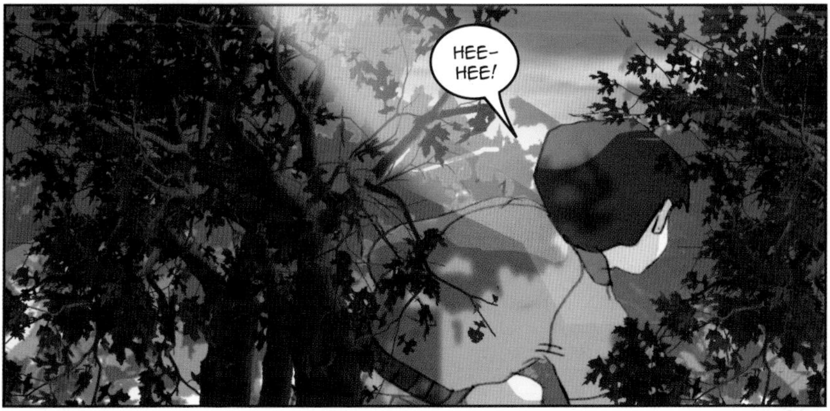
HEE-HEE!

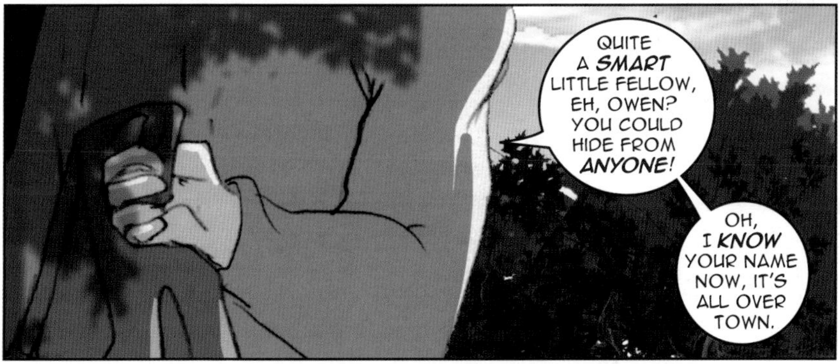
QUITE A SMART LITTLE FELLOW, EH, OWEN? YOU COULD HIDE FROM ANYONE!
OH, I KNOW YOUR NAME NOW, IT'S ALL OVER TOWN.

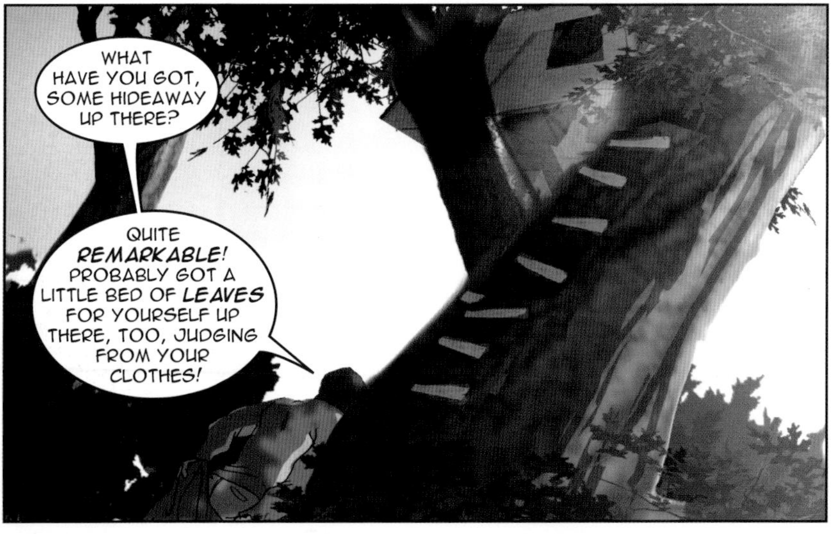
WHAT HAVE YOU GOT, SOME HIDEAWAY UP THERE?
QUITE REMARKABLE! PROBABLY GOT A LITTLE BED OF LEAVES FOR YOURSELF UP THERE, TOO, JUDGING FROM YOUR CLOTHES!

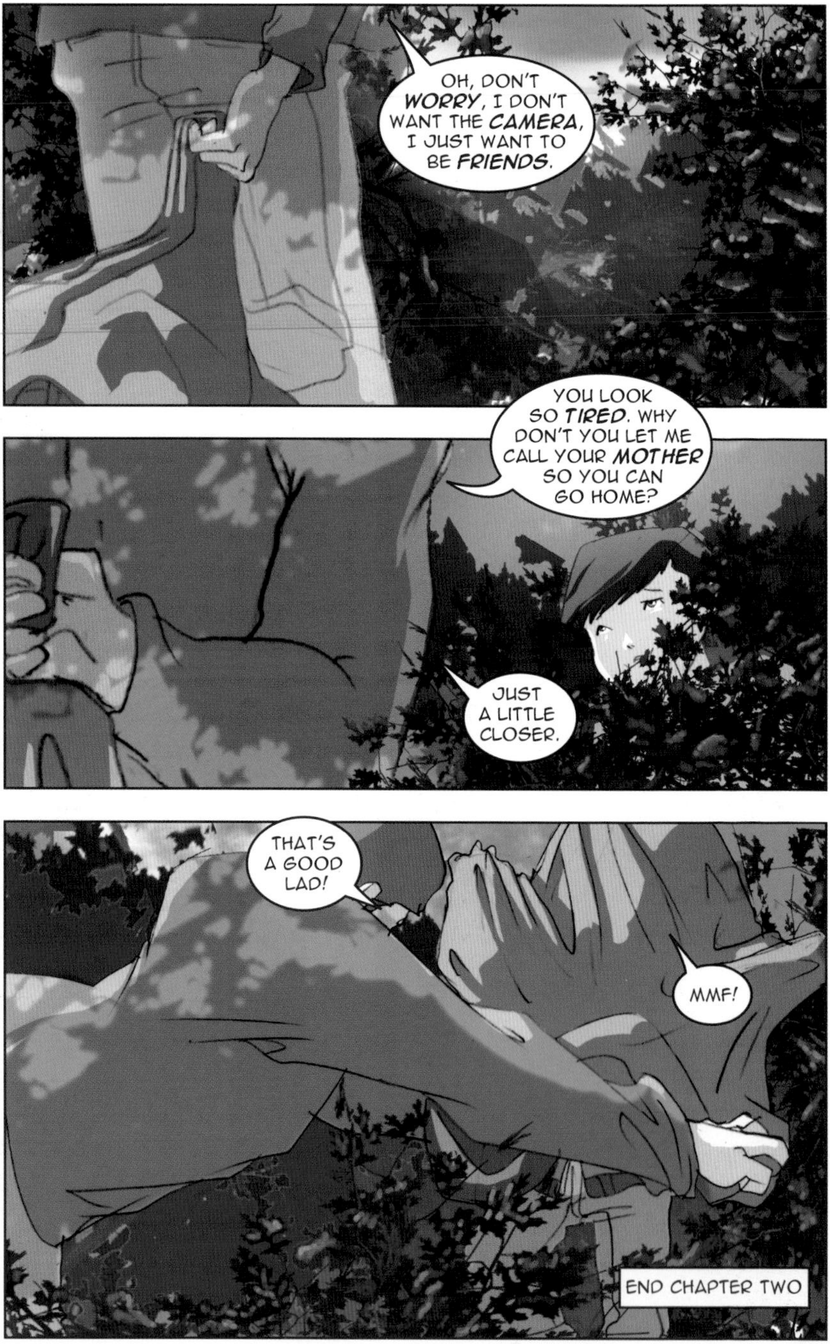
OH, DON'T WORRY, I DON'T WANT THE CAMERA, I JUST WANT TO BE FRIENDS.
YOU LOOK SO TIRED. WHY DON'T YOU LET ME CALL YOUR MOTHER SO YOU CAN GO HOME?
JUST A LITTLE CLOSER.
THAT'S A GOOD LAD!
MMF!
END CHAPTER TWO

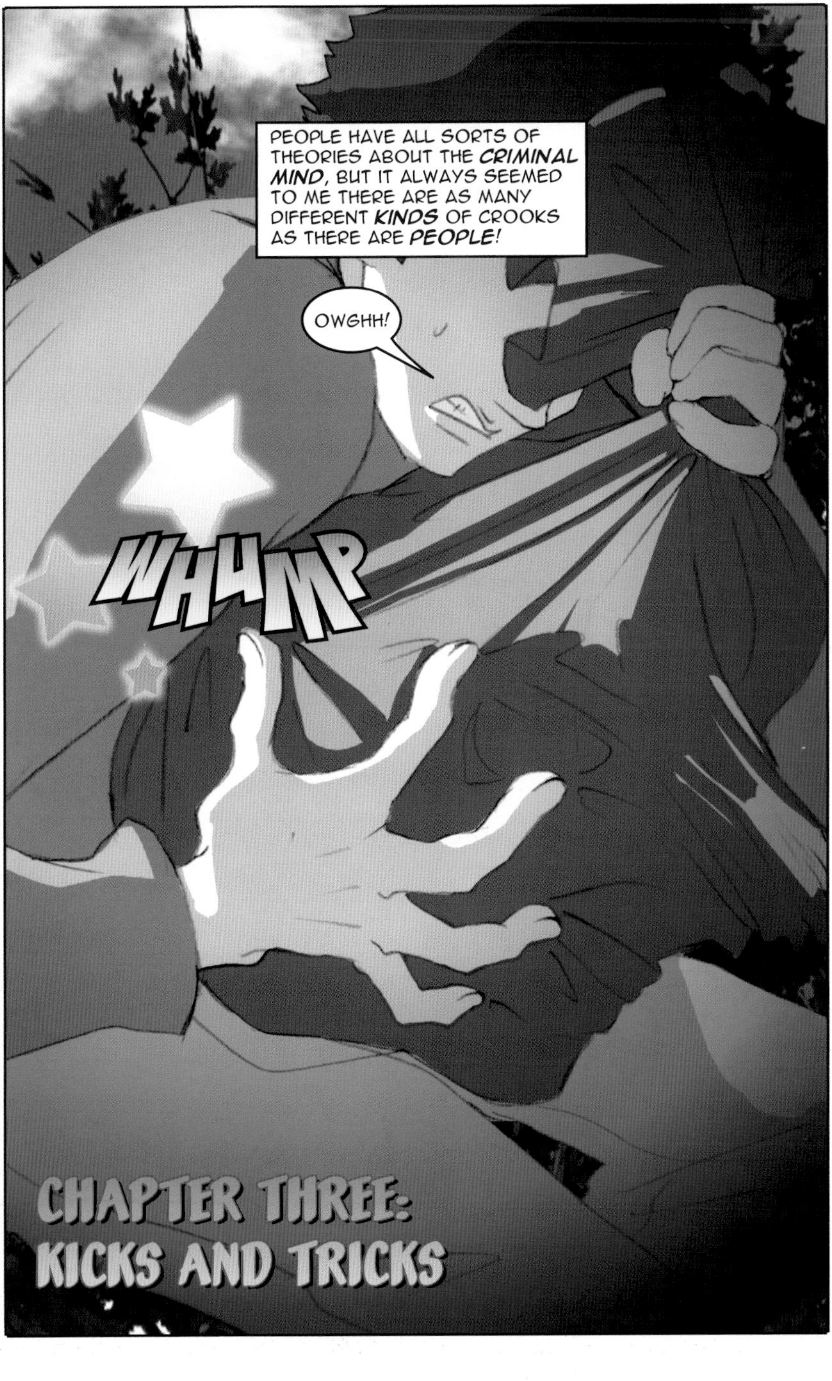
PEOPLE HAVE ALL SORTS OF THEORIES ABOUT THE CRIMINAL MIND, BUT IT ALWAYS SEEMED TO ME THERE ARE AS MANY DIFFERENT KINDS OF CROOKS AS THERE ARE PEOPLE!
OWGHH!
WHUMP
CHAPTER THREE:
KICKS AND TRICKS

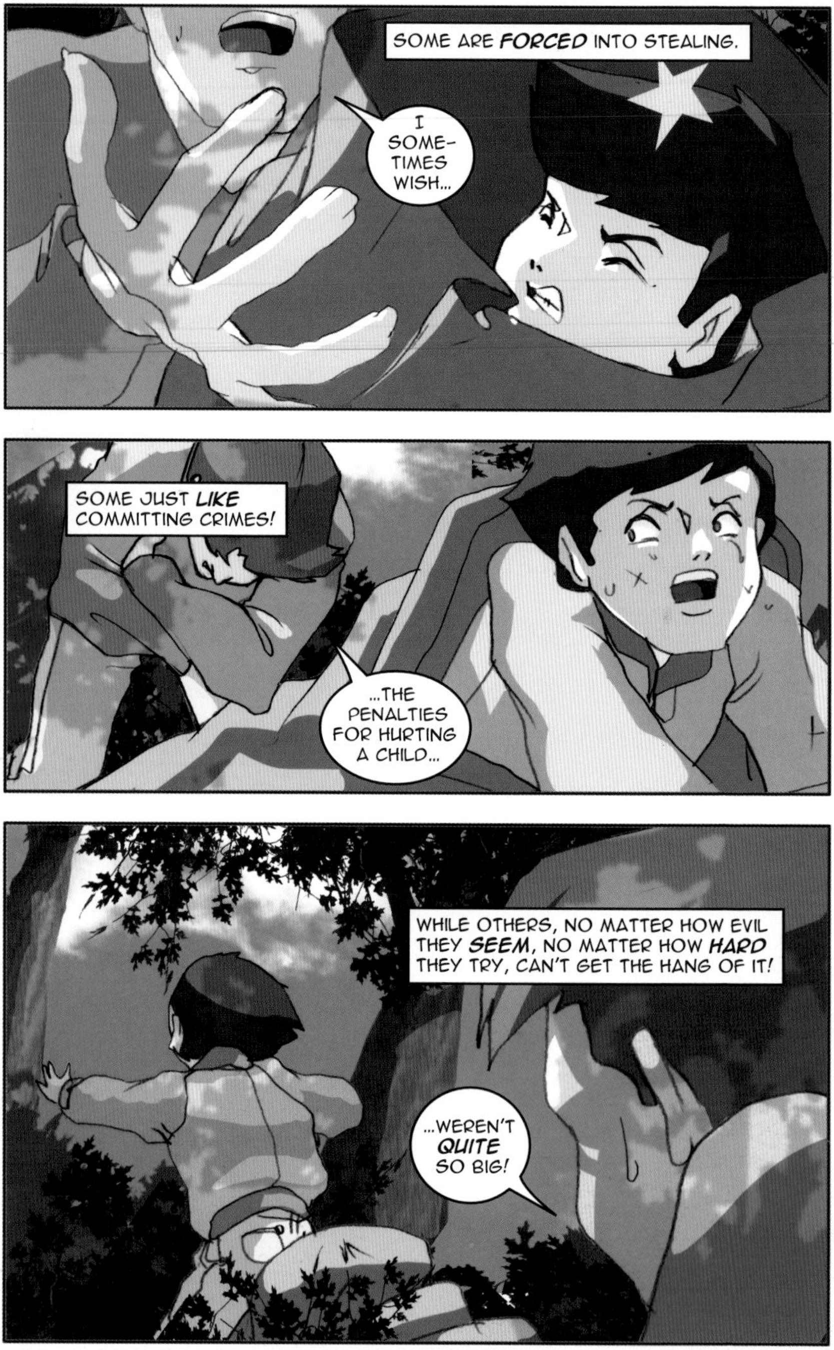
SOME ARE *FORCED* INTO STEALING.
I SOMETIMES WISH...
SOME JUST *LIKE* COMMITTING CRIMES!
...THE PENALTIES FOR HURTING A CHILD...
WHILE OTHERS, NO MATTER HOW EVIL THEY *SEEM*, NO MATTER HOW *HARD* THEY TRY, CAN'T GET THE HANG OF IT!
...WEREN'T *QUITE* SO BIG!

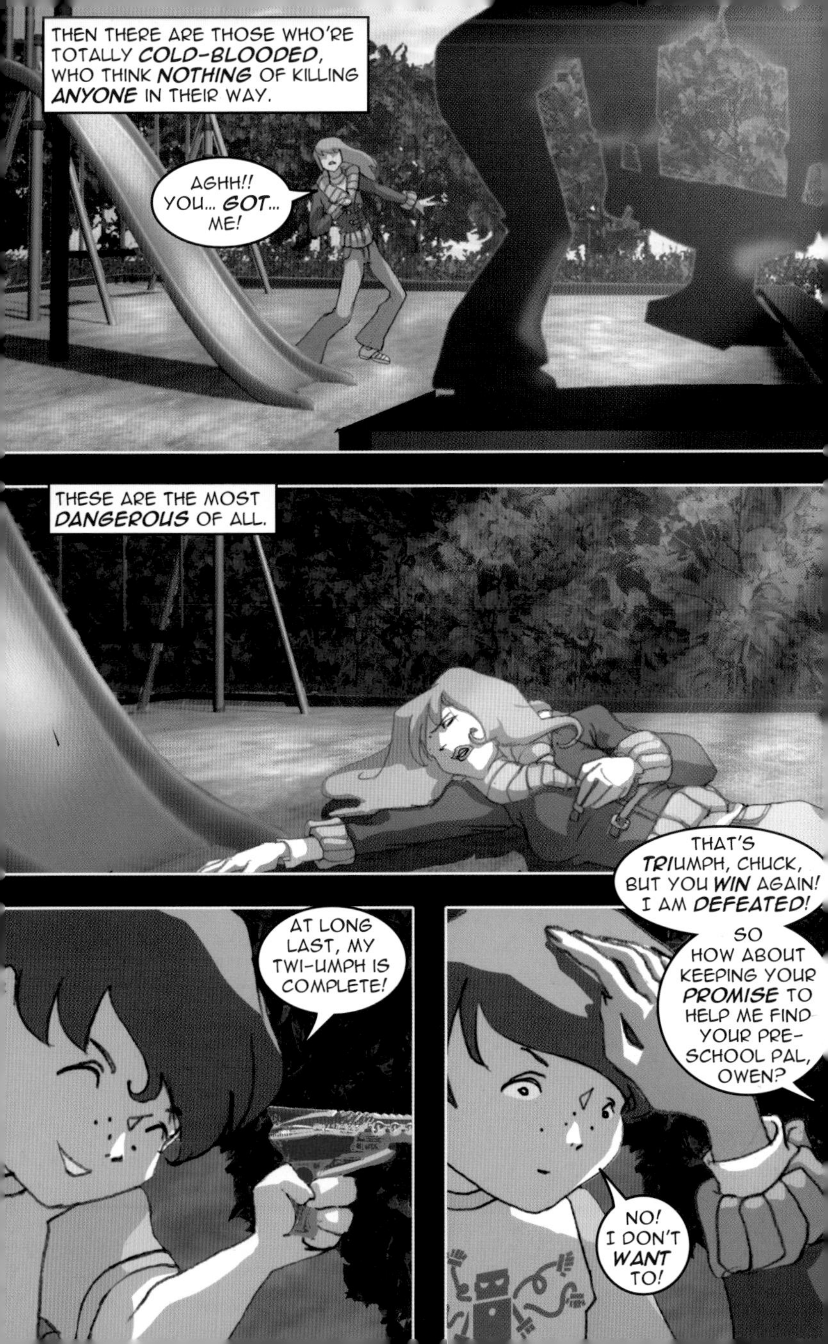
THEN THERE ARE THOSE WHO'RE TOTALLY COLD-BLOODED, WHO THINK NOTHING OF KILLING ANYONE IN THEIR WAY.
AGHH!! YOU... GOT... ME!
THESE ARE THE MOST DANGEROUS OF ALL.
AT LONG LAST, MY TWI-UMPH IS COMPLETE!
THAT'S TRIUMPH, CHUCK, BUT YOU WIN AGAIN! I AM DEFEATED!
SO HOW ABOUT KEEPING YOUR PROMISE TO HELP ME FIND YOUR PRE-SCHOOL PAL, OWEN?
NO! I DON'T WANT TO!

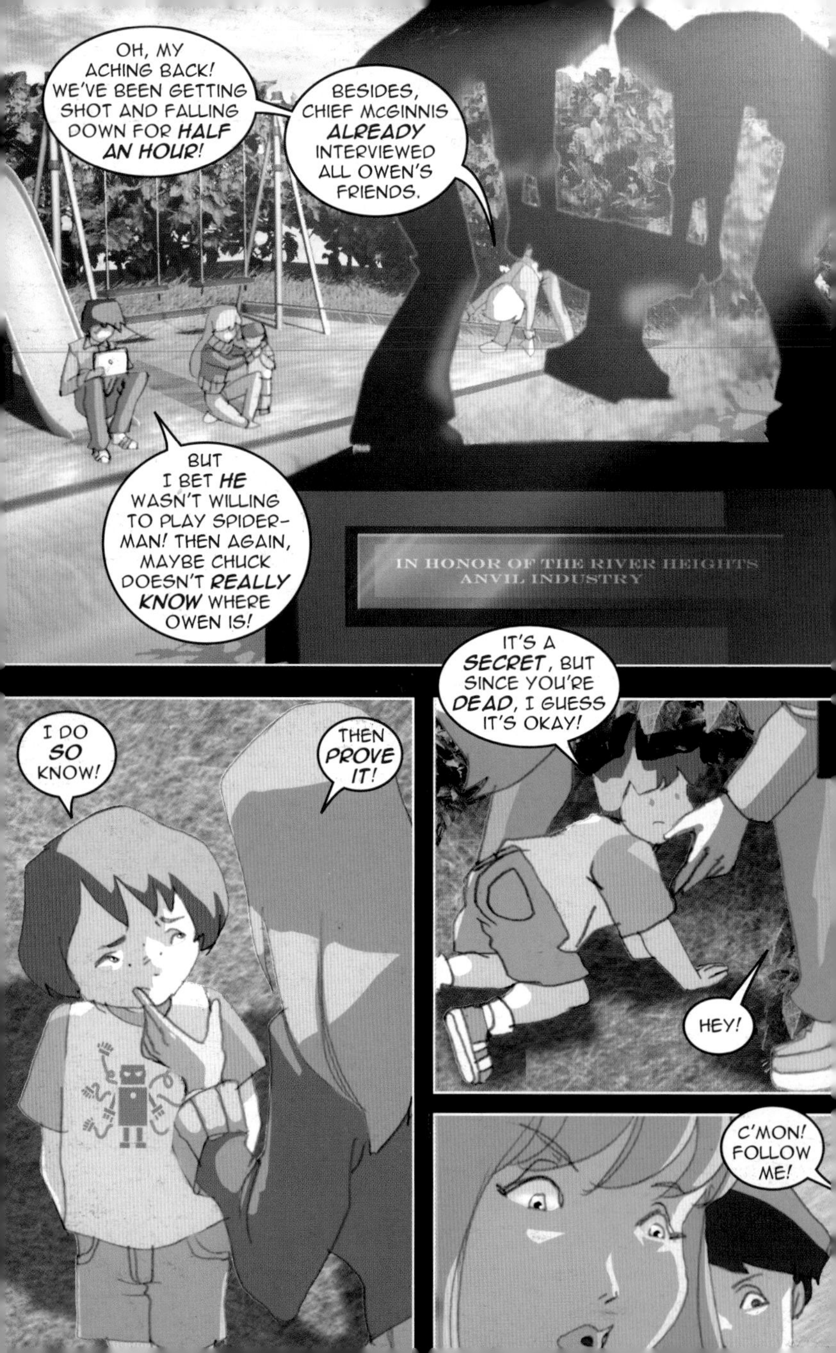
OH, MY ACHING BACK! WE'VE BEEN GETTING SHOT AND FALLING DOWN FOR HALF AN HOUR!
BESIDES, CHIEF McGINNIS ALREADY INTERVIEWED ALL OWEN'S FRIENDS.
BUT I BET HE WASN'T WILLING TO PLAY SPIDER-MAN! THEN AGAIN, MAYBE CHUCK DOESN'T REALLY KNOW WHERE OWEN IS!
IN HONOR OF THE RIVER HEIGHTS
ANVIL INDUSTRY
I DO SO KNOW!
THEN PROVE IT!
IT'S A SECRET, BUT SINCE YOU'RE DEAD, I GUESS IT'S OKAY!
HEY!
C'MON! FOLLOW ME!

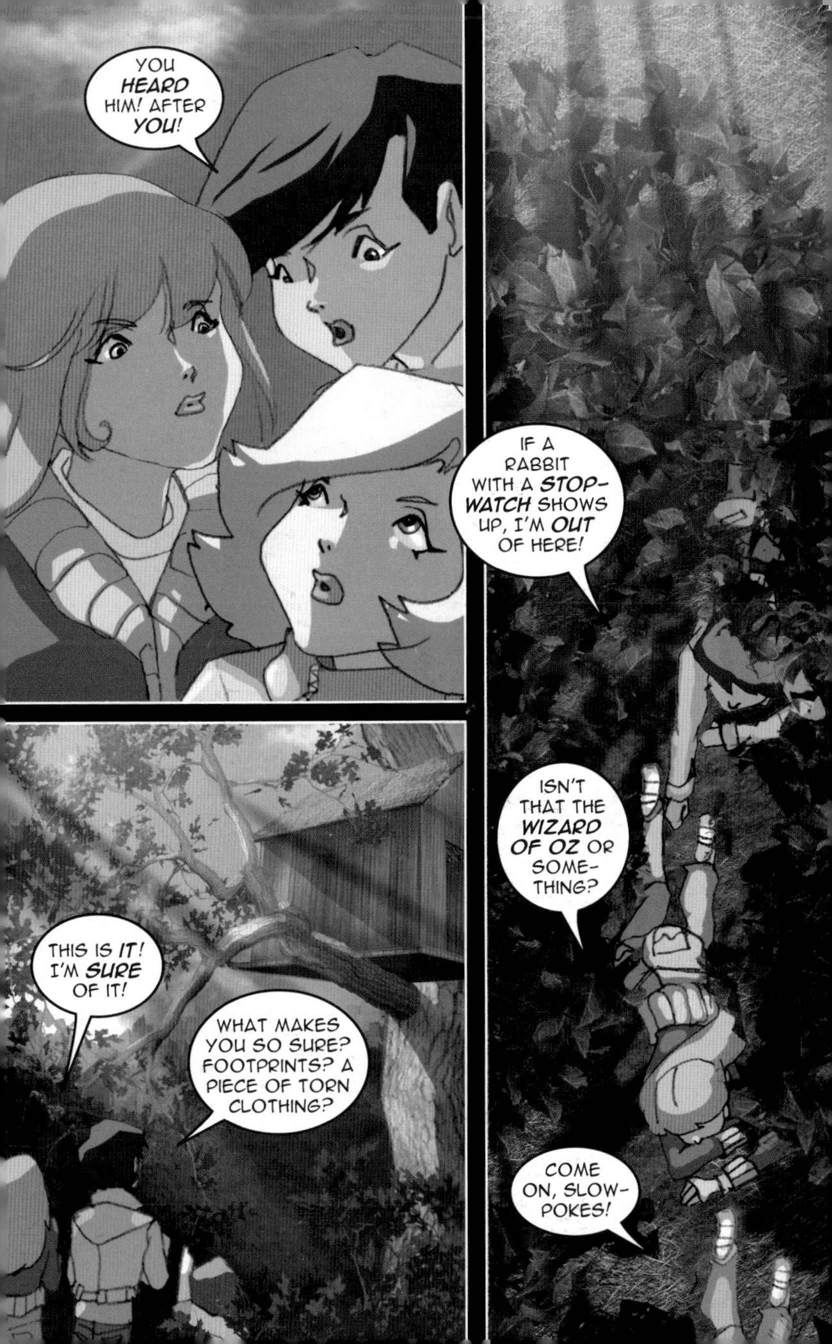
YOU HEARD HIM! AFTER YOU!
THIS IS IT! I'M SURE OF IT!
WHAT MAKES YOU SO SURE? FOOTPRINTS? A PIECE OF TORN CLOTHING?
IF A RABBIT WITH A STOP-WATCH SHOWS UP, I'M OUT OF HERE!
ISN'T THAT THE WIZARD OF OZ OR SOME-THING?
COME ON, SLOW-POKES!

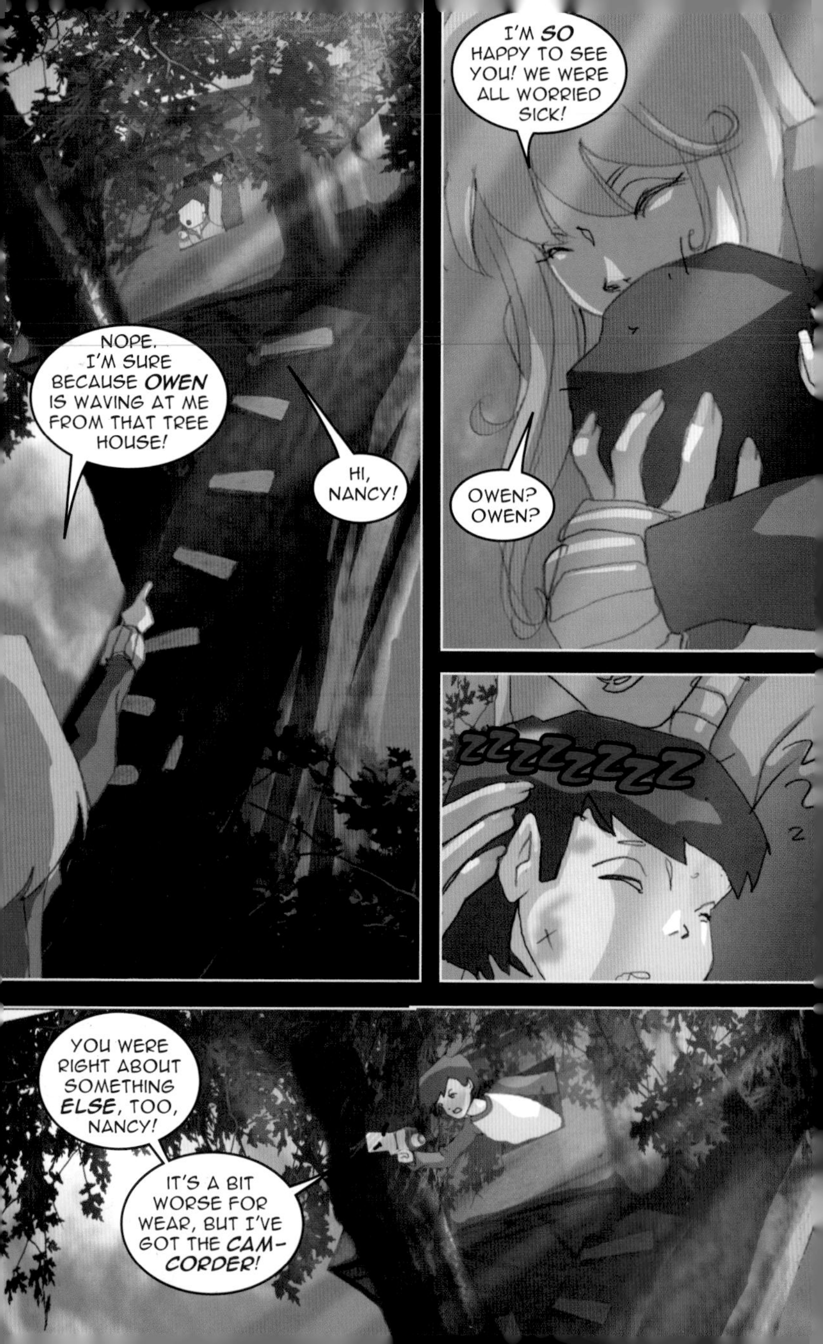
NOPE. I'M SURE BECAUSE OWEN IS WAVING AT ME FROM THAT TREE HOUSE!
HI, NANCY!
I'M SO HAPPY TO SEE YOU! WE WERE ALL WORRIED SICK!
OWEN? OWEN?
ZZZZZZZZ
YOU WERE RIGHT ABOUT SOMETHING ELSE, TOO, NANCY!
IT'S A BIT WORSE FOR WEAR, BUT I'VE GOT THE CAM-CORDER!

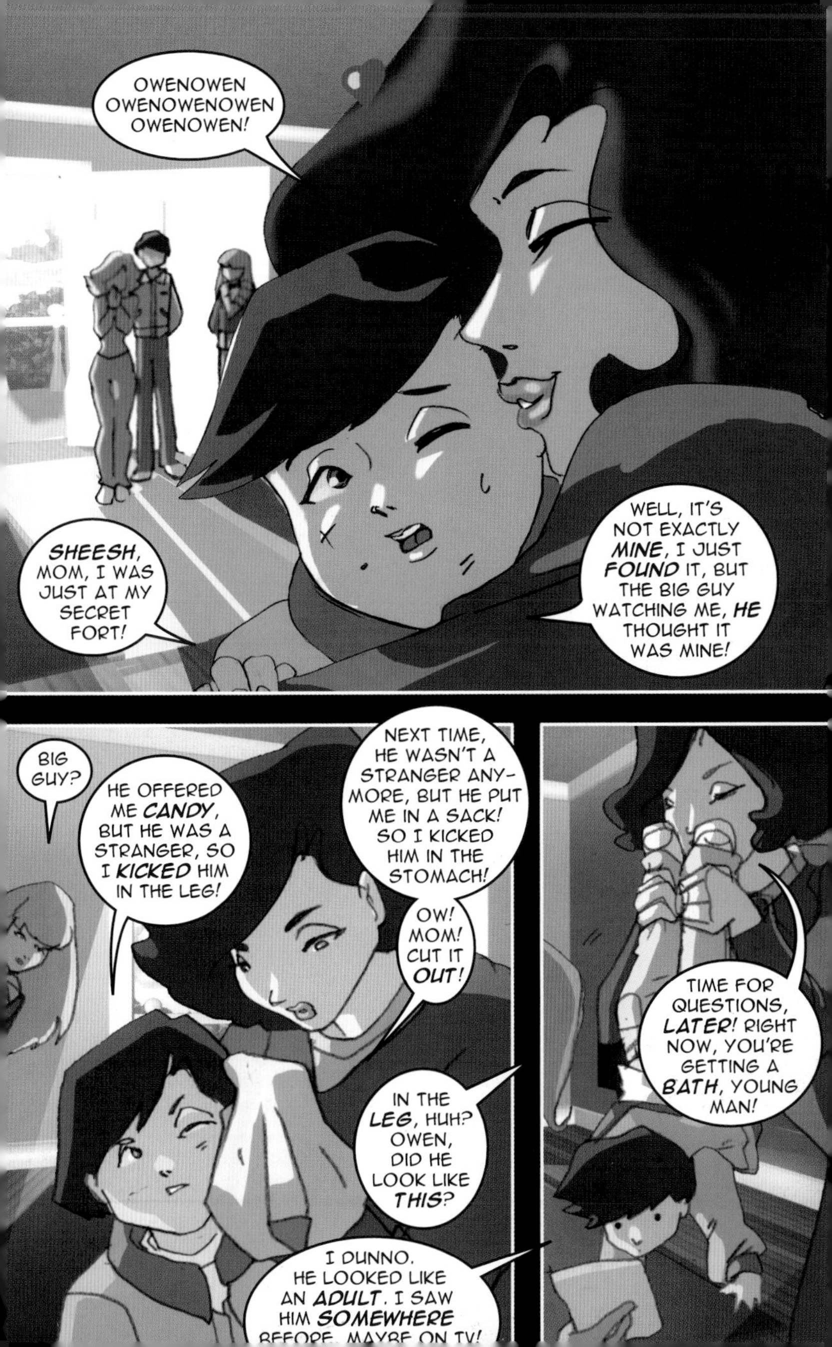
OWENOWEN OWENOWENOWEN OWENOWEN!
SHEESH, MOM, I WAS JUST AT MY SECRET FORT!
WELL, IT'S NOT EXACTLY MINE, I JUST FOUND IT, BUT THE BIG GUY WATCHING ME, HE THOUGHT IT WAS MINE!
BIG GUY?
HE OFFERED ME CANDY, BUT HE WAS A STRANGER, SO I KICKED HIM IN THE LEG!
NEXT TIME, HE WASN'T A STRANGER ANY-MORE, BUT HE PUT ME IN A SACK! SO I KICKED HIM IN THE STOMACH!
OW! MOM! CUT IT OUT!
IN THE LEG, HUH? OWEN, DID HE LOOK LIKE THIS?
I DUNNO. HE LOOKED LIKE AN ADULT. I SAW HIM SOMEWHERE BEFORE. MAYBE ON TV!
TIME FOR QUESTIONS, LATER! RIGHT NOW, YOU'RE GETTING A BATH, YOUNG MAN!

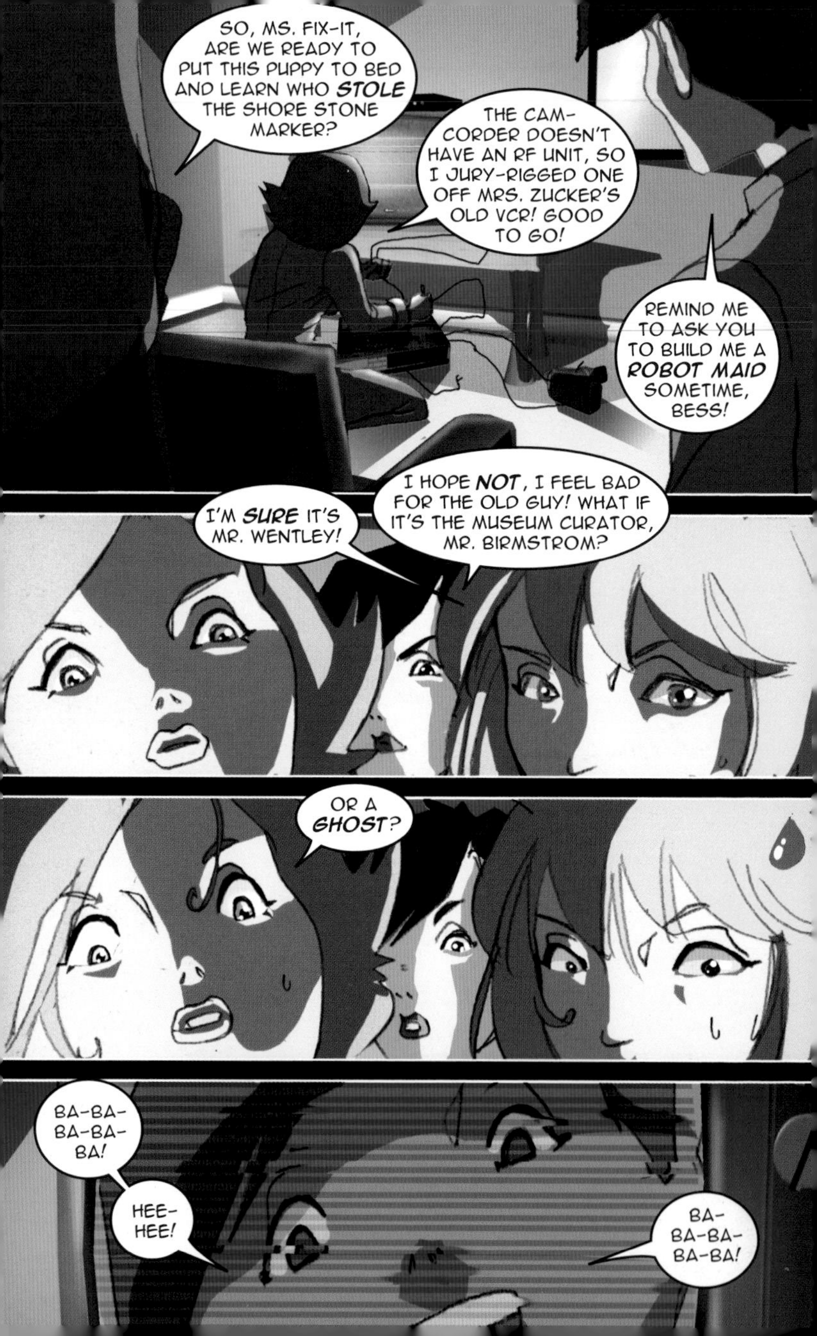
SO, MS. FIX-IT, ARE WE READY TO PUT THIS PUPPY TO BED AND LEARN WHO STOLE THE SHORE STONE MARKER?
THE CAM-CORDER DOESN'T HAVE AN RF UNIT, SO I JURY-RIGGED ONE OFF MRS. ZUCKER'S OLD VCR! GOOD TO GO!
REMIND ME TO ASK YOU TO BUILD ME A ROBOT MAID SOMETIME, BESS!
I'M SURE IT'S MR. WENTLEY!
I HOPE NOT, I FEEL BAD FOR THE OLD GUY! WHAT IF IT'S THE MUSEUM CURATOR, MR. BIRMSTROM?
OR A GHOST?
BA-BA-BA-BA-BA!
HEE-HEE!
BA-BA-BA-BA-BA!

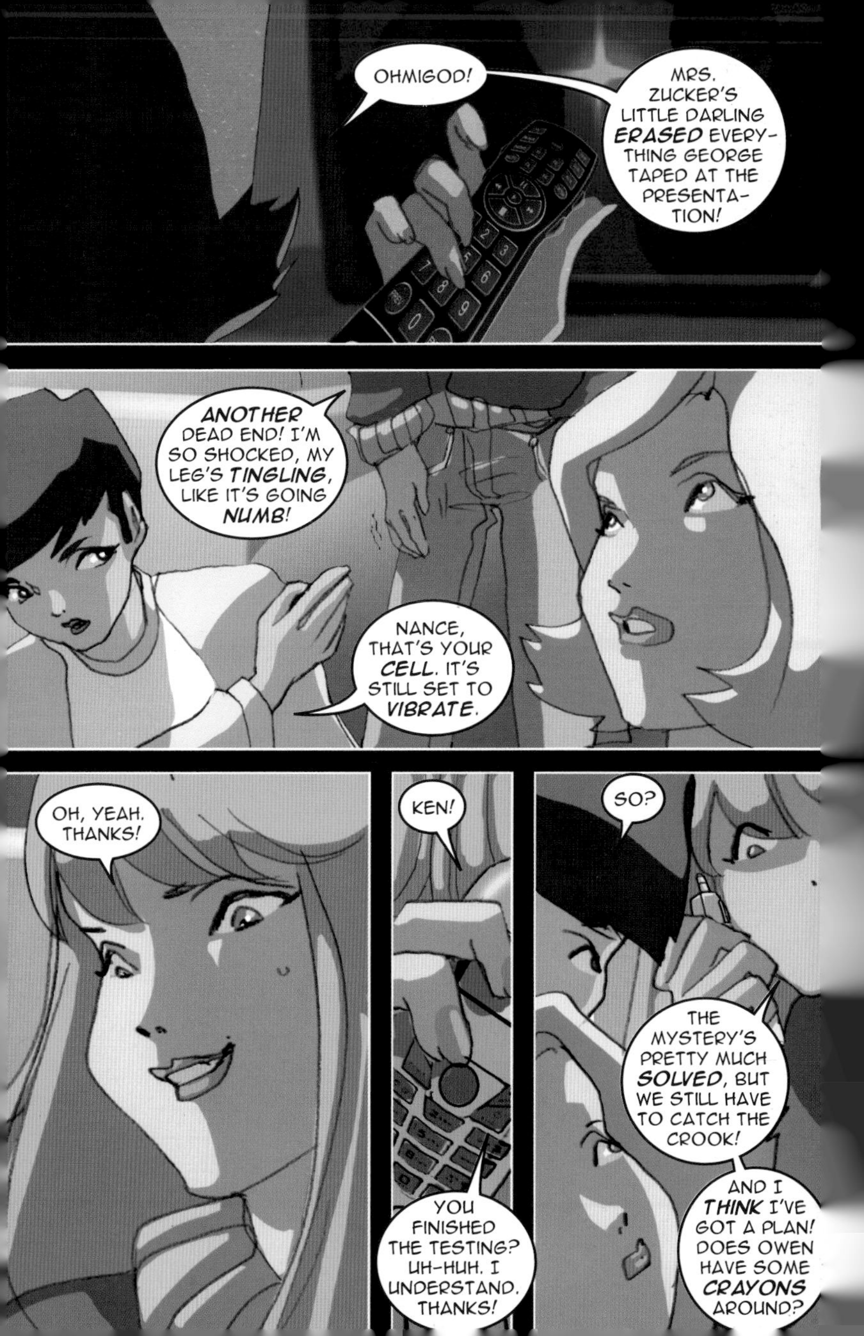
OHMIGOD!
MRS. ZUCKER'S LITTLE DARLING ERASED EVERY-THING GEORGE TAPED AT THE PRESENTA-TION!
ANOTHER DEAD END! I'M SO SHOCKED, MY LEG'S TINGLING, LIKE IT'S GOING NUMB!
NANCE, THAT'S YOUR CELL. IT'S STILL SET TO VIBRATE.
OH, YEAH. THANKS!
KEN!
YOU FINISHED THE TESTING? UH-HUH. I UNDERSTAND. THANKS!
SO?
THE MYSTERY'S PRETTY MUCH SOLVED, BUT WE STILL HAVE TO CATCH THE CROOK!
AND I THINK I'VE GOT A PLAN! DOES OWEN HAVE SOME CRAYONS AROUND?

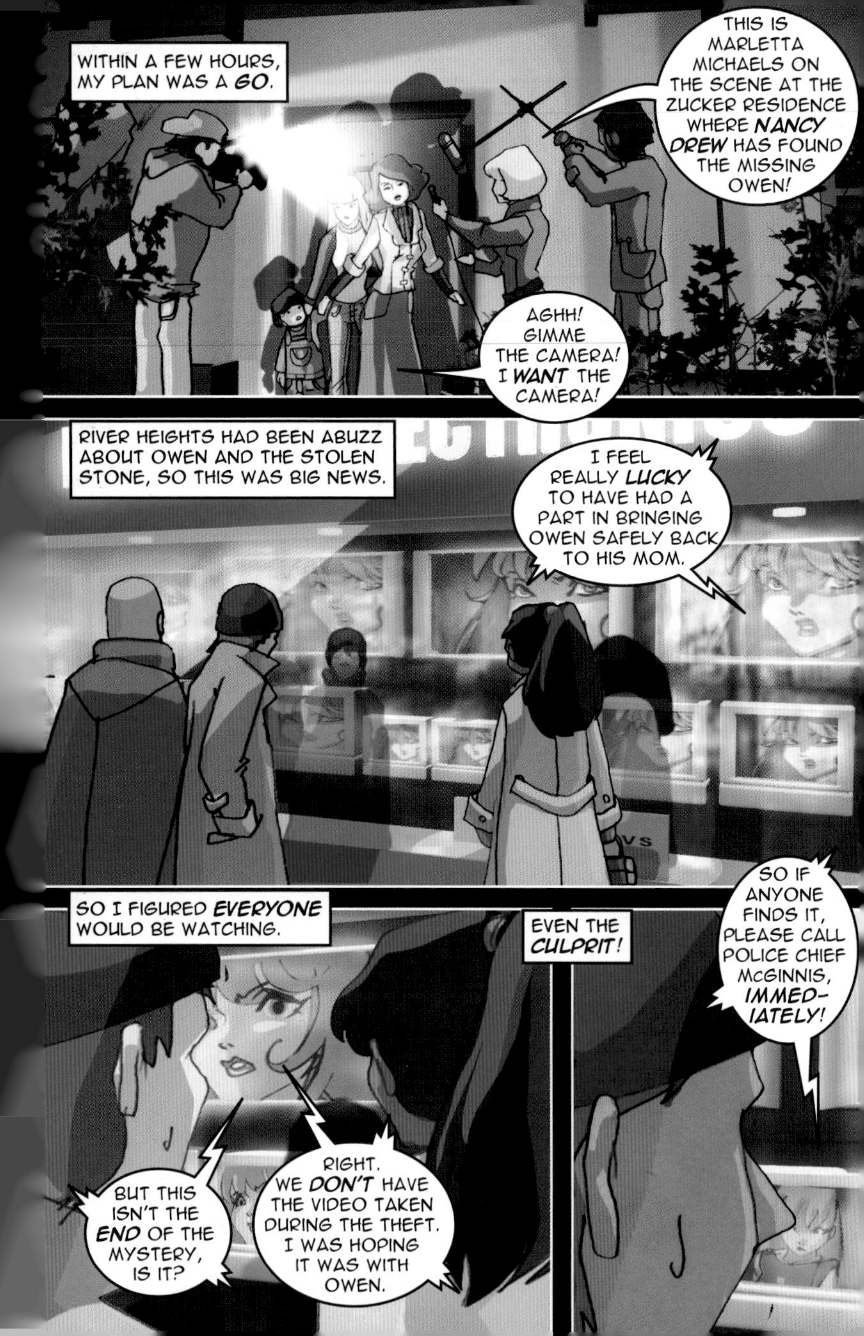

WITHIN A FEW HOURS, MY PLAN WAS A GO.
THIS IS MARLETTA MICHAELS ON THE SCENE AT THE ZUCKER RESIDENCE WHERE NANCY DREW HAS FOUND THE MISSING OWEN!
AGHH! GIMME THE CAMERA! I WANT THE CAMERA!
RIVER HEIGHTS HAD BEEN ABUZZ ABOUT OWEN AND THE STOLEN STONE, SO THIS WAS BIG NEWS.
I FEEL REALLY LUCKY TO HAVE HAD A PART IN BRINGING OWEN SAFELY BACK TO HIS MOM.
SO I FIGURED EVERYONE WOULD BE WATCHING.
EVEN THE CULPRIT!
BUT THIS ISN'T THE END OF THE MYSTERY, IS IT?
RIGHT. WE DON'T HAVE THE VIDEO TAKEN DURING THE THEFT. I WAS HOPING IT WAS WITH OWEN.
SO IF ANYONE FINDS IT, PLEASE CALL POLICE CHIEF McGINNIS, IMMEDIATELY!

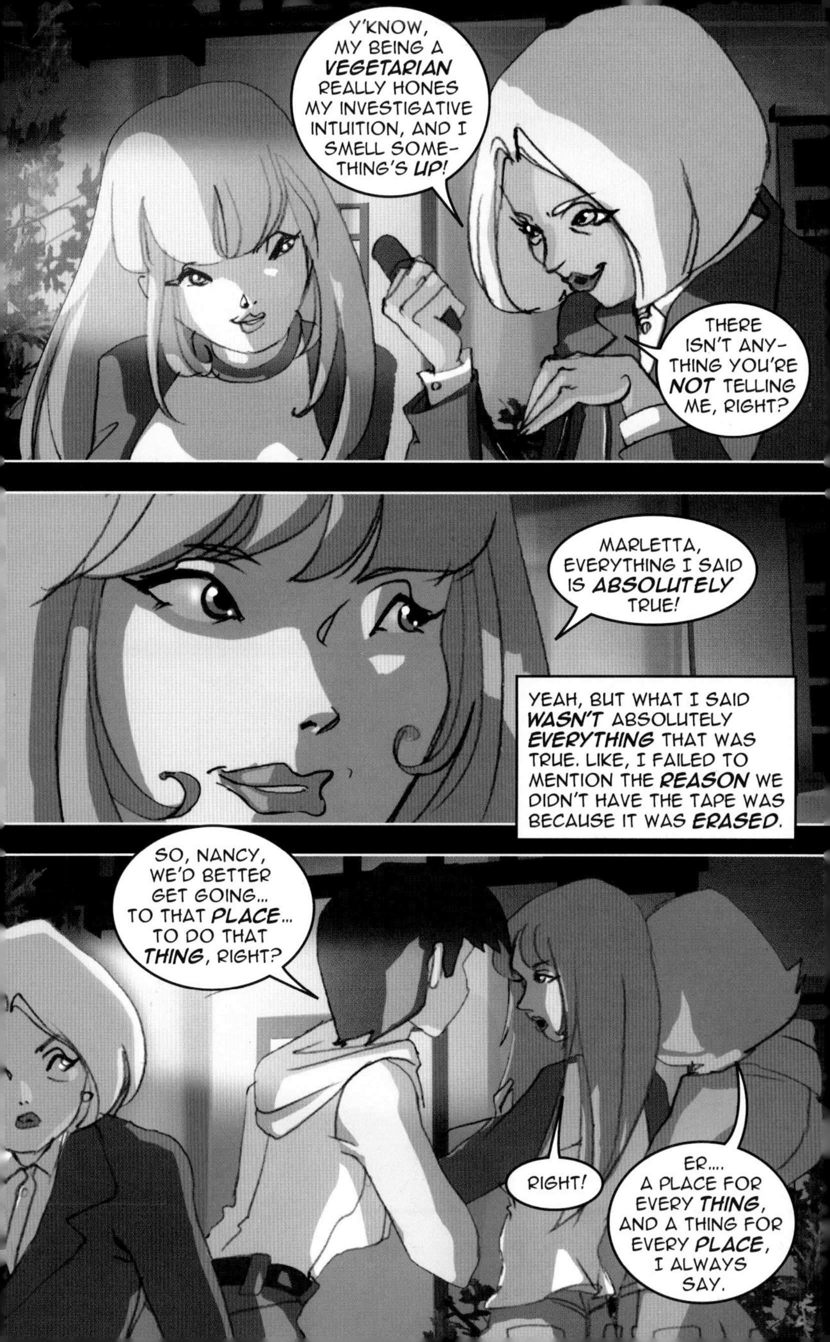
Y'KNOW, MY BEING A VEGETARIAN REALLY HONES MY INVESTIGATIVE INTUITION, AND I SMELL SOME-THING'S UP!
THERE ISN'T ANY-THING YOU'RE NOT TELLING ME, RIGHT?
MARLETTA, EVERYTHING I SAID IS ABSOLUTELY TRUE!
YEAH, BUT WHAT I SAID WASN'T ABSOLUTELY EVERYTHING THAT WAS TRUE. LIKE, I FAILED TO MENTION THE REASON WE DIDN'T HAVE THE TAPE WAS BECAUSE IT WAS ERASED.
SO, NANCY, WE'D BETTER GET GOING... TO THAT PLACE... TO DO THAT THING, RIGHT?
RIGHT!
ER.... A PLACE FOR EVERY THING, AND A THING FOR EVERY PLACE, I ALWAYS SAY.

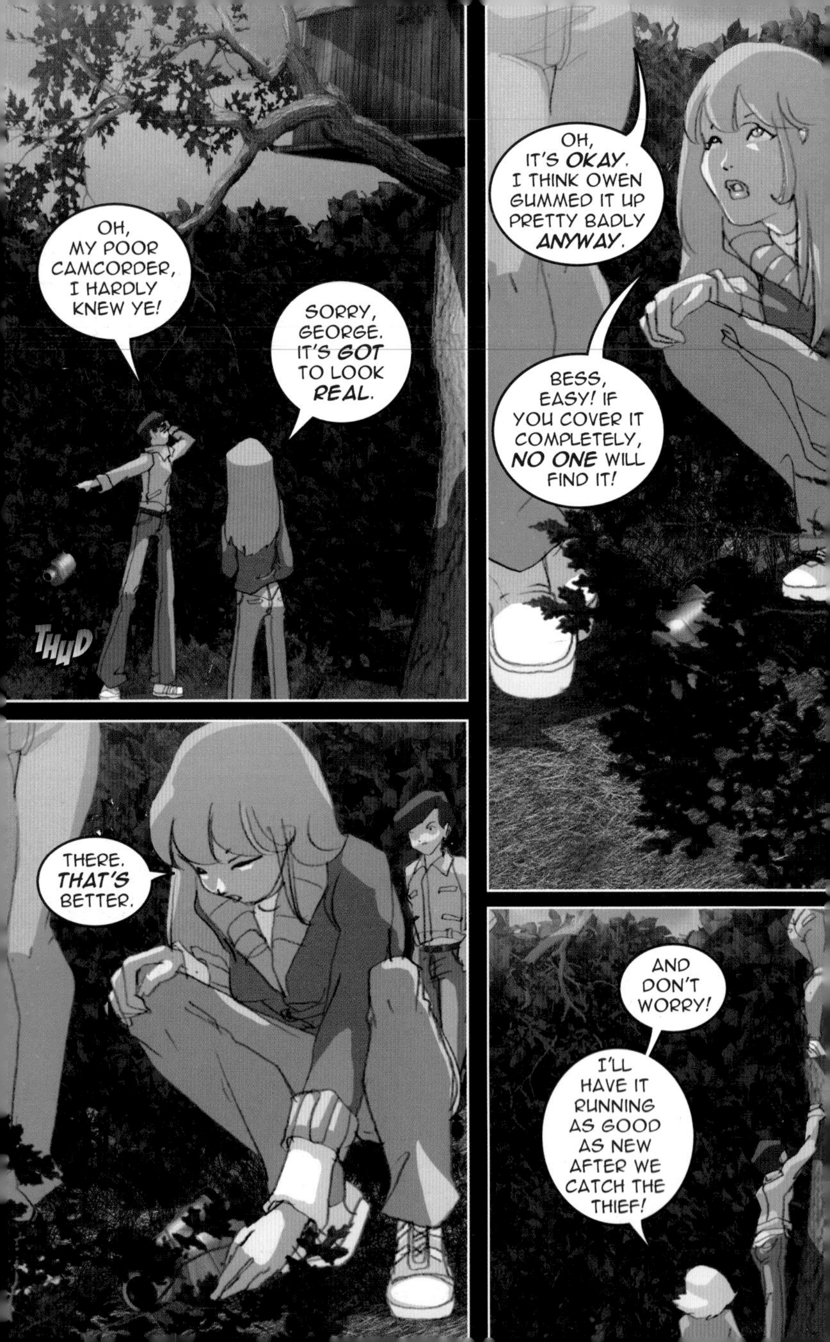
OH, MY POOR CAMCORDER, I HARDLY KNEW YE!
SORRY, GEORGE. IT'S *GOT* TO LOOK *REAL*.
THUD
OH, IT'S *OKAY*. I THINK OWEN GUMMED IT UP PRETTY BADLY *ANYWAY*.
BESS, EASY! IF YOU COVER IT COMPLETELY, *NO ONE* WILL FIND IT!
THERE. *THAT'S* BETTER.
AND DON'T WORRY!
I'LL HAVE IT RUNNING AS GOOD AS NEW AFTER WE CATCH THE THIEF!

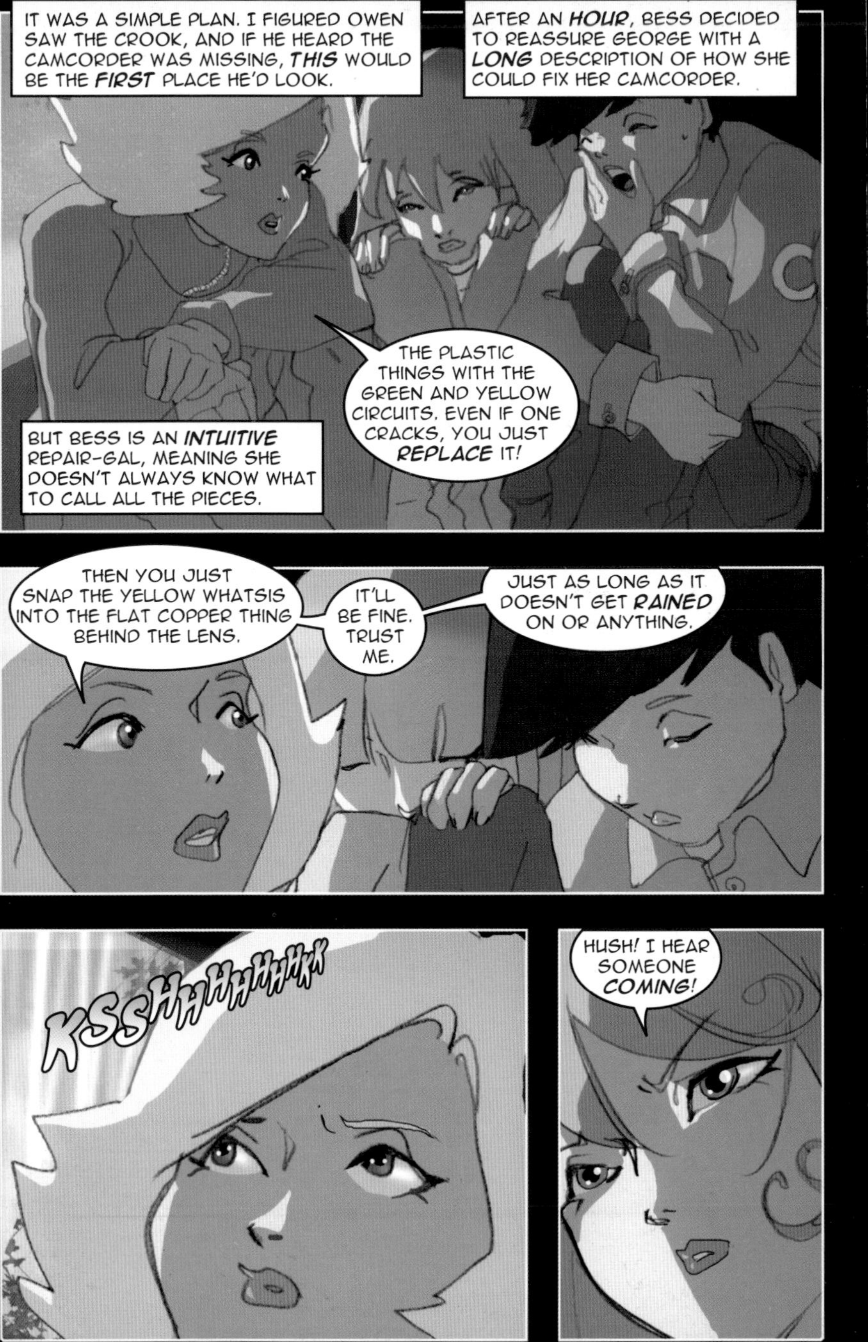
IT WAS A SIMPLE PLAN. I FIGURED OWEN SAW THE CROOK, AND IF HE HEARD THE CAMCORDER WAS MISSING, THIS WOULD BE THE FIRST PLACE HE'D LOOK.
AFTER AN HOUR, BESS DECIDED TO REASSURE GEORGE WITH A LONG DESCRIPTION OF HOW SHE COULD FIX HER CAMCORDER.
THE PLASTIC THINGS WITH THE GREEN AND YELLOW CIRCUITS. EVEN IF ONE CRACKS, YOU JUST REPLACE IT!
BUT BESS IS AN INTUITIVE REPAIR-GAL, MEANING SHE DOESN'T ALWAYS KNOW WHAT TO CALL ALL THE PIECES.
THEN YOU JUST SNAP THE YELLOW WHATSIS INTO THE FLAT COPPER THING BEHIND THE LENS.
IT'LL BE FINE. TRUST ME.
JUST AS LONG AS IT DOESN'T GET RAINED ON OR ANYTHING.
KSSHHHHHHHRK
HUSH! I HEAR SOMEONE COMING!

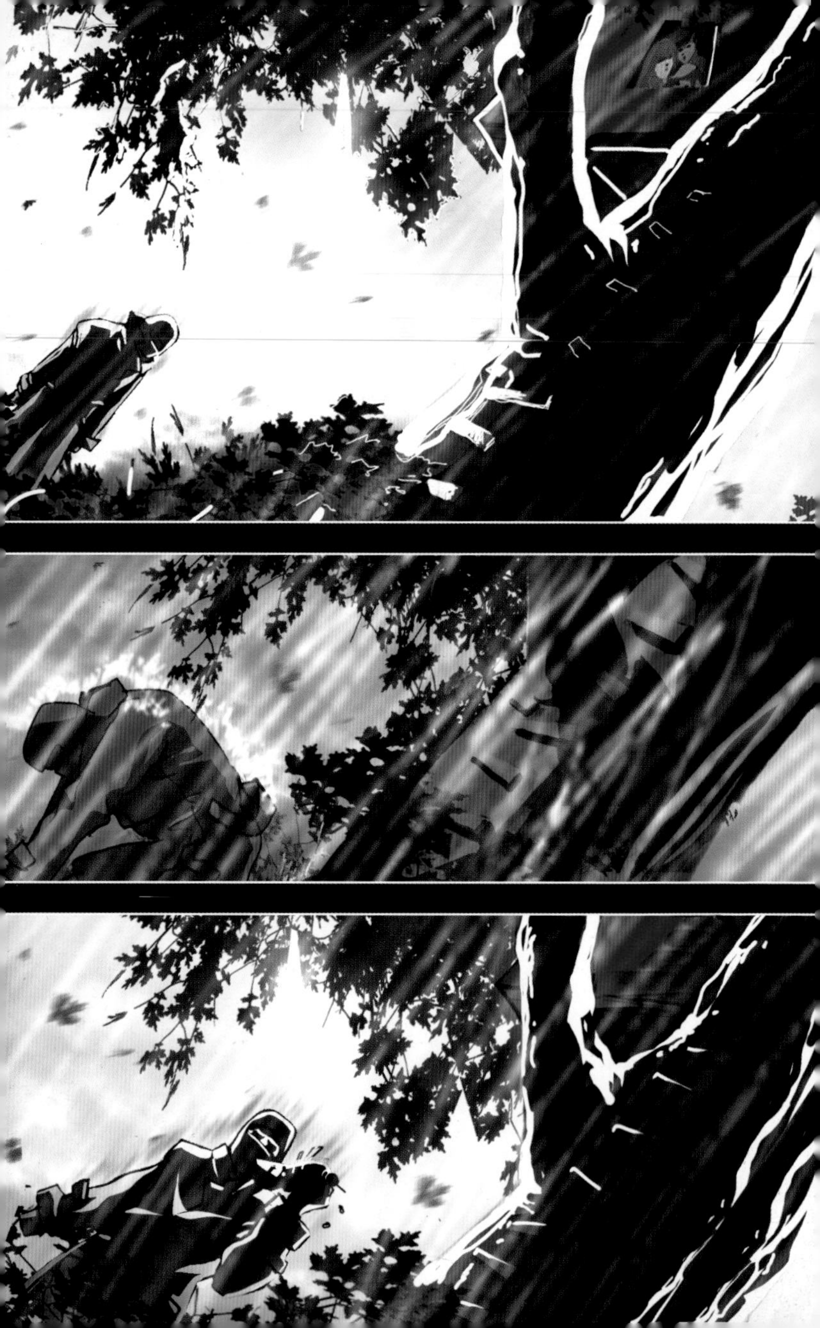

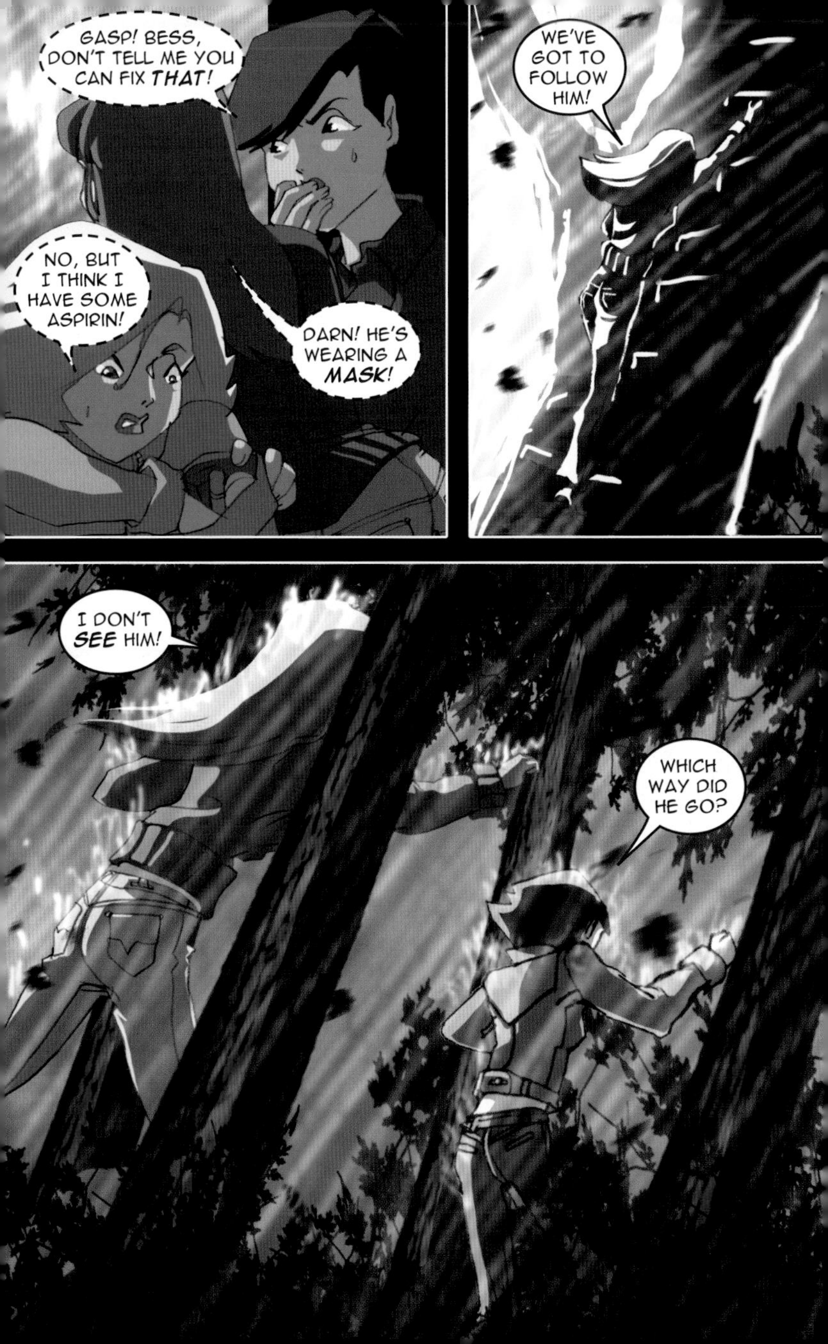
GASP! BESS, DON'T TELL ME YOU CAN FIX THAT!
NO, BUT I THINK I HAVE SOME ASPIRIN!
DARN! HE'S WEARING A MASK!
WE'VE GOT TO FOLLOW HIM!
I DON'T SEE HIM!
WHICH WAY DID HE GO?

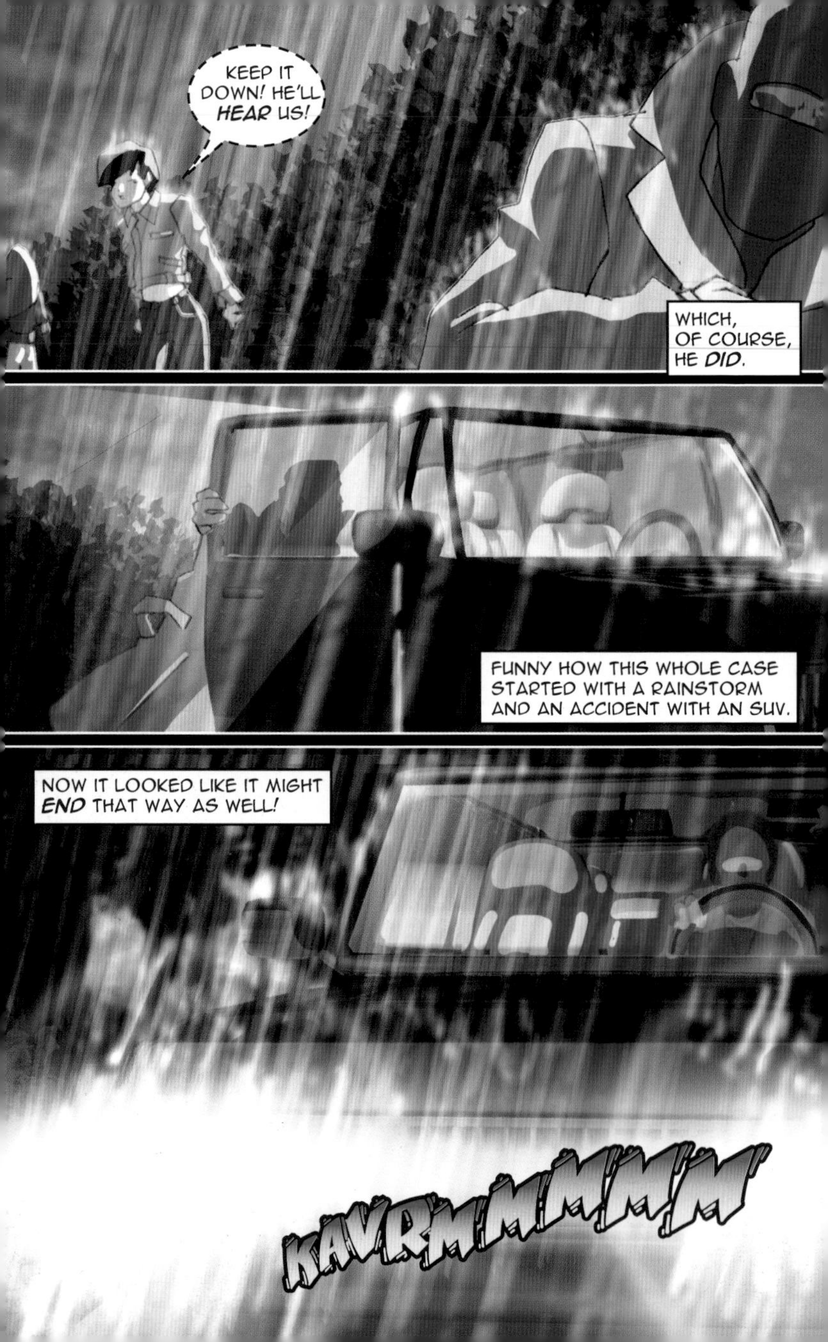
KEEP IT DOWN! HE'LL HEAR US!
WHICH, OF COURSE, HE DID.
FUNNY HOW THIS WHOLE CASE STARTED WITH A RAINSTORM AND AN ACCIDENT WITH AN SUV.
NOW IT LOOKED LIKE IT MIGHT END THAT WAY AS WELL!
KAVRMMMMMM

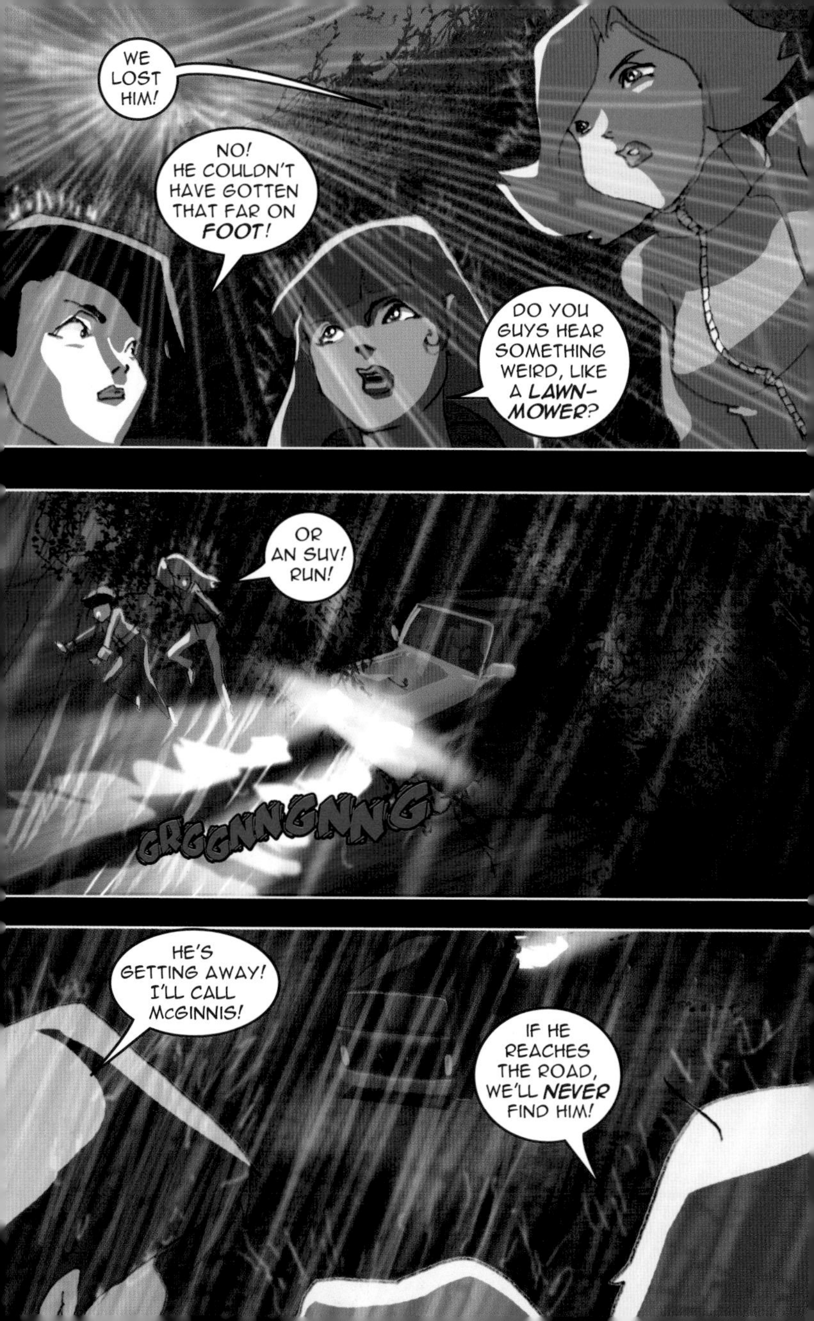
WE LOST HIM!
NO! HE COULDN'T HAVE GOTTEN THAT FAR ON FOOT!
DO YOU GUYS HEAR SOMETHING WEIRD, LIKE A LAWN-MOWER?
OR AN SUV! RUN!
GRGGNNGNNG
HE'S GETTING AWAY! I'LL CALL McGINNIS!
IF HE REACHES THE ROAD, WE'LL NEVER FIND HIM!

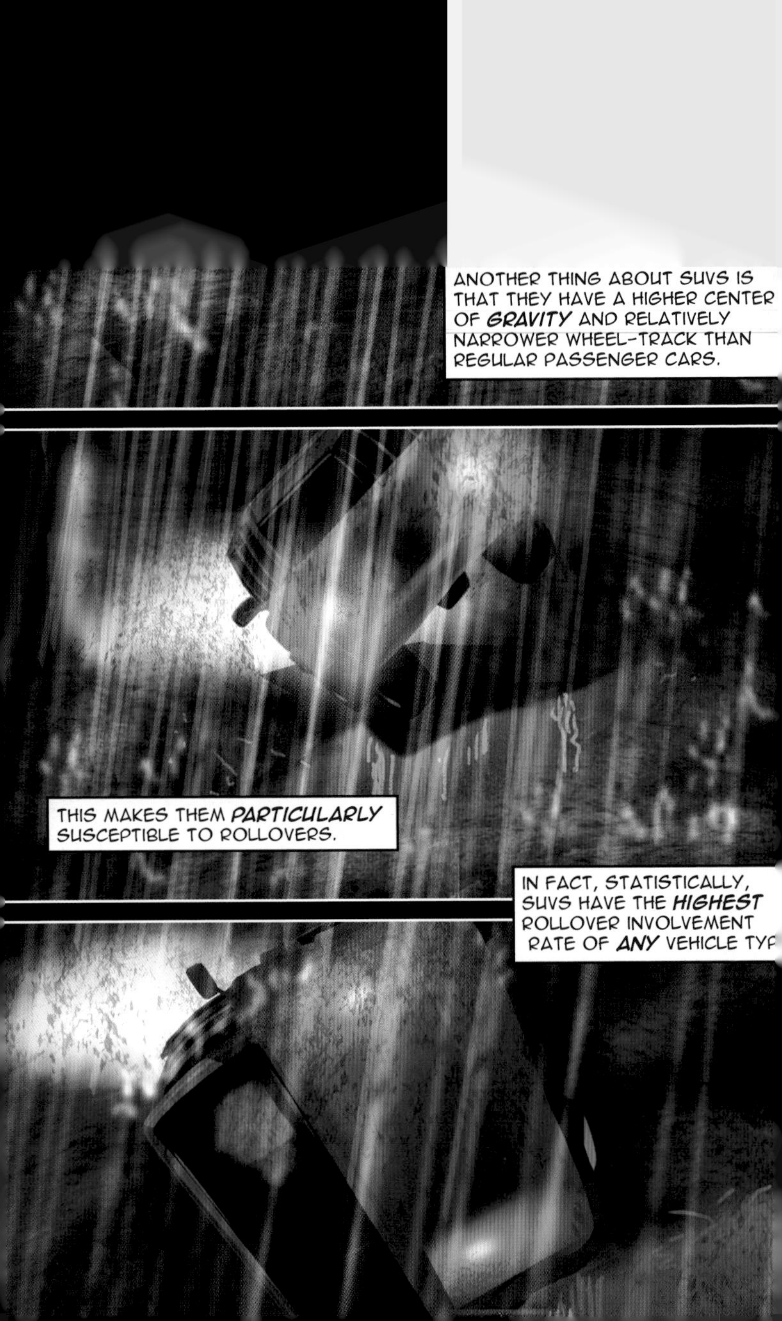
ANOTHER THING ABOUT SUVS IS THAT THEY HAVE A HIGHER CENTER OF GRAVITY AND RELATIVELY NARROWER WHEEL-TRACK THAN REGULAR PASSENGER CARS.
THIS MAKES THEM PARTICULARLY SUSCEPTIBLE TO ROLLOVERS.
IN FACT, STATISTICALLY, SUVS HAVE THE HIGHEST ROLLOVER INVOLVEMENT RATE OF ANY VEHICLE TYP

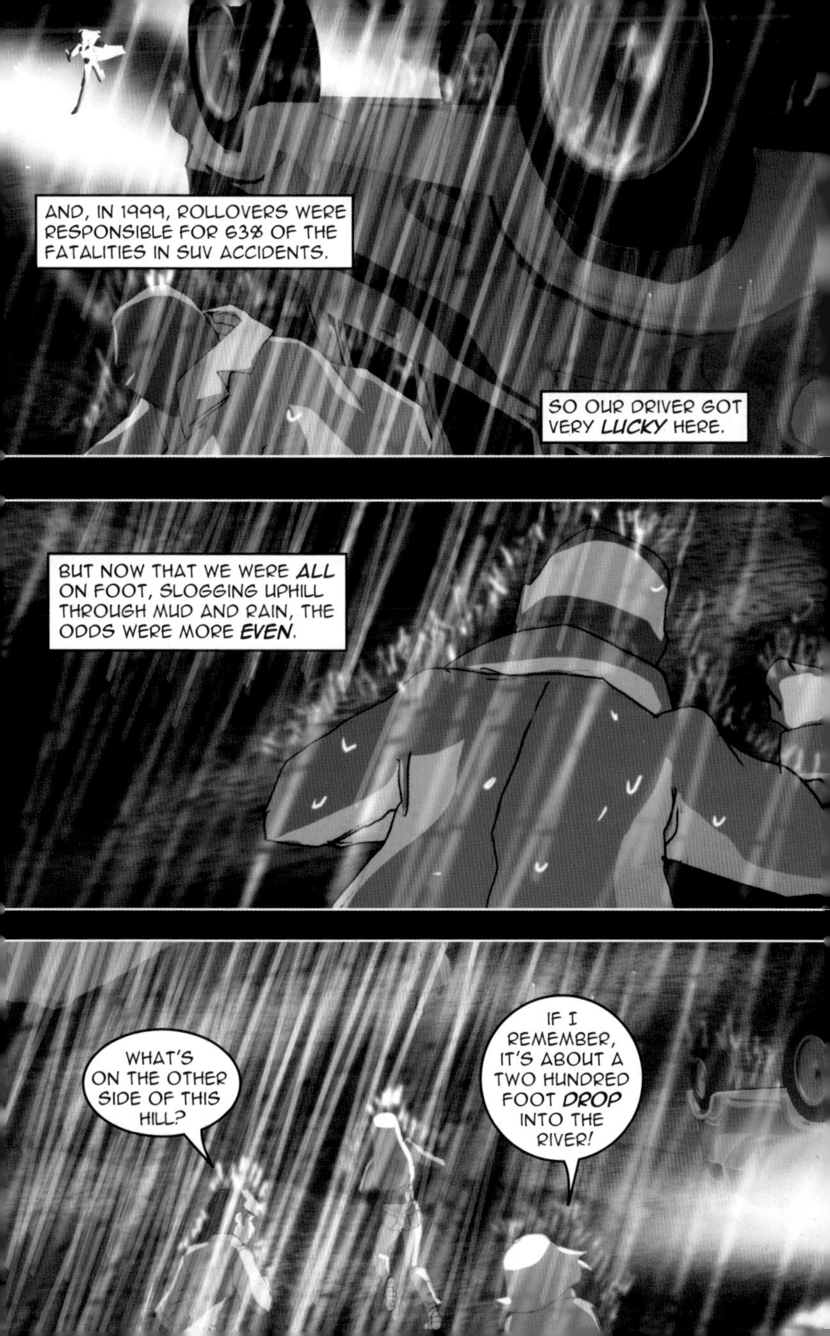
AND, IN 1999, ROLLOVERS WERE RESPONSIBLE FOR 63% OF THE FATALITIES IN SUV ACCIDENTS.
SO OUR DRIVER GOT VERY LUCKY HERE.
BUT NOW THAT WE WERE ALL ON FOOT, SLOGGING UPHILL THROUGH MUD AND RAIN, THE ODDS WERE MORE EVEN.
WHAT'S ON THE OTHER SIDE OF THIS HILL?
IF I REMEMBER, IT'S ABOUT A TWO HUNDRED FOOT DROP INTO THE RIVER!

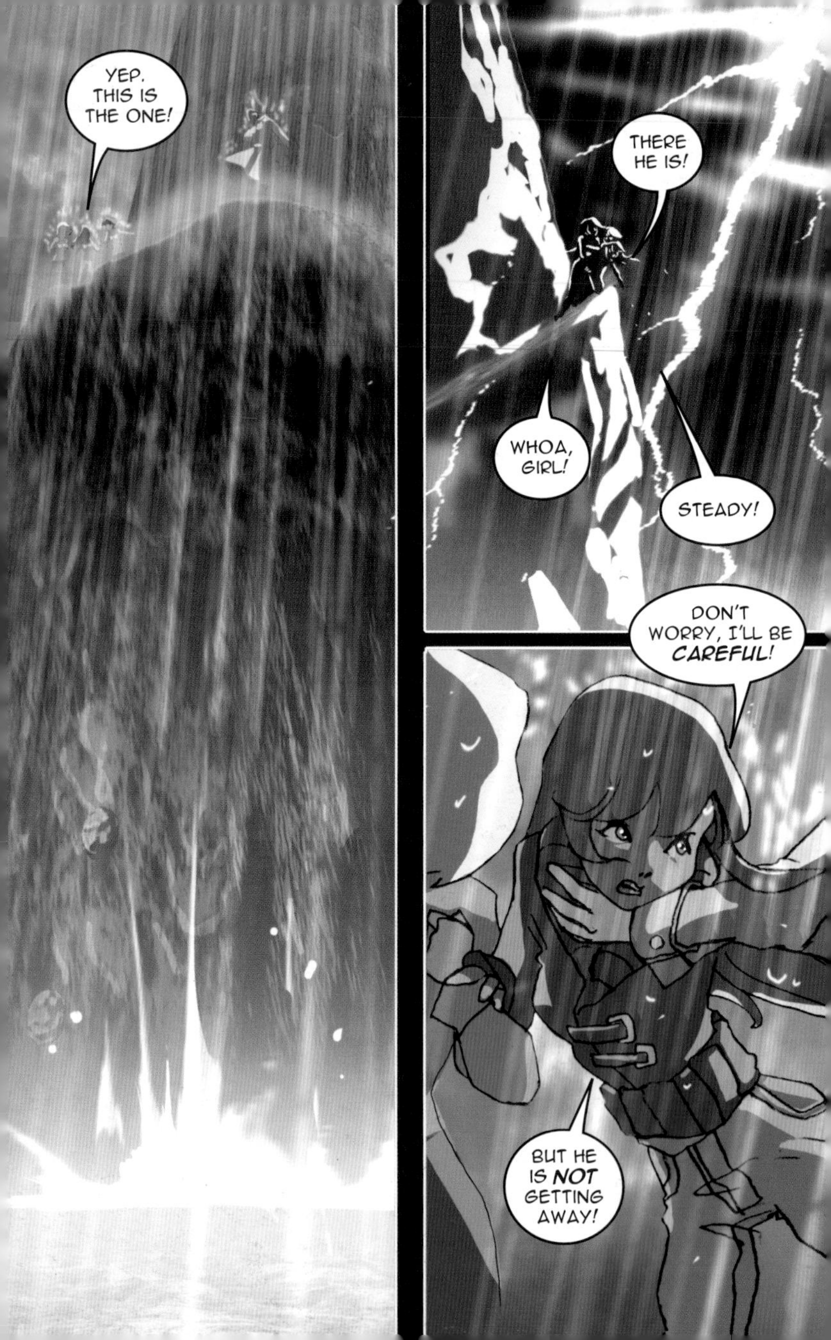
YEP. THIS IS THE ONE!
THERE HE IS!
WHOA, GIRL!
STEADY!
DON'T WORRY, I'LL BE **CAREFUL**!
BUT HE IS **NOT** GETTING AWAY!

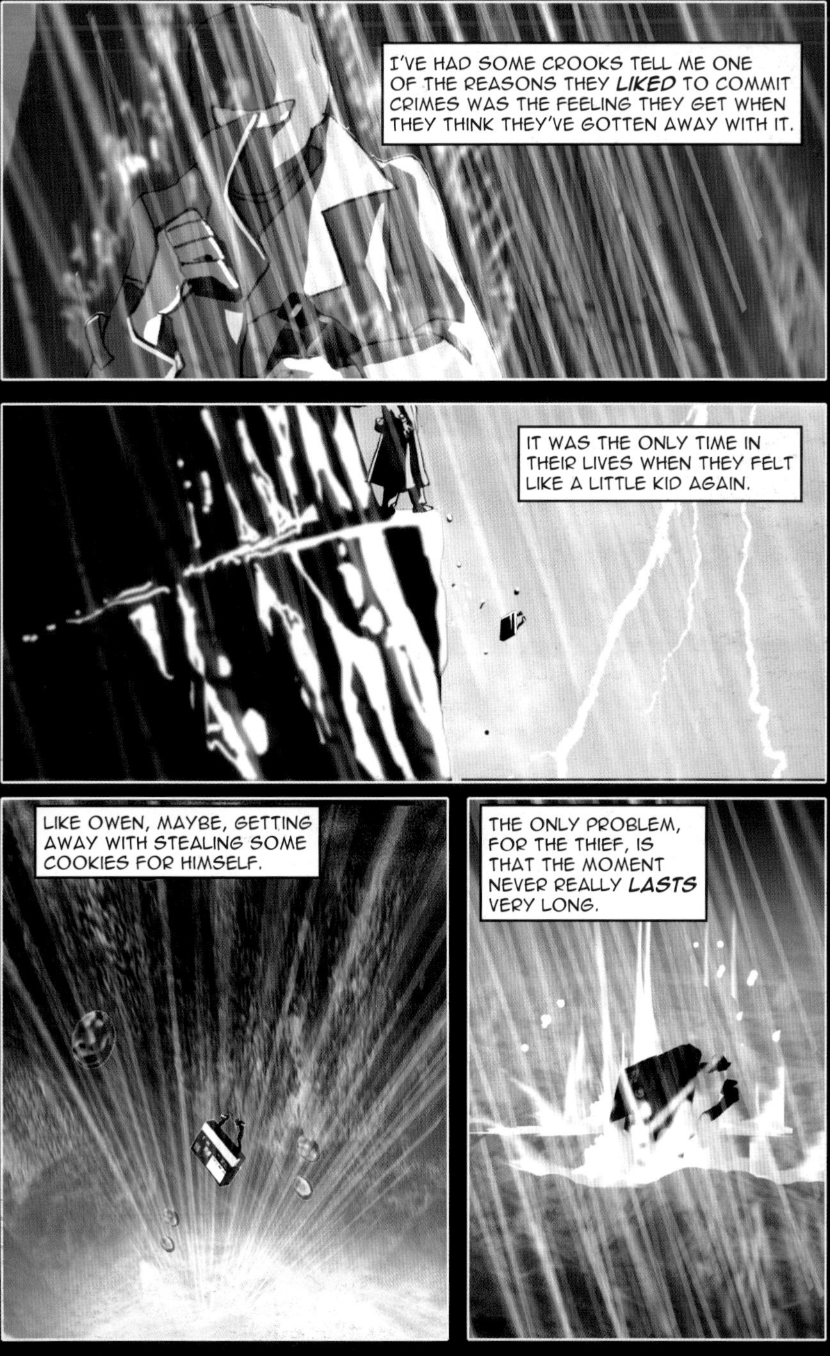
I'VE HAD SOME CROOKS TELL ME ONE OF THE REASONS THEY *LIKED* TO COMMIT CRIMES WAS THE FEELING THEY GET WHEN THEY THINK THEY'VE GOTTEN AWAY WITH IT.
IT WAS THE ONLY TIME IN THEIR LIVES WHEN THEY FELT LIKE A LITTLE KID AGAIN.
LIKE OWEN, MAYBE, GETTING AWAY WITH STEALING SOME COOKIES FOR HIMSELF.
THE ONLY PROBLEM, FOR THE THIEF, IS THAT THE MOMENT NEVER REALLY *LASTS* VERY LONG.

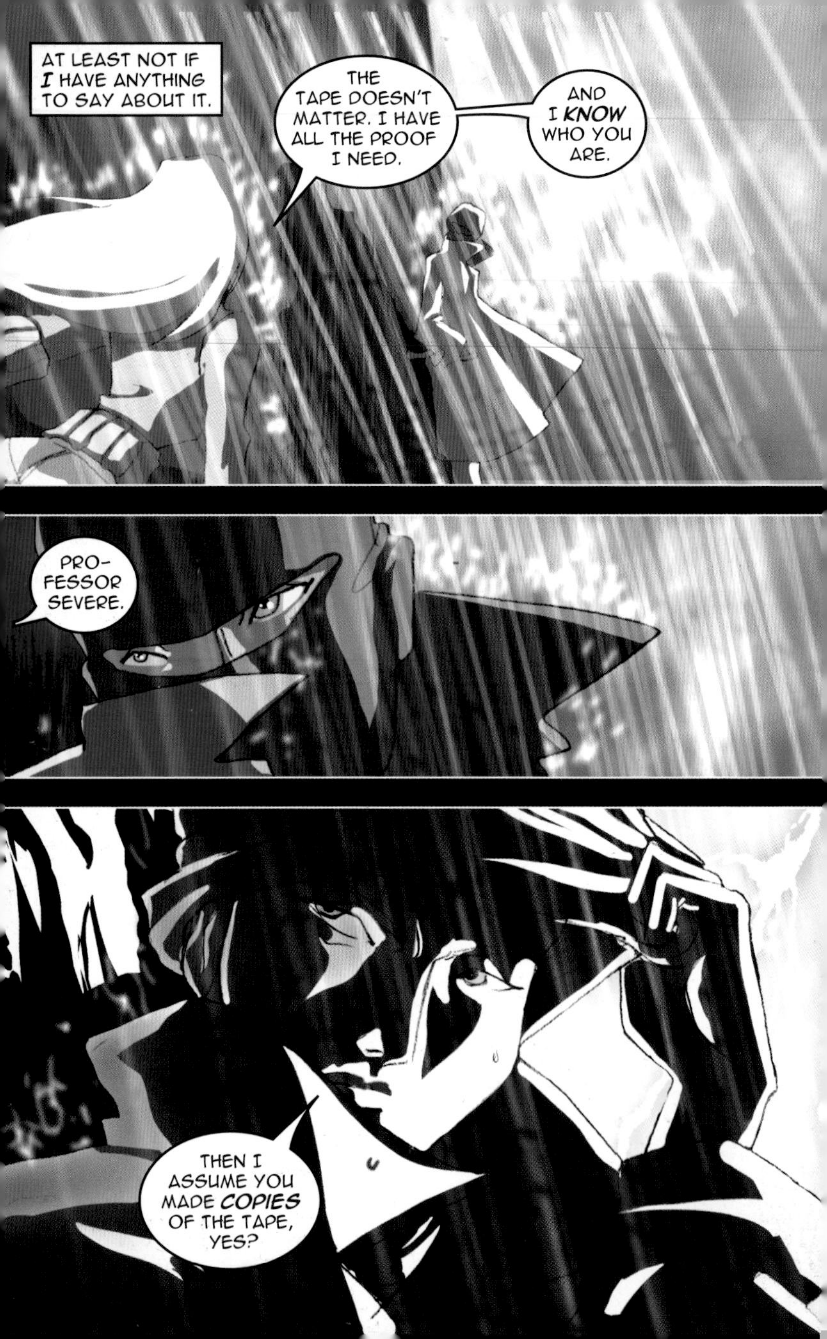
AT LEAST NOT IF I HAVE ANYTHING TO SAY ABOUT IT.
THE TAPE DOESN'T MATTER. I HAVE ALL THE PROOF I NEED.
AND I KNOW WHO YOU ARE.
PRO-FESSOR SEVERE.
THEN I ASSUME YOU MADE COPIES OF THE TAPE, YES?

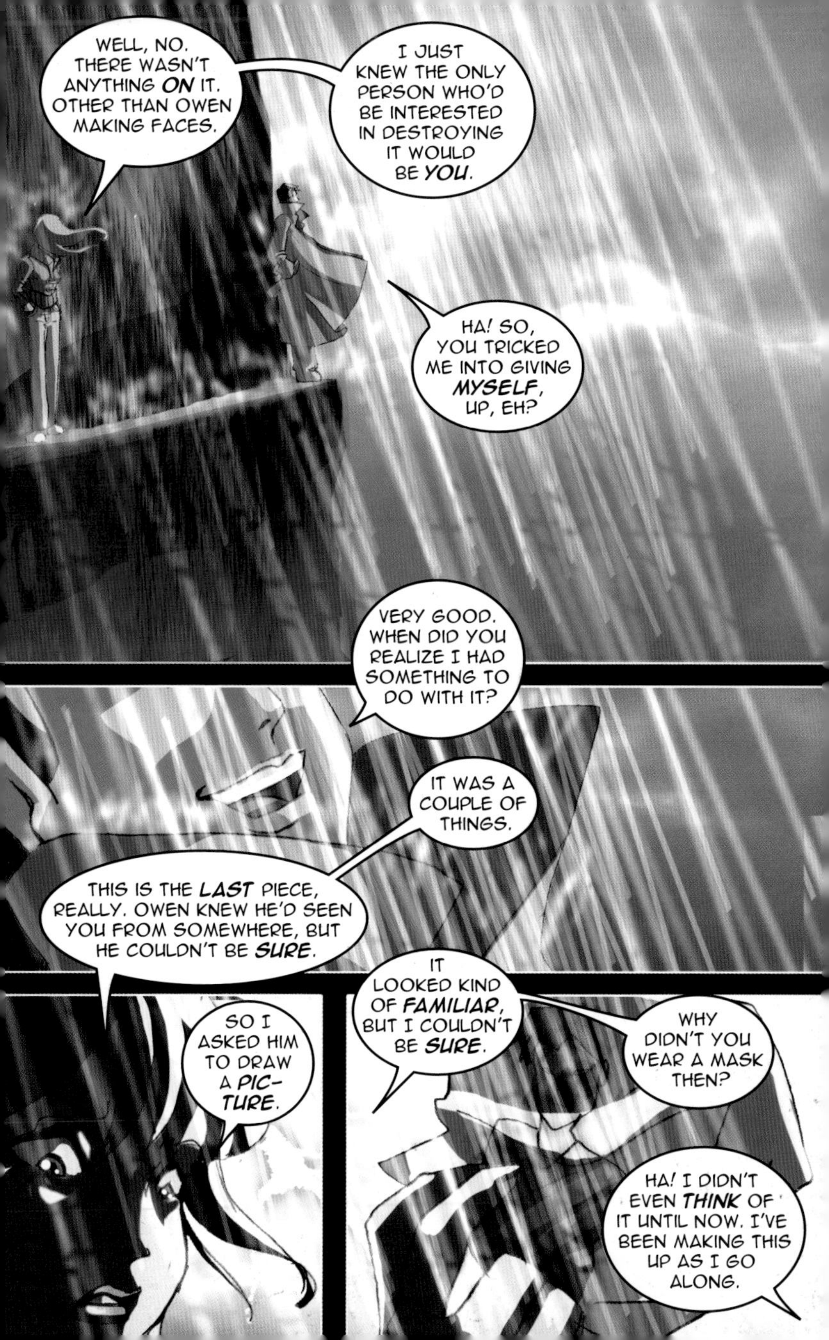
WELL, NO. THERE WASN'T ANYTHING ON IT. OTHER THAN OWEN MAKING FACES.
I JUST KNEW THE ONLY PERSON WHO'D BE INTERESTED IN DESTROYING IT WOULD BE YOU.
HA! SO, YOU TRICKED ME INTO GIVING MYSELF, UP, EH?
VERY GOOD. WHEN DID YOU REALIZE I HAD SOMETHING TO DO WITH IT?
IT WAS A COUPLE OF THINGS.
THIS IS THE LAST PIECE, REALLY. OWEN KNEW HE'D SEEN YOU FROM SOMEWHERE, BUT HE COULDN'T BE SURE.
SO I ASKED HIM TO DRAW A PIC-TURE.
IT LOOKED KIND OF FAMILIAR, BUT I COULDN'T BE SURE.
WHY DIDN'T YOU WEAR A MASK THEN?
HA! I DIDN'T EVEN THINK OF IT UNTIL NOW. I'VE BEEN MAKING THIS UP AS I GO ALONG.

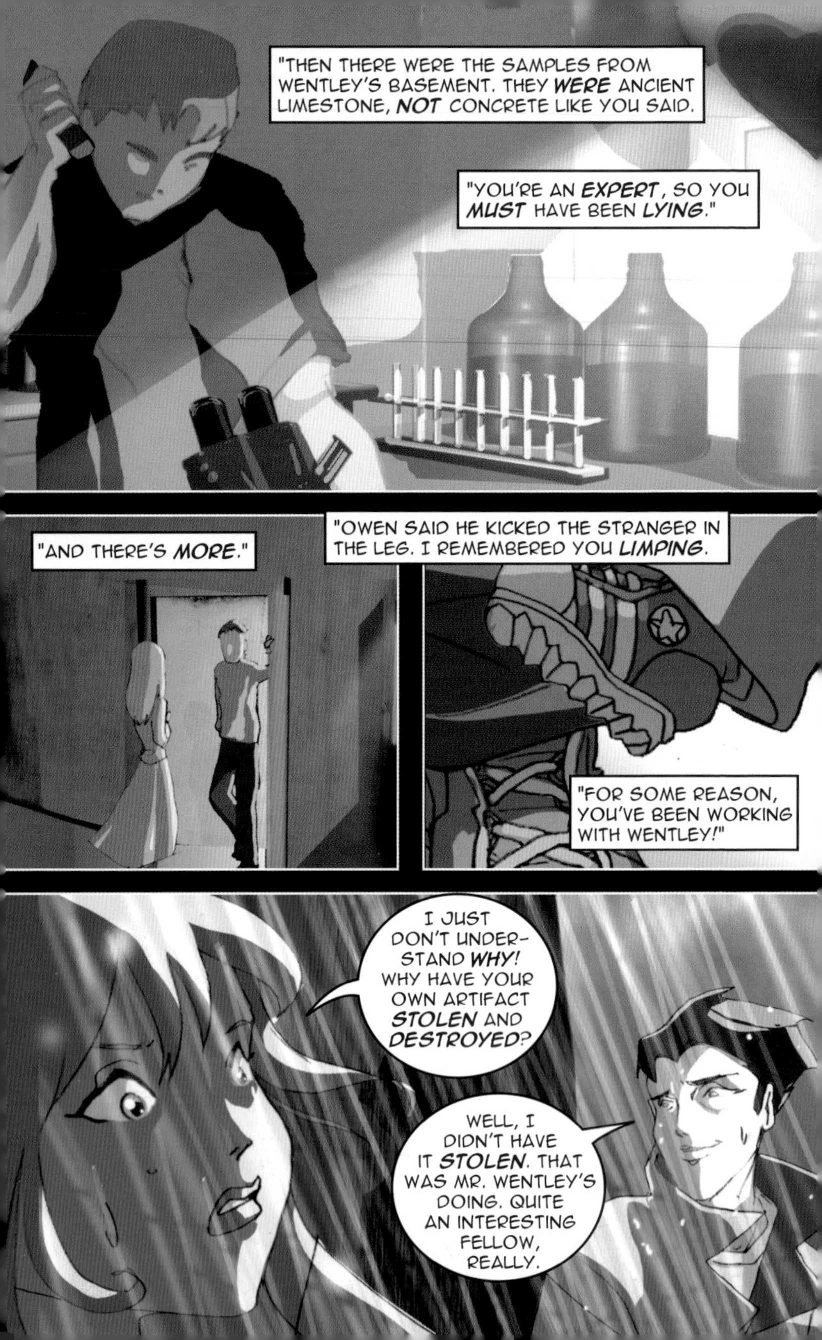
"THEN THERE WERE THE SAMPLES FROM WENTLEY'S BASEMENT. THEY **WERE** ANCIENT LIMESTONE, **NOT** CONCRETE LIKE YOU SAID.
"YOU'RE AN **EXPERT**, SO YOU **MUST** HAVE BEEN **LYING**."
"AND THERE'S **MORE**."
"OWEN SAID HE KICKED THE STRANGER IN THE LEG. I REMEMBERED YOU **LIMPING**.
"FOR SOME REASON, YOU'VE BEEN WORKING WITH WENTLEY!"
I JUST DON'T UNDER-STAND **WHY**! WHY HAVE YOUR OWN ARTIFACT **STOLEN** AND **DESTROYED**?
WELL, I DIDN'T HAVE IT **STOLEN**. THAT WAS MR. WENTLEY'S DOING. QUITE AN INTERESTING FELLOW, REALLY.

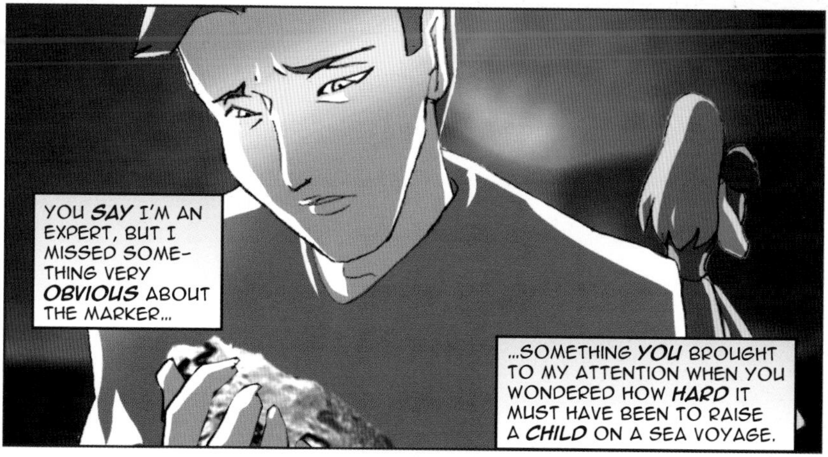
YOU SAY I'M AN EXPERT, BUT I MISSED SOME-THING VERY OBVIOUS ABOUT THE MARKER...
...SOMETHING YOU BROUGHT TO MY ATTENTION WHEN YOU WONDERED HOW HARD IT MUST HAVE BEEN TO RAISE A CHILD ON A SEA VOYAGE.

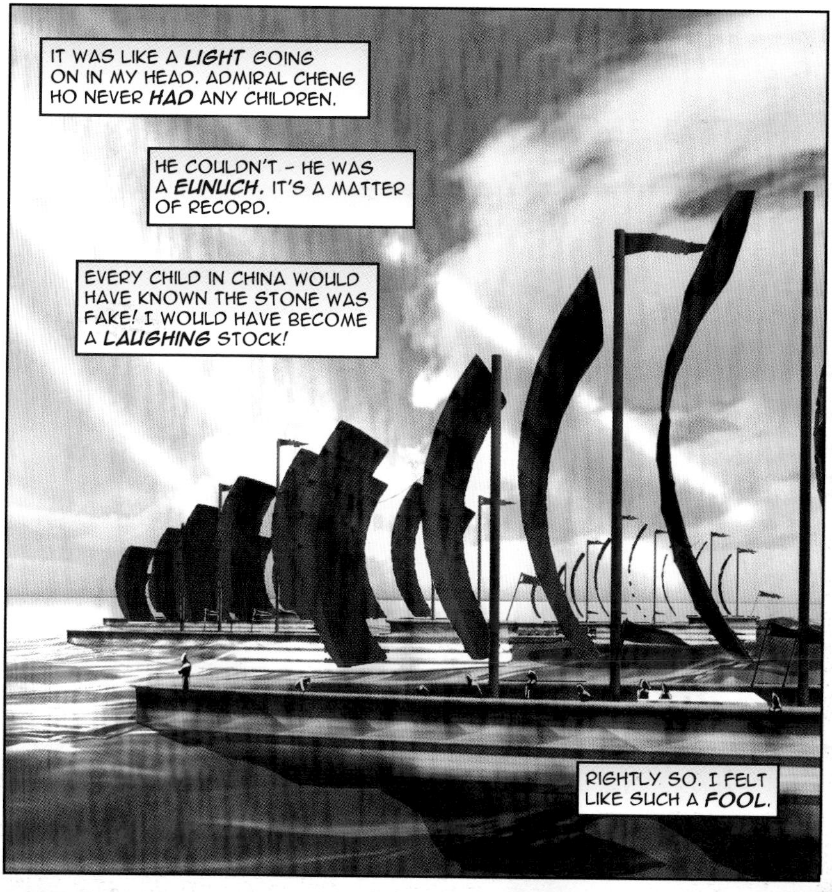
IT WAS LIKE A LIGHT GOING ON IN MY HEAD. ADMIRAL CHENG HO NEVER HAD ANY CHILDREN.
HE COULDN'T - HE WAS A EUNUCH. IT'S A MATTER OF RECORD.
EVERY CHILD IN CHINA WOULD HAVE KNOWN THE STONE WAS FAKE! I WOULD HAVE BECOME A LAUGHING STOCK!
RIGHTLY SO. I FELT LIKE SUCH A FOOL.

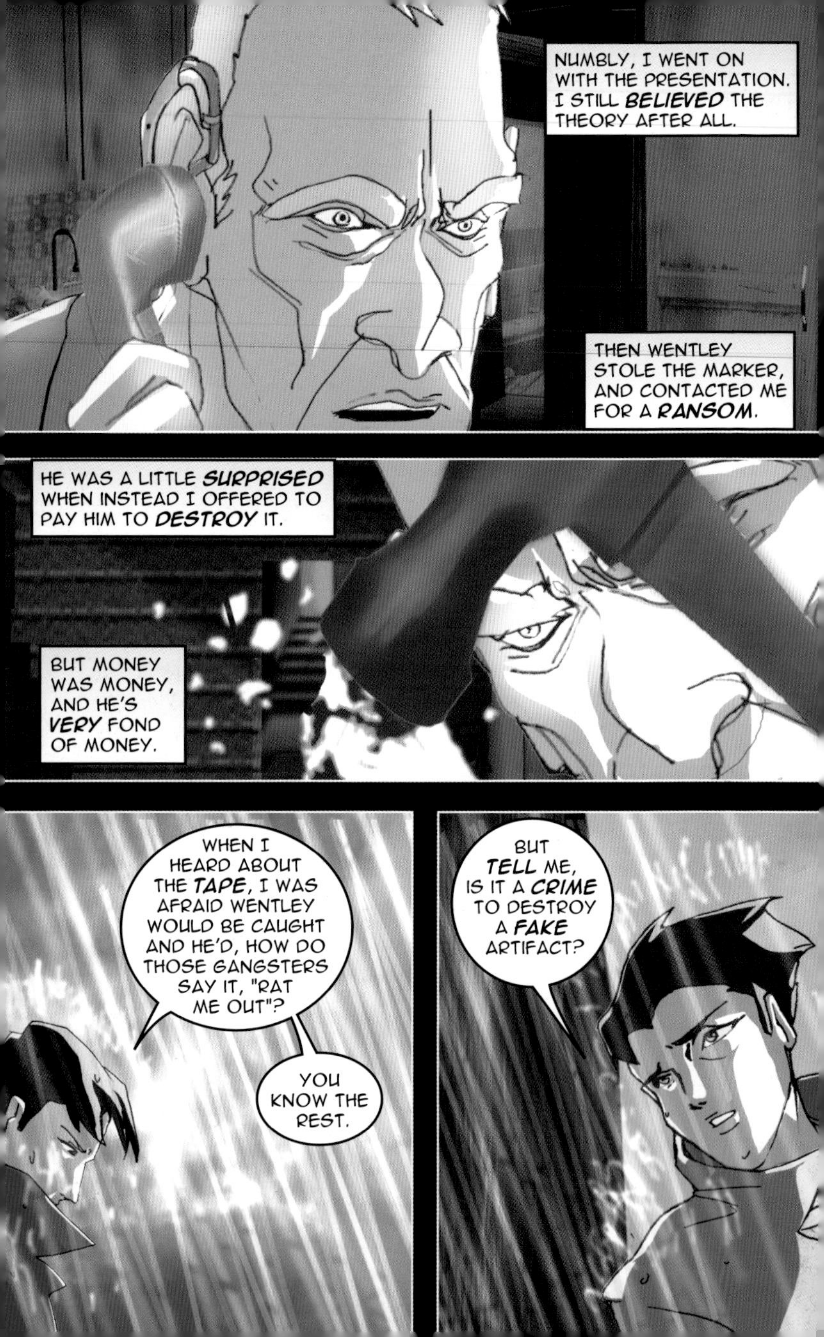
NUMBLY, I WENT ON WITH THE PRESENTATION. I STILL *BELIEVED* THE THEORY AFTER ALL.
THEN WENTLEY STOLE THE MARKER, AND CONTACTED ME FOR A *RANSOM*.
HE WAS A LITTLE *SURPRISED* WHEN INSTEAD I OFFERED TO PAY HIM TO *DESTROY* IT.
BUT MONEY WAS MONEY, AND HE'S *VERY* FOND OF MONEY.
WHEN I HEARD ABOUT THE *TAPE*, I WAS AFRAID WENTLEY WOULD BE CAUGHT AND HE'D, HOW DO THOSE GANGSTERS SAY IT, "RAT ME OUT"?
YOU KNOW THE REST.
BUT *TELL* ME, IS IT A *CRIME* TO DESTROY A *FAKE* ARTIFACT?

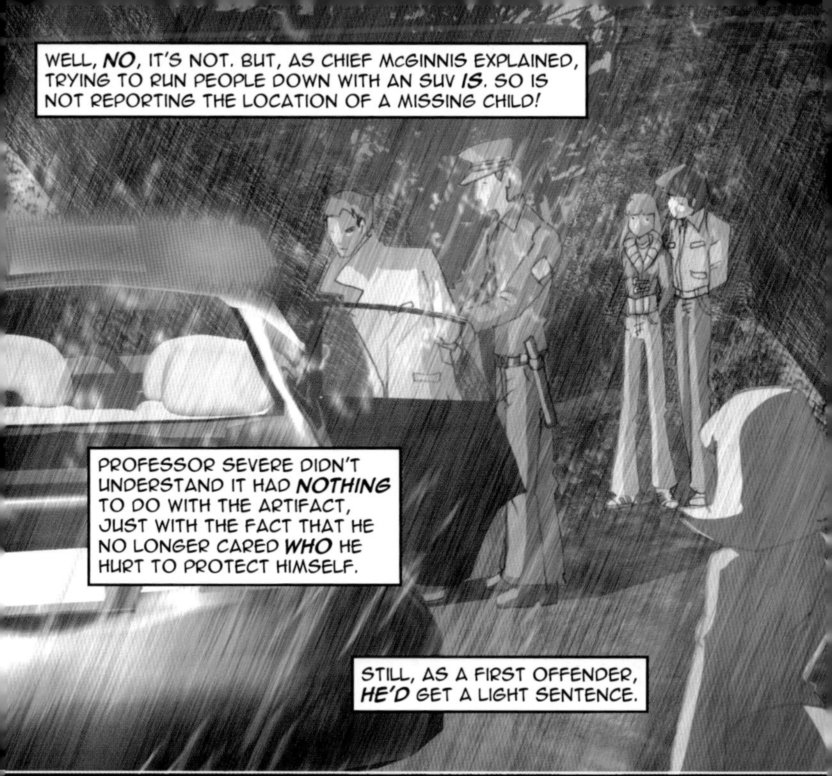
WELL, NO, IT'S NOT. BUT, AS CHIEF McGINNIS EXPLAINED, TRYING TO RUN PEOPLE DOWN WITH AN SUV IS. SO IS NOT REPORTING THE LOCATION OF A MISSING CHILD!
PROFESSOR SEVERE DIDN'T UNDERSTAND IT HAD NOTHING TO DO WITH THE ARTIFACT, JUST WITH THE FACT THAT HE NO LONGER CARED WHO HE HURT TO PROTECT HIMSELF.
STILL, AS A FIRST OFFENDER, HE'D GET A LIGHT SENTENCE.

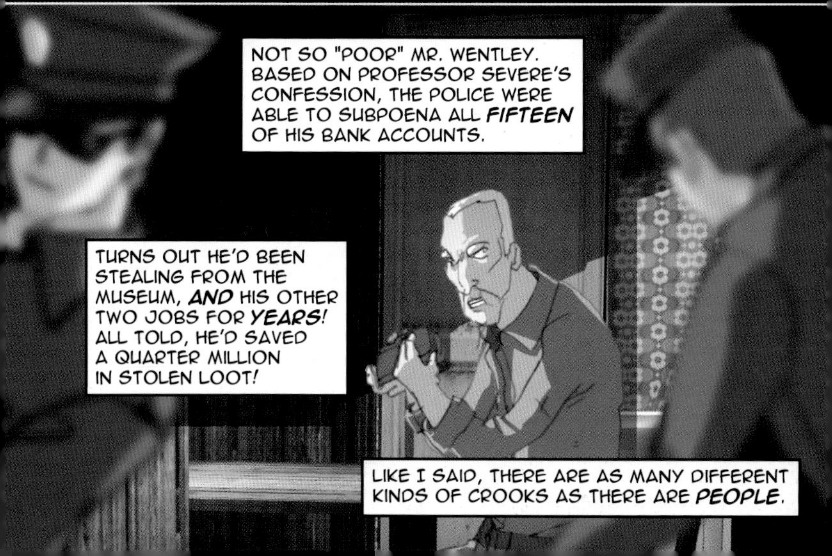
NOT SO "POOR" MR. WENTLEY. BASED ON PROFESSOR SEVERE'S CONFESSION, THE POLICE WERE ABLE TO SUBPOENA ALL FIFTEEN OF HIS BANK ACCOUNTS.
TURNS OUT HE'D BEEN STEALING FROM THE MUSEUM, AND HIS OTHER TWO JOBS FOR YEARS! ALL TOLD, HE'D SAVED A QUARTER MILLION IN STOLEN LOOT!
LIKE I SAID, THERE ARE AS MANY DIFFERENT KINDS OF CROOKS AS THERE ARE PEOPLE.

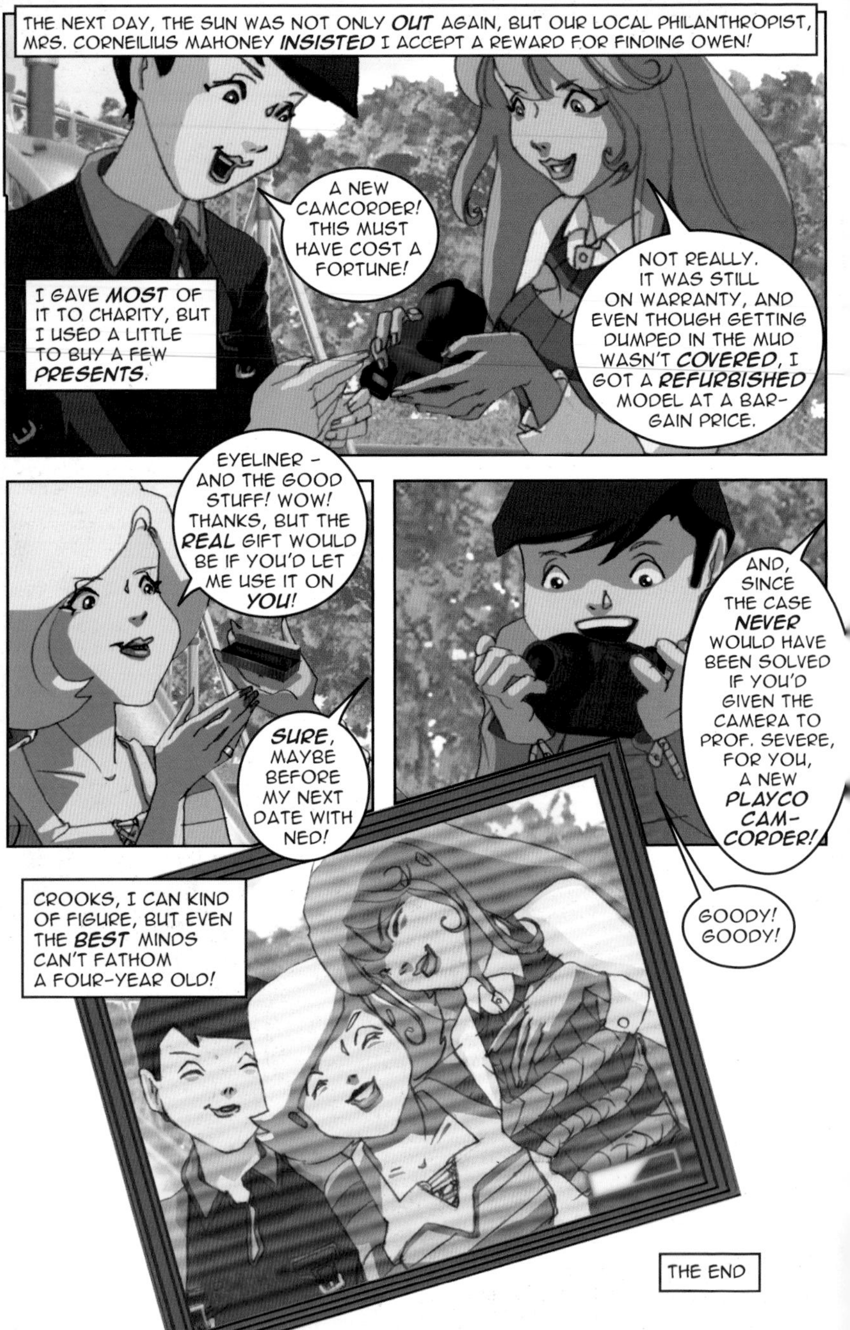
THE NEXT DAY, THE SUN WAS NOT ONLY OUT AGAIN, BUT OUR LOCAL PHILANTHROPIST, MRS. CORNEILIUS MAHONEY INSISTED I ACCEPT A REWARD FOR FINDING OWEN!
A NEW CAMCORDER! THIS MUST HAVE COST A FORTUNE!
I GAVE MOST OF IT TO CHARITY, BUT I USED A LITTLE TO BUY A FEW PRESENTS.
NOT REALLY. IT WAS STILL ON WARRANTY, AND EVEN THOUGH GETTING DUMPED IN THE MUD WASN'T COVERED, I GOT A REFURBISHED MODEL AT A BAR-GAIN PRICE.
EYELINER - AND THE GOOD STUFF! WOW! THANKS, BUT THE REAL GIFT WOULD BE IF YOU'D LET ME USE IT ON YOU!
SURE, MAYBE BEFORE MY NEXT DATE WITH NED!
AND, SINCE THE CASE NEVER WOULD HAVE BEEN SOLVED IF YOU'D GIVEN THE CAMERA TO PROF. SEVERE, FOR YOU, A NEW PLAYCO CAM-CORDER!
GOODY! GOODY!
CROOKS, I CAN KIND OF FIGURE, BUT EVEN THE BEST MINDS CAN'T FATHOM A FOUR-YEAR OLD!
THE END

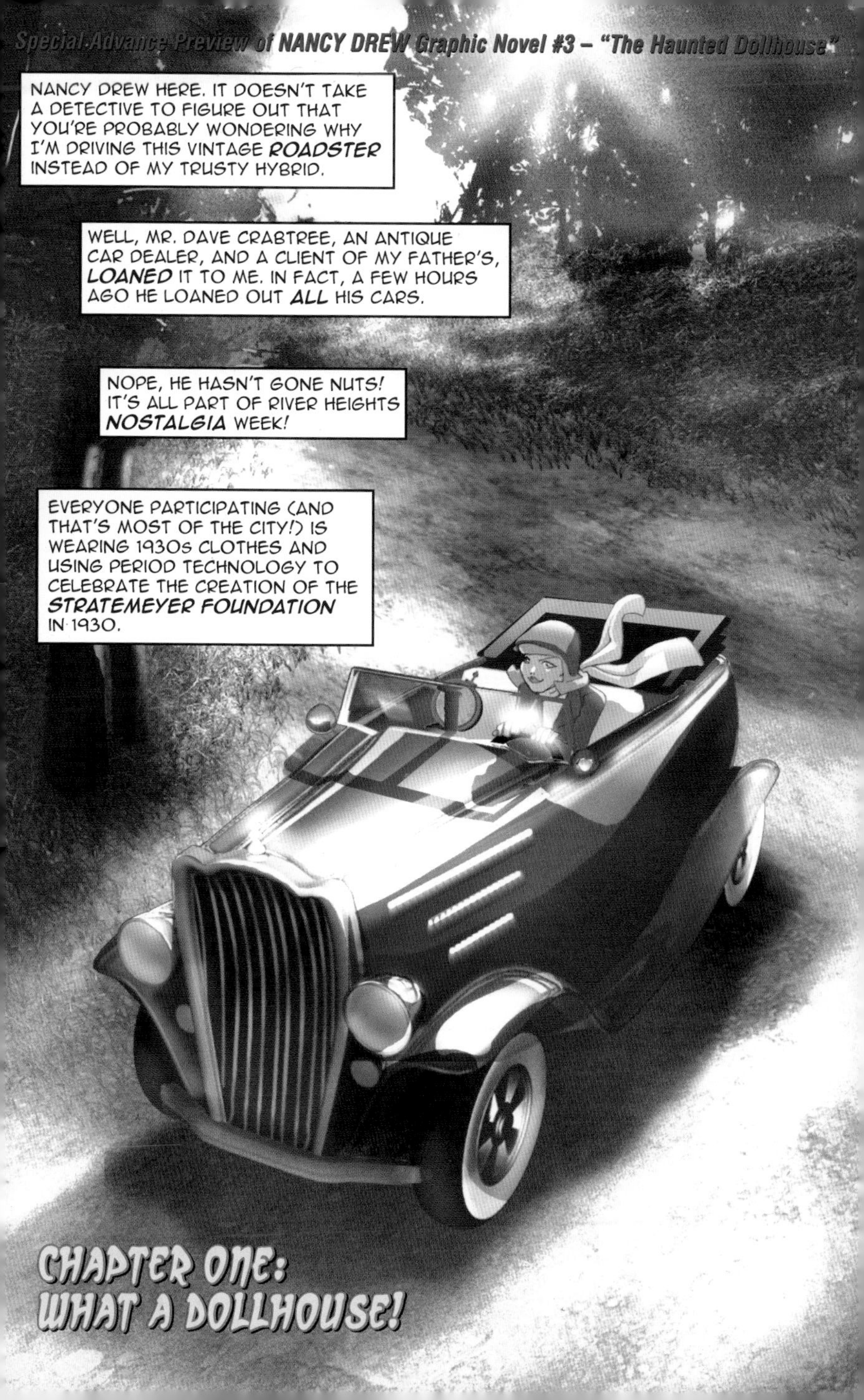
Special Advance Preview of NANCY DREW Graphic Novel #3 – "The Haunted Dollhouse"
NANCY DREW HERE. IT DOESN'T TAKE A DETECTIVE TO FIGURE OUT THAT YOU'RE PROBABLY WONDERING WHY I'M DRIVING THIS VINTAGE ROADSTER INSTEAD OF MY TRUSTY HYBRID.
WELL, MR. DAVE CRABTREE, AN ANTIQUE CAR DEALER, AND A CLIENT OF MY FATHER'S, LOANED IT TO ME. IN FACT, A FEW HOURS AGO HE LOANED OUT ALL HIS CARS.
NOPE, HE HASN'T GONE NUTS! IT'S ALL PART OF RIVER HEIGHTS NOSTALGIA WEEK!
EVERYONE PARTICIPATING (AND THAT'S MOST OF THE CITY!) IS WEARING 1930s CLOTHES AND USING PERIOD TECHNOLOGY TO CELEBRATE THE CREATION OF THE STRATEMEYER FOUNDATION IN 1930.
CHAPTER ONE:
WHAT A DOLLHOUSE!

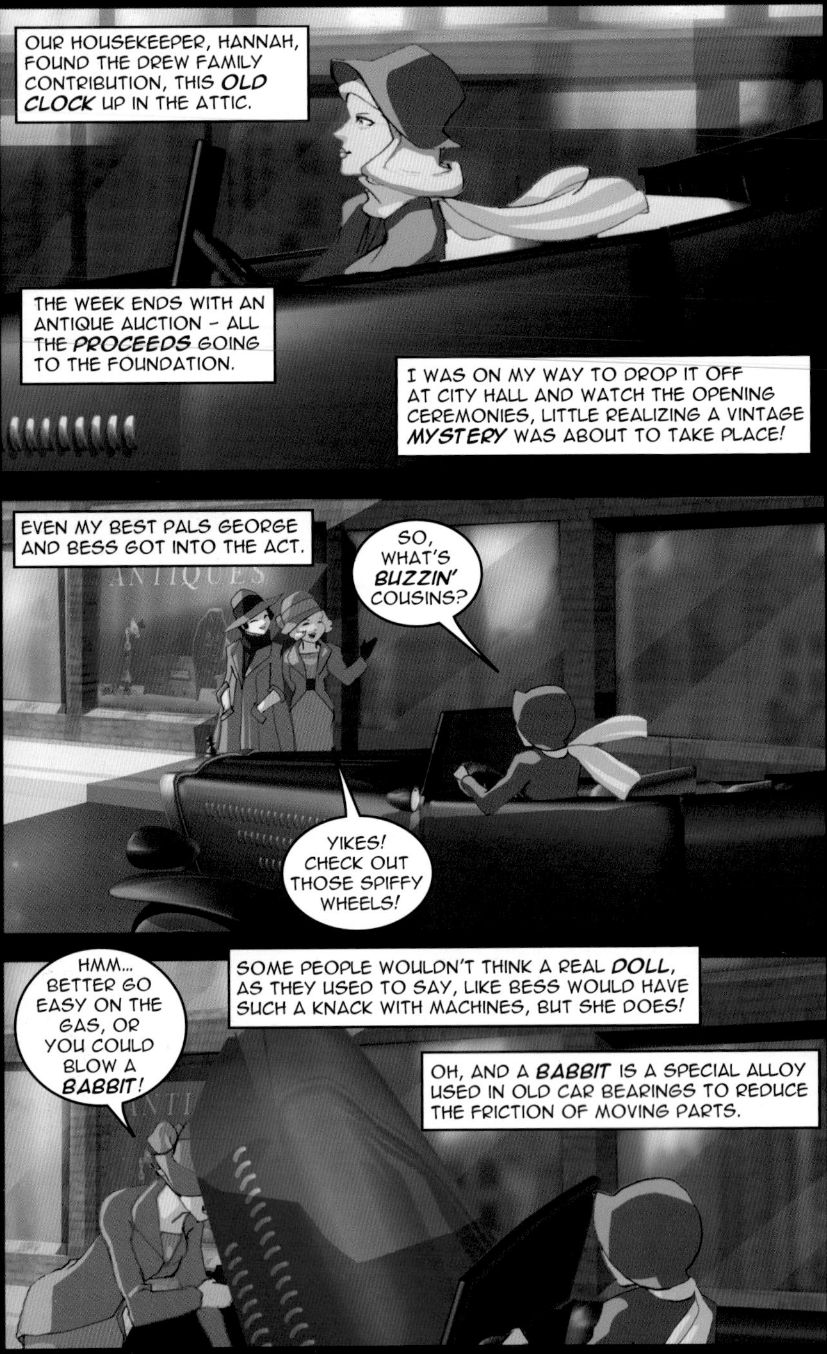
OUR HOUSEKEEPER, HANNAH, FOUND THE DREW FAMILY CONTRIBUTION, THIS OLD CLOCK UP IN THE ATTIC.
THE WEEK ENDS WITH AN ANTIQUE AUCTION - ALL THE PROCEEDS GOING TO THE FOUNDATION.
I WAS ON MY WAY TO DROP IT OFF AT CITY HALL AND WATCH THE OPENING CEREMONIES, LITTLE REALIZING A VINTAGE MYSTERY WAS ABOUT TO TAKE PLACE!
EVEN MY BEST PALS GEORGE AND BESS GOT INTO THE ACT.
ANTIQUES
SO, WHAT'S BUZZIN' COUSINS?
YIKES! CHECK OUT THOSE SPIFFY WHEELS!
HMM... BETTER GO EASY ON THE GAS, OR YOU COULD BLOW A BABBIT!
SOME PEOPLE WOULDN'T THINK A REAL DOLL, AS THEY USED TO SAY, LIKE BESS WOULD HAVE SUCH A KNACK WITH MACHINES, BUT SHE DOES!
OH, AND A BABBIT IS A SPECIAL ALLOY USED IN OLD CAR BEARINGS TO REDUCE THE FRICTION OF MOVING PARTS.

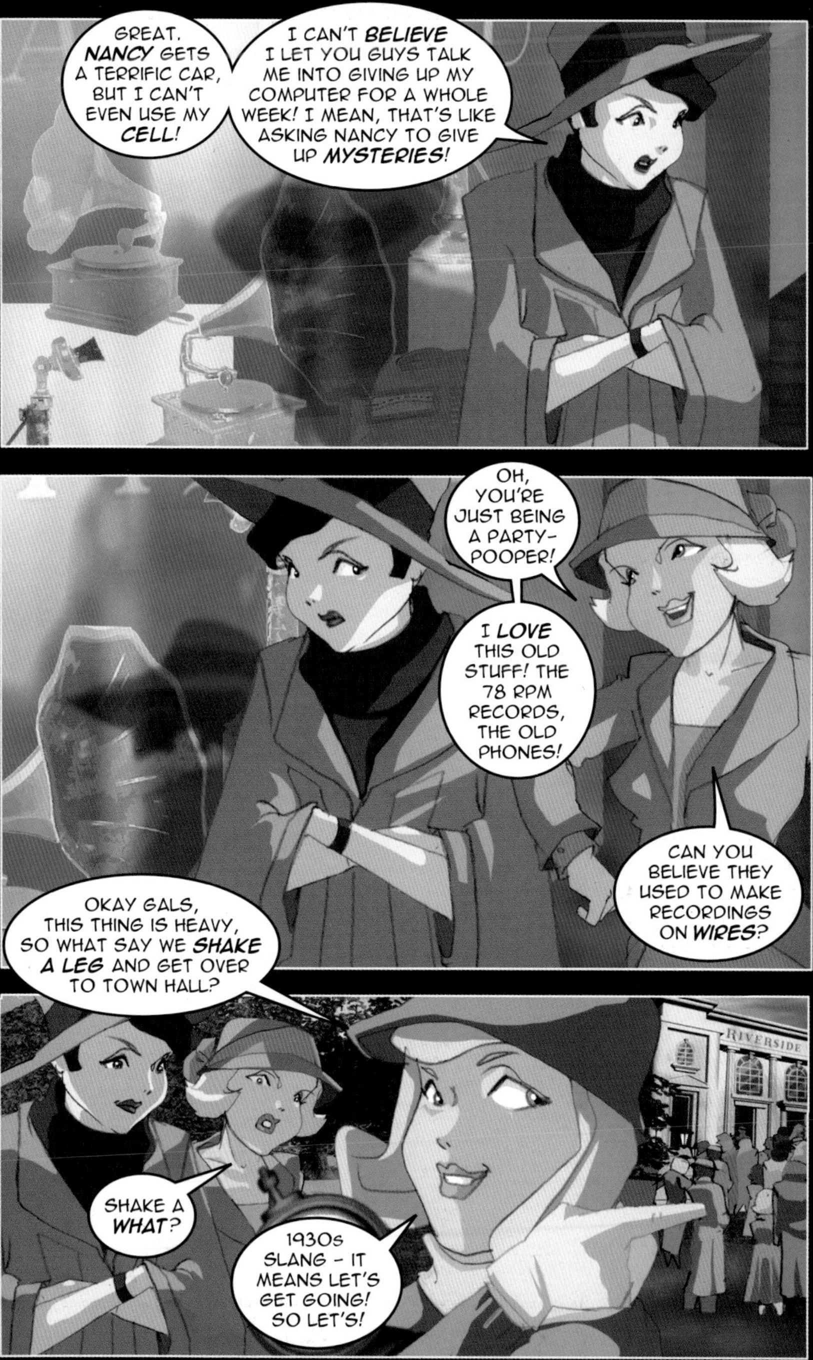
GREAT. NANCY GETS A TERRIFIC CAR, BUT I CAN'T EVEN USE MY CELL!
I CAN'T BELIEVE I LET YOU GUYS TALK ME INTO GIVING UP MY COMPUTER FOR A WHOLE WEEK! I MEAN, THAT'S LIKE ASKING NANCY TO GIVE UP MYSTERIES!
OH, YOU'RE JUST BEING A PARTY-POOPER!
I LOVE THIS OLD STUFF! THE 78 RPM RECORDS, THE OLD PHONES!
CAN YOU BELIEVE THEY USED TO MAKE RECORDINGS ON WIRES?
OKAY GALS, THIS THING IS HEAVY, SO WHAT SAY WE SHAKE A LEG AND GET OVER TO TOWN HALL?
RIVERSIDE
SHAKE A WHAT?
1930s SLANG - IT MEANS LET'S GET GOING! SO LET'S!

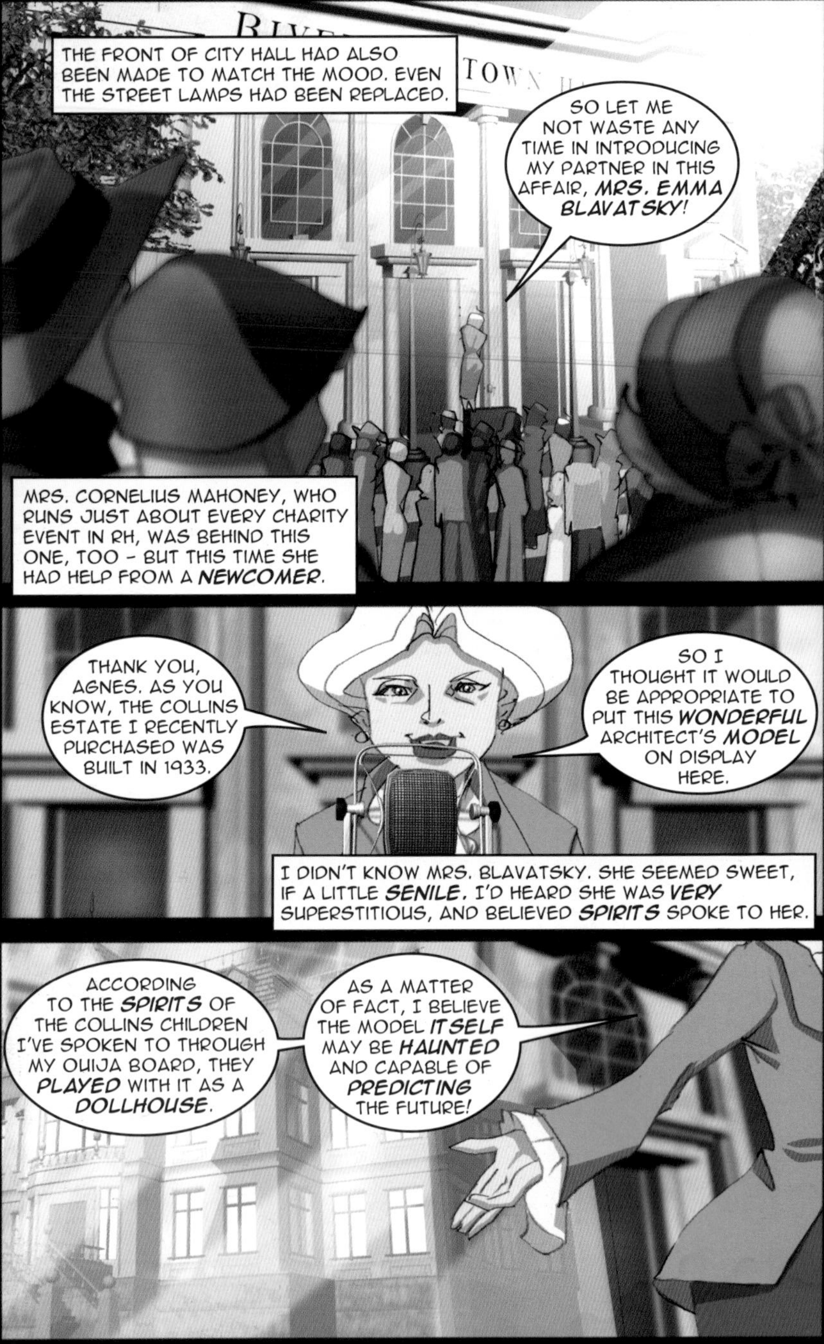
RIVER
TOWN H
THE FRONT OF CITY HALL HAD ALSO BEEN MADE TO MATCH THE MOOD. EVEN THE STREET LAMPS HAD BEEN REPLACED.
SO LET ME NOT WASTE ANY TIME IN INTRODUCING MY PARTNER IN THIS AFFAIR, *MRS. EMMA BLAVATSKY*!
MRS. CORNELIUS MAHONEY, WHO RUNS JUST ABOUT EVERY CHARITY EVENT IN RH, WAS BEHIND THIS ONE, TOO - BUT THIS TIME SHE HAD HELP FROM A *NEWCOMER*.
THANK YOU, AGNES. AS YOU KNOW, THE COLLINS ESTATE I RECENTLY PURCHASED WAS BUILT IN 1933.
SO I THOUGHT IT WOULD BE APPROPRIATE TO PUT THIS *WONDERFUL* ARCHITECT'S *MODEL* ON DISPLAY HERE.
I DIDN'T KNOW MRS. BLAVATSKY. SHE SEEMED SWEET, IF A LITTLE *SENILE*. I'D HEARD SHE WAS *VERY* SUPERSTITIOUS, AND BELIEVED *SPIRITS* SPOKE TO HER.
ACCORDING TO THE *SPIRITS* OF THE COLLINS CHILDREN I'VE SPOKEN TO THROUGH MY OUIJA BOARD, THEY *PLAYED* WITH IT AS A *DOLLHOUSE*.
AS A MATTER OF FACT, I BELIEVE THE MODEL *ITSELF* MAY BE *HAUNTED* AND CAPABLE OF *PREDICTING* THE FUTURE!

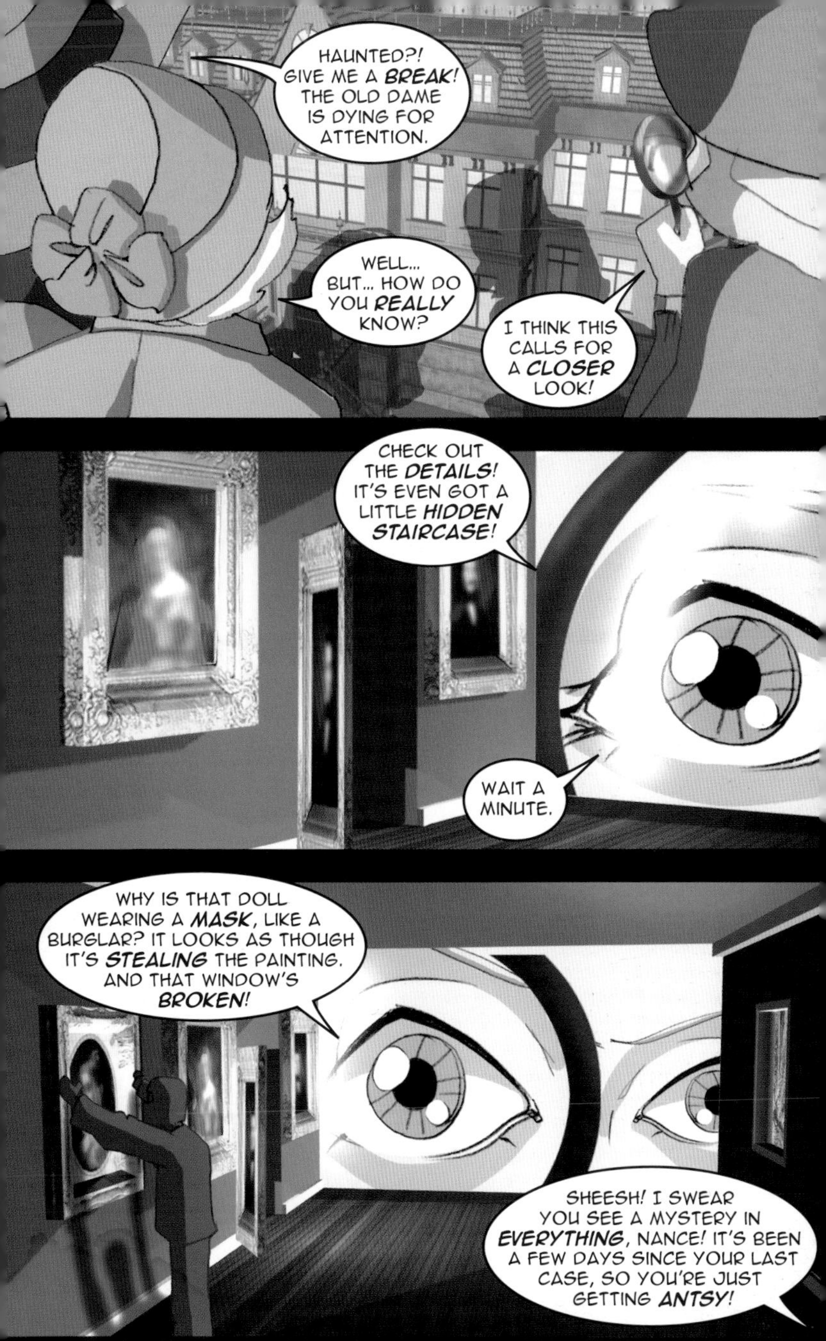
HAUNTED?! GIVE ME A BREAK! THE OLD DAME IS DYING FOR ATTENTION.
WELL... BUT... HOW DO YOU REALLY KNOW?
I THINK THIS CALLS FOR A CLOSER LOOK!
CHECK OUT THE DETAILS! IT'S EVEN GOT A LITTLE HIDDEN STAIRCASE!
WAIT A MINUTE.
WHY IS THAT DOLL WEARING A MASK, LIKE A BURGLAR? IT LOOKS AS THOUGH IT'S STEALING THE PAINTING. AND THAT WINDOW'S BROKEN!
SHEESH! I SWEAR YOU SEE A MYSTERY IN EVERYTHING, NANCE! IT'S BEEN A FEW DAYS SINCE YOUR LAST CASE, SO YOU'RE JUST GETTING ANTSY!